Christopher stared at her in surprise.

He was unable, or unwilling, to believe what his brain was telling him—that the pretty, slender, soft, delicate woman who had drawn a response from him that he hadn't experienced in a very long time was Shelley Evans. She can't be Shelley Evans, he thought irrationally. She's a reporter. How can I possibly want to make love to a reporter?

"What do you think you're doing?" Shelley demanded, her eyes on the notes—*her* notes— he was holding.

He flushed. Now she'd think he was not only a spy but a common crook as well. It surprised him that he cared what she thought. "I'm reading," he finally replied.

"Find anything interesting?"

"Just you." As he made the flippant comment, he realized that it was true. "Do me a favor," he said coolly.

She looked wary. "What?"

"Tell me you're not Shelley Evans. Tell me you're her neighbor or her roommate or even her sister. Just tell me you're not her."

"But I am," she said flatly.

Dear Reader,

When two people fall in love, the world is suddenly new and exciting, and it's that same excitement we bring to you in Silhouette Intimate Moments. These are stories with scope, with grandeur. The characters lead the lives we all dream of, and everything they do reflects the wonder of being in love.

Longer and more sensuous than most romances, Silhouette Intimate Moments novels take you away from everyday life and let you share the magic of love. Adventure, glamour, drama, even suspense— these are the passwords that let you into a world where love has a power beyond the ordinary, where the best authors in the field today create stories of love and commitment that will stay with you always.

In coming months look for novels by your favorite authors: Maura Seger, Parris Afton Bonds, Linda Howard and Nora Roberts, to name just a few. And whenever you buy books, look for all the Silhouette Intimate Moments, love stories *for* today's women *by* today's women.

Leslie J. Wainger
Senior Editor
Silhouette Books

Marilyn Pappano
Guilt
by Association

Silhouette Intimate Moments

Published by Silhouette Books New York

America's Publisher of Contemporary Romance

SILHOUETTE BOOKS
300 East 42nd St., New York, N.Y. 10017

Copyright © 1988 by Marilyn Pappano

ISBN: 0-373-07233-3

First Silhouette Books printing April 1988

America's Publisher of Contemporary Romance

Printed in the U.S.A.

Books by Marilyn Pappano

Silhouette Intimate Moments

Within Reach #182
The Lights of Home #214
Guilt by Association #233

MARILYN PAPPANO

has been writing as long as she can remember, just for the fun of it, but recently she decided to take her life-long hobby seriously. She was encouraging a friend to write a romance novel and ended up writing one herself. It was accepted, and she plans to continue as an author for a long time. When she's not involved in writing, she enjoys camping, quilting, sewing and, most of all, reading. Not surprisingly, her favorite books are romance novels.

Her husband is in the navy, and in the course of her marriage she has moved all over the U.S. Currently she lives in South Carolina with her husband and son.

To my husband, Bob

With love and unending gratitude
for getting me through the
rough spots.

Prologue

It was a rare night when Christopher Morgan found himself at home with nothing on his calendar—no meetings or parties to attend, no dates, no social obligations to fulfill. Tonight, though, he was alone, with nothing to do unless he wanted to do it. He could watch television, read the newspaper and the magazines that had accumulated on the hall table, or even indulge himself by going to bed early for once. The prospect, the lack of demands on his time, was so novel that, after he changed from the suit he'd worn to work into more comfortable trousers and a sweater, he took a few minutes with a drink just to enjoy the freedom.

The doorbell rang before he was half finished with his drink. Two men waited outside. One was dark, and one was fair, and both wore somber, grim expressions. The fair one spoke first. "Christopher Morgan?"

He switched the glass to his other hand. "Yes?"

The dark one raised his hand. In it was a small black wallet, flipped open to reveal the contents. Christopher glanced at the picture in the bottom half of the wallet, noticed that it matched the face of the man before him, then looked at the top half. The words in bold black type on the upper card faded as the shadow printing registered in Christopher's mind. FBI. Federal Bureau of Investigation.

"We're FBI agents, Mr. Morgan," the blond man said. He offered Christopher a folded piece of paper. "We have a warrant to search the buildings that house Morgan Industries. We'd like you to come down there with us."

Christopher looked at the warrant, but none of the words made any sense. "Why? What's happened?" He looked from one man to the other, but neither seemed willing to answer him.

"Will you please come with us?" The dark one asked it as a question, but the cool tone of his voice left no doubt that Christopher had no choice in the matter.

"Just a minute," he said quietly. "Let me get my keys." He went into the house, downing the rest of his drink in one swallow. He wished he could have another, but he didn't think the blond agent who was on his heels would appreciate it if he stopped to refill his glass. "Can I take my car?"

"We'd prefer that you come with us."

They were good, Christopher thought as he slid into the back seat of a black sedan, at making polite requests out of steely orders. As soon as the car pulled out of the driveway, he turned his thoughts to the company. What had happened at M.I. that involved the FBI? If there had been a break-in at one of the buildings where the Defense Department research was done, of course the FBI would be brought in, but Christopher should have been notified first, not the other way around.

What else could possibly have happened? A breach in security? He dismissed that. Morgan Industries had an excellent security setup. He employed a top-notch security firm, all of whose procedures had been reviewed and approved by the Defense Investigative Service agent who had been assigned to the company before the government contracts had been granted.

So what was wrong?

The complex had never seen so much activity after six o'clock. The dark agent maneuvered his car through a parking lot filled with similar cars and vans. Dozens of men and women, wearing nondescript, dark windbreakers that read "FBI" in gold letters and bore laminated badges, were gathered near the door of the main building, where the executive offices were located. The half-dozen security guards on duty that night stood in a group nearby.

Christopher was led from the car to the agent in charge, a tall, rugged-looking man with gray hair, who introduced himself as Special Agent Taylor. "Thank you for coming out, Mr. Morgan," Taylor said. "Let's go inside."

Christopher followed him in. "What are you doing? What's going on?"

Taylor gestured to a corner of the reception area, where they would be out of the way for the time being. "Let's sit down. Did you read the warrant?"

Christopher looked down at the paper crumpled in his hands. In the car, he'd forgotten about it. Now he smoothed it out and concentrated on reading it. A moment later he looked up. "It says you can search all the buildings and all the offices. Why? What are you looking for?"

"Evidence." Taylor hesitated, his eyes moving away from the man beside him to watch his agents go about the jobs they'd been assigned. They were well trained. Methodical. Meticulous. After a moment he turned back to Christopher, his expression grave. "Tonight we arrested one of the officers of this company on charges of espionage, Mr. Morgan. We'll confiscate whatever material we find that could pertain to the investigation. We'll also take everything that concerns the defense research projects your company has been handling. All work on those contracts will, of course, be stopped immediately."

The loss of the defense contracts meant hundreds of thousands of dollars, but Christopher was too numbed by the first part of Taylor's speech to care about the contracts. One of his employees a spy? It was impossible! He had handpicked every one of them. They weren't just employees, they were friends—and he'd bet his life on their loyalty and honesty.

Taylor was looking at him curiously. He was waiting for him to ask who it was, Christopher realized sickeningly. He didn't want to know. He didn't want to hear that one of his officers, one of his friends, had betrayed him, the company and the United States.

He didn't want to know, but if he didn't ask, Taylor was going to tell him anyway. He opened his mouth, then had to clear his throat before he could get the words out. "Who? Who is it?"

There was no way to soften the blow, so Taylor answered bluntly. "Gary Morgan. We arrested your brother, Mr. Morgan."

They asked him questions—Taylor and a female agent. Were he and his brother very close? Why had he offered Gary a job in his company? What kind of work had Gary done before he came to M.I.? Had he ever been married? Did he have a girlfriend? What were his responsibilities in the company? What materials did he have access to? How much was he paid? Did he have any income other than his salary? Did he spend a lot of money?

The questions went on and on through the night, some of them repeated a second and third time. Christopher answered many of them with "I don't know." He racked his brain for anything that might be of importance to them, but there was nothing. The strangers interrogating him knew more about his brother than he did.

He was so tired. A couple of times, when they stopped their questioning briefly, he dozed off in his chair, but each time some noise startled him awake—a new voice, a closing door, the clatter from the search, which had moved upstairs.

It was eight-fifteen in the morning when an agent, another woman, came to the door, calling Taylor away. The woman who had questioned Christopher remained with him.

Half an hour later Taylor returned, accompanied by the two agents who had picked Christopher up at his house. All three of them looked grimmer than ever. Standing directly in front of Christopher, Taylor spoke in a quiet, solemn voice. "Christopher Morgan, you're under arrest for violation of the espionage laws of the United States." Taylor turned to the two men.

The dark one stepped forward. "Place your hands against the door, please."

Christopher looked helplessly at each of the four people in the office, then got to his feet and placed his hands flat against the door. As the dark man began a brief but thorough search, the fair one tonelessly recited the Miranda warning. "Before we ask you any questions, it is my duty to advise you of your rights. You have the right to remain silent. Anything you say can be used against you in court or any other proceedings. You have the right to consult..."

Christopher heard the words—he'd heard similar versions so many times on television. That was what it seemed like—television. Fiction. Fantasy. It couldn't possibly be real. He was so exhausted that his mind was distorting the events taking place around him. Once he'd gotten some rest, he would find out that none of this had ever happened.

"Do you understand each of these rights?"

Christopher realized that the blond man was waiting for a response. Although he hadn't heard most of what the man had said, he nodded anyway and said yes.

The first man finished the search, pulled Christopher's hands behind his back and fastened a pair of handcuffs around his wrists. The steel was cold and uncomfortable, but at that moment it seemed like the only thing in his life that was real.

He was led from the office and outside to the same black sedan. Just like on TV, he thought numbly as the blond agent pushed Christopher's head down and he awkwardly climbed into the back seat, with the agent right behind him. A moment later Taylor got in on the other side.

Christopher bowed his head as they drove away from Morgan Industries, and his lips moved in silent prayer. *Dear God, please help me.*

Chapter 1

Shelley Evans chewed her lower lip as she worked. It was an annoying habit—one that she'd been trying to break for most of her thirty-one years without much success. At least now she only did it when she was frustrated, and today she was definitely frustrated.

It was the change, she kept telling herself. San Diego was a pretty big change from Mobile, Alabama, where she'd lived all her life, and the *Chronicle* made the Mobile paper where she'd worked since graduation look like small potatoes. Pretty soon, though, she would become familiar with the routine at the *Chronicle*. Pretty soon she would make some friends, maybe even meet her neighbors. And sometime in the near future, she hoped, she would know enough about the city to be able to go somewhere besides work without getting lost. Lord, she was tired of getting lost. She'd been in San Diego nearly three weeks, and she'd spent at least half that time asking for directions or studying street maps.

The nearly empty computer screen in front of her glowed softly, waiting for her to display a flash of genius and fill it with brilliant thoughts. It had been waiting for almost half an hour and still held only three sentences. Forty-one words. Not much to show for a morning's work. At this rate, she thought sourly, her editor would wonder why he'd bothered to hire her. Maybe she wasn't cut out for the big city.

She shut that thought firmly out of her mind. She had come willingly to the *Chronicle* and to San Diego, and she was going to make a go of things or die trying. In her ten years as a reporter she'd never given up yet, and she wasn't about to start now.

Massaging the inside of her lip with her tongue, she sat straighter in her chair, placed her hands above the keyboard and began typing. The words meant little, but they would get her started, and soon the ideas would be flowing.

The ideas did come, and she finished the story on San Diego's mayor in record time. Pleased with her success, she looked up to see Brad Davis, her boss, watching her. "Finished?"

She nodded.

"Come on into my office, Shelley. I want to talk to you."

Warily she followed him into the corner office and sat down in a leather chair when he asked her to. He leaned against the windowsill. "Are you getting settled in okay?"

She nodded. She still didn't feel very comfortable with the man who had hired her so unexpectedly. She had been looking for a way to get out of the rut her life had dumped her into—and a way to escape the uneasy situation she'd found herself in at work—when, out of the blue, came a telephone call from Brad Davis. Based on the recommendation of a college professor they had both studied under, Brad wanted to hire her. It had taken Shelley about a minute to assess the problems in her life—the restlessness, the frustration, the feeling that her life was going nowhere. Kevin. She had accepted the job offer right then, with no time to think it over. No time to change her mind.

"Where are you living?"

"I found an apartment out on the . . ." She paused to get her bearings. "I think on the east side of town. I'm not sure. I'm a couple miles from the university."

Brad smiled. "We have several universities."

"Oh. San Diego State." She flushed, the color hiding the freckles across her nose. There wasn't a place in the entire city of Mobile that she wasn't familiar with. She wondered if she would ever know her new home as well.

Enough small talk. Brad sat down at his desk and picked up a file folder, but instead of giving it to her, he simply held it in his hands. "About eleven months ago," he began slowly, "San Diego had a pretty big scandal—not our usual run-of-the-mill investment fraud or city government thing."

That was one thing that Shelley had already learned: San Diego was a beautiful city, but it *did* seem to attract trouble. In recent years it had had more than its share of scandals, all dealing in some form or other with money.

"This one involved one of our biggest companies—one that did a lot of defense research. One of the company officers was selling secrets to the Russians. The president and owner of the company—who also happens to be the spy's brother—was also a suspect, but no charges were ever filed against him. His company was destroyed. After all, in a military town, who wants to do business with a suspected spy? He lost everything he had and disappeared, just fell off the face of the earth."

Shelley listened quietly, making mental notes as Brad continued.

"Their name is Morgan. Gary was the one who was definitely spying, and Christopher is the alleged spy."

"Gary *was*?"

"He was killed the day after he was arrested. They'd taken him to MCC . . ." He saw her puzzled look. "The Metropolitan Correctional Center. Jail. Anyway, the FBI and the marshals left him there, and they were going to pick him up for his arraignment that afternoon. Unfortunately one of the other prisoners got to him first. He'd made a knife from the handle of a spoon and stabbed Morgan. Gary died immediately.''

Shelley leaned slightly forward in her chair, her interest growing with each detail. ''Why did the guy do it? Did someone hire him to keep Gary from talking?''

''That's what I think, and so does just about everyone else, but it'll never be proven. There was a struggle between the prisoner and the deputy on duty, and the deputy shot the man. He died, too.''

''So what happened to Christopher?''

''Like I said, he disappeared. He sold everything he owned and left San Diego. No one has seen him since.'' He looked down at the file, then back up at Shelley. ''I used to cover financial stories back before I took this job. I had a lot of contacts in banks, investment firms, credit-reporting agencies. If a business dealt with money, I had someone inside who would help me.'' He grinned. ''In a city that has as many schemers as this one, you need all the sources you can cultivate.''

Shelley waited for him to get to the point. She wanted to hear the whole story, to get her hands on that file folder of clippings that he was holding on to so protectively, but she hid her impatience well and let him proceed at his own pace.

''I haven't done anything for the financial section in a couple of years now, but I still keep in touch with some of the people out there—never know when I might need them. Last week one of them gave me a call. She works at the bank where Gary Morgan had his personal accounts. Are you familiar with banking procedures?''

She shook her head. ''I know how to write checks and to make deposits and withdrawals. That's about it.''

''Before Gary was arrested, the FBI got copies of his records, planning to use them against him, I guess. When they did, they put a flag on them. That means that if anyone requests Gary's records, no matter who it is, the bank is supposed to notify the FBI. Now, theoretically, because they're flagged, you can only get them with a judge's okay, but lucky for us and others, things don't always work out the way theory says they should. According to my friend, someone got Gary Morgan's records a few months ago. He didn't have any authorization, but he somehow convinced one of her coworkers to give him copies. He also convinced her not to tell the FBI that he'd been around."

"Do you think he paid her?"

Brad shrugged, setting the folder down, and leaned back. "It's possible. For all I know, he might just have charmed her out of them."

"Was it Christopher?"

"I don't know. The woman who gave him the copies denies that it ever happened. My friend only caught a glimpse of him, but all she can say is that he was tall and had dark hair. Christopher is tall and has dark hair, but I just don't think he'd do it. If the woman hadn't cooperated with him and had called the FBI the way she was supposed to, he would have been in a world of trouble."

"Then who could it have been?"

"*I* think it was a buddy of his, Gabriel Rodriguez. Rodriguez is a cop with the SDPD—a detective. He's tall, dark, has black hair. He knows the proper procedure for getting those kinds of records, and he also knows that there's no way in hell any judge is going to let him meddle in an FBI case. And, from what I hear, he could charm the rattles off a sidewinder. I'm betting it was him." Brad opened the file, giving Shelley a tantalizing glimpse of what was inside, then closed it again and stood up. "Of course, I don't have any proof that it's Rodriguez, but it makes sense. Who besides Christopher would be interested in Gary so long after his death? And who would Christopher turn to for help? His best friend, who happens to be a cop."

Shelley caught herself chewing her lower lip again. She had to stop to speak. "I can see why the FBI would still be interested. They'd still like to know who Gary was working for, and the records might provide a connection. But why would Christopher and Rodriguez want them? Unless...''

Brad was smiling when she looked up. ''Right. I don't know if Christopher was guilty or not. He swore he was innocent, but that means nothing. Still, maybe he was. Maybe he honest to God didn't know what was going on in his own company. Or maybe he was the one Gary was working for, the one who ordered his death.''

''Assuming he *is* innocent...''

''That's a dangerous thing to do.''

Shelley smiled for the first time that morning. ''But assuming that he is, then he could be looking for the man who *was* responsible—for Gary's spying, and especially for his murder. But he would need a lot more than bank records. He'd have to have telephone and credit card records, too, and names of friends.'' She stared thoughtfully. If Christopher Morgan was looking for vengeance, though maybe he saw it as justice, he had a hard job ahead of him. ''If the FBI couldn't find any trace of another man—a contact or something—what makes Morgan think he can?''

''Arrogance?''

''Does he have the background to conduct this kind of an investigation?''

''No, but Rodriguez does—he has a background in military intelligence, plus almost ten years as a cop. If they're working together, I imagine he's giving the orders and Morgan's simply carrying them out. Remember, too, that Christopher's got a couple of things going for him that the FBI didn't: unlimited time; a personal desire to see his brother's killer punished; and a determination to clear his own name.''

''Do you think he's innocent?''

Brad refused to answer. ''I'd prefer that you make up your own mind about that, based on the facts. I don't want to influence you.''

''Facts can be interpreted in different ways. Based simply on the fact that the FBI arrested him, and admitting that making assumptions can be dangerous, I would assume that he's guilty. It wouldn't be the first time that a guilty person got off because of lack of evidence.''

He picked up the file and offered it to her. "That's everything the *Chronicle*'s ever done on Christopher and Gary Morgan. Read it over. If you want more information, you can check the clip files at the library for the *Tribune* and *Union* stories and get copies of the magazine articles.''

"And do what?'' She had a fair idea, but she wanted to hear it put into words.

"Find him. Find out if he's guilty. Find out what he's doing these days. If he's the one investigating Gary, see what he's learned.''

She accepted the file, resisting the impulse to open it and start reading immediately. "Wouldn't you rather give this to one of your better reporters—someone who's already familiar with San Diego and has their own sources?''

"You *are* one of my better reporters,'' he replied with a grin. "And nothing will get you familiar with San Diego like this case will.''

"What if I fail? What if Christopher has covered his tracks so well and is so careful that he never slips up and I never find him?''

"Then we'll at least get an anniversary story out of it. Something short and not so sweet. Get started on it today, okay?''

She stood up, clutching the folder tightly. "All right.''

When she reached the door, he spoke again. "If you have any problems, Shelley, let me know. I'm here to help.''

She acknowledged his offer with a smile.

"One other thing: keep this to yourself. I know you'll have to interview some people, but don't tell anyone what we suspect—not even anyone here at the paper. Just say that we're doing an anniversary article. If Morgan is checking out his brother, he might drop way out of sight if he finds out someone is on to him. And if it's not him snooping around, you might be safer if you don't know who it is. So be careful, and if you don't mind, work on this at home.''

He looked out the window. Sensing that there was more on his mind, Shelley waited quietly. At last he turned back to her. "One last warning: Christopher Morgan doesn't like reporters. Frankly, he's got good reason not to. Finding him will be hard enough, but it will still be the easy part. Getting him to trust you will be tough.''

She nodded once, left the office and closed the door behind her. She stopped at her desk and got her handbag and the lightweight jacket she'd worn to work, then left the office.

The drive to work each morning took twenty-one minutes in rush-hour traffic and left her wide-eyed and white-knuckled. At midmorning, she discovered, she could make it in eleven minutes without breaking the speed limit once.

Her apartment was located only a few blocks from the freeway that led straight to the office. That, plus the fact that it had two bedrooms and a relatively private patio, was the primary reason she'd chosen it. She certainly couldn't say that the rent was reasonable—it was more than double what she'd paid for a comparable apartment in Mobile—but a higher cost of living could be expected with the higher salary of her new job.

The second bedroom had been turned into an office, where she spent a large part of her free time. It was no wonder she hadn't met her neighbors yet, she thought with a scowl as she seated herself at the desk. Maybe if she'd get out of this office... No. The only neighbor she currently had any interest in meeting was the man upstairs. He owned two mint-condition Porsches, one of which he insisted on parking in the space assigned to her. She'd left a polite note on the windshield, but it had brought no response. He would be put out when he came home today and found that Shelley had beaten him to the coveted parking space.

She switched on the stereo next to her desk, inserted a cassette of soft, instrumental jazz and turned her attention to the file.

Most of the articles Brad had put together for her dealt with the spy case, although a fair number of them had been written about Christopher Morgan before the arrests. He had been a successful businessman, an art collector, a member of the social elite. His name had turned up as frequently in the society pages as it had in the business and local news sections. There were several pictures, mostly grainy newsprint, but Brad had found one black-and-white original.

Shelley set the stories aside and picked up the photograph. She cleared the bulletin board on the wall above her desk, then used a pushpin to attach the photo.

It showed a handsome man wearing a grave expression. His hair was thick and black, with a few strands of gray at the temples, parted slightly off center and combed back from his features. The style drew attention to his face, with its square jaw and clean lines, straight nose and intelligent dark eyes.

She leaned on the desk and cupped her chin in her hands. The picture had been taken four months before his arrest, probably at one of the many social functions he had attended; the barely visible black jacket and tie and ruffled white shirt suggested a tuxedo. Why had he looked so solemn? Had he known then what was going on at Morgan Industries? Had he known that his brother was a spy?

She found it hard to pull her gaze away. The picture was lifeless, a flat, empty reflection of the man, but even so, it held her. What was he like? How had the past eleven months changed him? How had his brother's death and his own arrest affected him?

And the most important question of all: was he guilty? Was Christopher Morgan a spy?

By seven o'clock that night Shelley was ready to leave the room, close the door and forget about Christopher Morgan until the next day, but she found that forgetting was hard. She was intrigued by his story—and by him.

All the prearrest stories were about Christopher, with only occasional mentions of his brother. How had Gary felt about the attention Christopher got? she wondered. Had Gary deliberately stayed out of the limelight, or had he resented the attention being lavished on his younger brother? Jealousy, or sibling rivalry, could provide a powerful enough motivation to do almost anything.

The stories seemed to be fair and objective, for the most part. There was only one that raised any questions for Shelley. Written the day after Gary's death, it seemed too intimately detailed. After everything Christopher had been through in the previous twenty-four hours, she thought it strange that he would talk so candidly to a reporter. She made a mental note to ask Brad about Mike Jennings, the man who had written the story. It might tell her why Christopher disliked reporters. It also might give her a clue on how to deal with his hostility when they met.

She laughed aloud at her choice of words. Lack of confidence had never been a problem for her. She hadn't even started looking yet, but she was certain that she could find Christopher Morgan. It was just a matter of time.

Wednesday morning, the first thing on Shelley's list was a trip to the library downtown. There she got copies of articles on the Morgans that had appeared in the other two local papers and in the San Diego County edition of the *Los Angeles Times*, along with a dozen or so from nationwide newsmagazines.

Back at home, she settled in at her desk, another jazz tape playing softly, and began sorting through the copies, adding them to the ones Brad had given her. There were neat piles—those dealing with his business interests and those of a more personal nature side by side with those covering his arrest. That done, she began reading again, this time taking notes—names, dates, events. Nothing was overlooked, no matter how insignificant it seemed.

She wrote on a legal pad—page after page of scribbled notes. Later she would transcribe them into something neat and legible that made sense. Now she just wanted the information at hand.

Periodically she stopped to think or to rest her cramped fingers. Each time she looked up, the picture of Christopher was in front of her, commanding her attention. It was his eyes that drew her, she decided. They were so dark, so piercing. Compelling. It was as if the picture was willing her to look at it. No matter how she shifted in her chair, his eyes followed her.

What was he like? According to reports, he was a shrewd businessman. Intelligent. Charming. Generous. Loyal to his friends and employees. Honest. Even kind.

Shelley wanted to know more. Was he angry? Bitter? Did he have friends? Could he still laugh and smile? Was he happy? Did he have someone to share his problems, someone to love, or was he alone?

Someone to love.

She turned her chair until her back was to the desk and the picture, bent her head and rubbed her eyes with her hands. The idea of Christopher Morgan in love with some woman was vaguely disturbing, and she found *that* fact disturbing, too. She had no right to care about his personal life. She didn't even know him!

He was the subject of an assignment, and she had to see him as such. Not a man but a name, a photograph, a character in a story that had taken place long ago. Just part of her job.

Hadn't Kevin taught her anything? Getting personally involved—even a one-sided involvement like this—with a man in any way connected with her work was an invitation to trouble. Her friends back in Mobile had tried to tell her that about Kevin, but she had ignored them—and the results had been both predictable and painful. She wouldn't make that mistake again.

Forcing her attention back to the stories on the desk, Shelley read the final articles covering Christopher's disappearance, one printed by each of San Diego's three newspapers. According to the reporters, Christopher Morgan was a broken man, unable to recover from the blows of recent weeks, unable to continue his life in San Diego. "Without a trace" was a phrase that appeared in two of the three stories. She knew better. Wherever Morgan had gone, he had to have money and a place to live. He had to buy groceries, needed to pay for electricity and water, and to own some means of transportation. All of that meant bills, taxes, contact with other people, and anyone who paid bills and taxes and had contact with other people could be found.

Was he guilty? She tried to consider the question coolly, logically. As she'd told Brad in his office, her first inclination had been to believe that he was. After all, the FBI had arrested him, and they seldom made mistakes. Even if they'd made one this time, if he'd been truly, completely innocent, he should have been able to clear himself long ago.

But the more she learned about him, the more certain she became of his innocence. She corrected that: the more she learned, the more she *wanted* to believe in his innocence. She wished she could convince herself that it was the intuitions and instincts of an experienced, well-trained reporter making that decision, but she was very much afraid that it was based on pure emotion.

Logically. Study it logically, she instructed herself. There were three common reasons for espionage: money, ideology and revenge. Shelley suspected that Gary Morgan had done it for the money, although she didn't discount the third possibility. If he had been jealous of his brother, it wasn't unreasonable that he might have tried to jeopardize Christopher's company and possibly even Christopher himself by selling secrets from M.I.'s research.

But Christopher hadn't needed money—he'd been a wealthy man. There was nothing in his background to suggest that he shared the ideology of the Soviet Union, and no reason to believe that he held a grudge against anyone who could be hurt if he sold classified documents.

So logic bore out her emotions—so far. She found that reassuring.

She spent the rest of the day making up lists of people who'd been associated with Christopher in the news stories. Her next step involved finding addresses and phone numbers for them.

At the top of the list was Gabriel Rodriguez. A quick look in the phone book revealed one Gabriel and a half-dozen G. Rodriguezes, but Shelley doubted that any of them were the right one. Most of the policemen she'd known in Mobile had had unlisted phone numbers; Rodriguez probably did, too. But finding him would be no problem. He was a policeman; policemen worked at police stations.

He refused to take her call. The detective she talked to claimed that Sergeant Rodriguez was out, but Shelley had heard a deep voice instruct him to say that. "When will the sergeant be back?" she asked patiently.

"I really can't say."

"If I leave a message for him, will he get it?"

"Yeah, sure," the man said.

Shelley didn't doubt that; Rodriguez was probably sitting right next to the other officer. She repeated her name and that of the paper, then gave her home phone number. Instinct told her that it would do no good. Gabriel Rodriguez wasn't going to call her back. But that was all right. He'd find that she wasn't so easy to avoid.

Rodriguez fit the description that Brad had given Shelley: tall, dark, black-haired. Brad had left out slender, graceful, arrogant and handsome as sin, she thought dryly as he approached.

After his refusal to take her call yesterday, she'd decided that the best way to see him was to catch him at work. It had involved one small deception, giving a false name to the officer at the desk. If Rodriguez wouldn't talk to Shelley Evans of the *Chronicle* on the phone, she doubted that he would talk to her in person. She would soon find out.

"Miss Edwards? I'm Sergeant Rodriguez. They said you wanted to see me."

It was the same voice she'd heard yesterday in the background over the phone—deep, warm, friendly. There was a smile on his lips, polite but rather vague. He was curious about who she was and what she wanted. He was also interested. She saw it in his eyes.

"Yes, I do. But ... my name isn't Edwards. I'm Shelley Evans, and I'm with the *Chronicle*."

The interest immediately disappeared, replaced by suspicion and distrust, and his voice became hard. "What do you want?"

"I'd like to talk."

"I have nothing to say to you."

"How do you know until you hear what I want to talk about?"

Gabriel's eyes narrowed. "You're a reporter. That's all I need to hear."

Where was the charm that Brad had told her about? He was behaving more like the rattler Brad had mentioned, she thought sourly. "Do you dislike all reporters, or is it something about me in particular?"

He looked her over, his gaze moving slowly from head to toe. "I don't talk to reporters. They interfere. They create problems."

"Did they create problems for Christopher Morgan?"

He changed right before her eyes. A stiffness spread through him, and the distrust in his eyes turned to outright hostility. He was cold all the way through.

"You didn't answer my question, Sergeant. Did reporters cause problems for Morgan?"

He walked away from her. Shelley fully expected him to keep walking. She was surprised when he stopped in front of an open door and gestured to her to enter. When she did, he closed the door behind him and sat down at the table that filled the room. She sat across from him, studying him.

The white shirt he wore was brilliant against the bronze of his skin and the black of his trousers. His tie had been loosened, the top button of his shirt was undone and the long sleeves were rolled to his elbows. He looked more like a businessman who had been interrupted at his work than a cop fighting crime.

Amused by her perusal, he waited until she was finished before speaking. "What do you want?"

"It's been almost a year since Christopher's and Gary's arrests. The *Chronicle* is going to run a story about the case—just a brief report on what's happened since then."

"What *has* happened since then?" he asked, sounding lazy and bored.

"That's what I'm going to find out. I'd like to talk to Christopher before I write the story."

"I bet you would."

"You know where he is, don't you?"

He leaned back in his chair. "I know a lot of things."

"And Christopher's location is one of them."

He didn't answer.

"You've kept in touch with him, haven't you?"

He simply looked at her. He didn't flinch, didn't blink, didn't look away. Nor did he speak. It was effective, Shelley thought, his technique of staring coolly at his inquisitor while remaining stubbornly, maddeningly silent.

"Is he still in San Diego?"

"You're from the South."

She nodded once. She never noticed the soft drawl in her voice until it was pointed out by someone. "Do you see him very often?"

"What part?" he asked, ignoring her.

"Alabama. Mobile." She smiled faintly. "If you're going to check with the Mobile police, I can tell you now that I don't have an arrest record. And if you happen to talk to Lieutenant Jackson, tell him hello for me. He's my uncle. Why did Christopher disappear? Did he receive threats on his life?"

"What are you doing in San Diego? You're a long way from home."

She hid her impatience. If he wanted to play games, she could do that, but he wasn't going to distract her from her purpose in interviewing him. "I'm working here. Will you give Christopher a message for me?"

"What makes you think I'll see him?"

"Because you're his friend. Of the entire bunch, you're probably the only real friend he had." She rose from the table. "Tell him that I'd like to talk to him. Tell him about the story. I'd like to hear his side before I write it."

Gabriel watched her walk to the door. He didn't agree to deliver her message, nor did he refuse.

"I *do* have one other question." She paused for a long moment before asking it. "Was Christopher friends with a reporter named Mike Jennings?"

Gabriel's scowl came before he could stop it. Although he said nothing, the grimace was answer enough for Shelley. She nodded once, opened the door and walked away.

So that was why Christopher didn't like reporters. She had thought his statements in Jennings's article were too intimate to be made to a reporter, and she'd been right. He hadn't been talking to a reporter; he'd been confiding in a friend, and that friend had sold him out for the sake of a story. The idea left a sour taste in her mouth.

Shelley Evans. The name sounded...wholesome. Innocent. It sounded so sweet that it didn't even hint of the danger she represented to him.

Christopher Morgan sighed softly. His hand was still on the phone, even though he'd ended the conversation with

Gabriel several minutes earlier. Slowly he drew his hand back and returned to the task he'd started when the phone had interrupted him. He laced the running shoe, tying it tightly but comfortably, then turned to the other one.

Shelley Evans. Brown hair, brownish eyes and freckles. She sounded as wholesome and innocent as her name, but Christopher was certain that the description was deceiving. Shelley Evans was a reporter; therefore she could not be wholesome, innocent, sweet or even human. He would have to do something about her. He couldn't afford one more worry added to the burden he already carried.

He felt as if he had spent most of his life worrying—about himself, Gary, his company. A year ago he had come close to going to prison, where he would have had a whole new set of worries—like staying alive. That was something that Gary hadn't succeeded at. The FBI agents questioning Christopher that day had told him that the makeshift knife had penetrated his brother's heart, that he had died instantly. But Christopher had always wondered about that. Surely there had been an instant—maybe only a second or two—when Gary had realized that he was dying. Had he been scared? Had he been sorry? Had he regretted destroying Christopher's life along with his own? Had he even known that he'd destroyed Christopher?

Why had he done it? What on God's earth had been so important to Gary that he would betray his own country to get it? Money? Christopher would have given him enough to last a lifetime. The thrill of playing spy? The power that came from knowing that he was outsmarting them all— Christopher, the researchers, the security at the plant, the entire U.S. intelligence network?

Christopher would never know.

He walked to the window. All he could see beyond the clearing where the house sat was trees. This house had been his haven when business was booming and his life was full. This was where he came to relax, to unwind, to regain his sanity. Now it was his sanctuary.

Sighing softly, he went out onto the deck. The house had a total of six decks at varying levels connected by stairs and walkways. The highest deck, out of sight on the other side, held the satellite dish that enabled him to pick up more television channels than he could ever watch.

It was time for his run. He laid his towel on the rail, then started down the steps. He didn't bother to lock the door. Up here, miles from his nearest neighbor, there was no need.

Running in the city had been a chore; he'd had to settle for the monotony of a track or take his chances with the traffic and exhaust fumes. But here in the mountains it had become pure pleasure. Months of following the same route day after day had packed the dirt into the hard surface that he preferred. The trail wound through the trees, joined an old dirt road, then disappeared into the trees again, uphill and down. It was ironic that at a time in his life when everything else was a mess, he was in better physical condition than ever before. The hours-long runs saw to that.

He used the time to think, to concentrate on his newest problem. Shelley Evans had to be stopped. After all the months of work that he and Gabriel had done, he couldn't let her destroy things now. But how could he get her out of the way?

When he returned to the house, he'd found no answers but he'd gotten a good workout. He was drenched with sweat despite the cold temperature, and his breathing was labored. For a few minutes every breath he forced into his lungs was painful, but it was a natural pain—a good one, so different from the pain that he lived with every day. He walked slowly around the house, circling it several times, until his breathing slowed and his heart rate was back to normal.

The answer came to him as he stretched the taut muscles of his legs before going inside. He would follow Gabriel's first rule of investigation: look for the obvious. People often overlooked the obvious because it was *too* obvious, too simple. The obvious way to deal with Shelley Evans was the simplest: he would talk to her. He would make a deal with her. He would explain the problems that she was causing him, and he would be charming and persuasive, and she would agree to back off, temporarily at least.

And if that didn't work, he thought with a grin, he'd just out-and-out threaten her.

The numbers were mind-boggling. Whatever else he was, Christopher Morgan had been a financial genius. He hadn't needed to sell out the government, not when he'd made money hand over fist without even trying.

She spent most of Monday morning in the tax assessor's office going over the records for all of the property Morgan had owned in San Diego County. It included the complex of office buildings, two houses, two planes, a helicopter... The list went on and on.

For the first time in a week Shelley began to get discouraged. There was so much information available on Morgan, but most of it pertained to his life before the arrest. None of it would lead her to him now.

Back home, she started calling the people who had bought Morgan's property. From each one she got the same answers. Yes, they had bought their property from Morgan. No, they hadn't met him; they had dealt with his attorneys. No, they had no idea where he could be reached. No, they'd had no further contact with him or his attorneys.

There was one call, one buyer, left. Shelley looked at the name for a moment. Gabriel Rodriguez. He had purchased the mountain property. Sighing softly, she closed the file. Rodriguez would tell her nothing about Christopher Morgan.

The face of the man in her thoughts was in front of her, solemn-eyed. Shelley stared at the photograph. Turning away wouldn't help. She had memorized every line, every detail. If she saw him in a crowd of tall, dark-haired men, she would recognize him in an instant.

"Where are you, Christopher?" she whispered. "Damn it, where are you?"

Slowly rising to her feet, she snapped off the desk lamp, then left the room, closing the door behind her. She was tired and hungry, and there was no food in the apartment. She had neglected to do her shopping, cleaning, laundry— all the little things that were necessary to keep life running smoothly. She had neglected everything but Christopher. It was time to forget him. Time to return to reality.

Christopher parked in a space marked Visitor, shut off the engine and glanced around. The apartment complex was typical of San Diego. In the center, behind a tall fence, were a pool and a Jacuzzi. Mailboxes were in front of the club-house, and garbage Dumpsters were discreetly placed at the ends of the reserved parking lots. The lavish landscaping included tall, spindly pines, ice plants, cacti and shrubs, some as tall as Christopher himself. It looked overdone to him.

Gabriel had gotten the address for him with a warning not to do anything stupid. Aware that his friend would con- sider this visit incredibly stupid, Christopher had said nothing. He wouldn't mention it until later, when it was too late for Gabriel to do anything about it.

The parking space assigned to Shelley Evans was empty. One part of Christopher was relieved; he didn't relish mak- ing deals with a reporter. But he kept walking around the building toward the back. He wanted to make sure that she wasn't home.

Footsteps sounded ahead of him. Reacting instinctively, Christopher stepped off the sidewalk and into the shadows. It was dark enough, and the bushes were thick enough, to provide him with protective cover.

It was a woman. She wore jeans, with a lavender sweater, and her hands were stuck inside her pockets. She walked slowly, her head down, chewing her lower lip. Unaware of him, she walked past, giving him a clear view of her profile.

Lord, she was pretty, he thought, catching his breath. Pretty and slender and soft and delicate.

And he wanted her. The swift, unexpected tightening of his jeans left no doubt about that.

Christopher gave a shake of his head, surprised by his response. How long had it been since he'd looked at a woman with enough interest to notice if she was pretty? How long since he'd touched a woman, held her, kissed her, loved her? How long since he'd wanted to do any of those things? Longer than he cared to admit, which naturally explained why the effect of this woman was so sudden, so strong.

As she passed, a soft breeze picked up the scent of her perfume, carrying it to him. It was light, subtle—a hint, there and gone, of something vague. Insubstantial. Sensual.

He waited until she was out of sight, until the sound of her footsteps could no longer be heard; then he stepped out of his hiding place and went in search of Shelley Evans's apartment.

Number 7C was on the far side of the building, a downstairs apartment. There was a light burning inside, but no one answered his knock. He knocked again and waited a moment before turning away.

He didn't know what drew him to the patio. He had to push his way through more of the tall, thick shrubbery to reach the square cement pad. A gas grill was in one corner, a pastel-blue wire chair with blue pads in another. Next to the screen door was a stack of firewood, recently delivered.

The sliding glass door was locked when Christopher tried it. But it would be easy to open.

He shoved his hands into his jacket pockets. It would be easy, but it would also be illegal. He didn't want to talk to her that badly.

But if he went in when she wasn't there, he could do more than just talk to her. He could see her notes. He could read through everything that she'd found so far, and he could find out just how much of a threat she was to him. He could find out how to handle her.

Christopher glanced around to make sure that no one could see him, then stepped closer to the door. It was a standard sliding glass door. He'd had several like it in his La Jolla house. In fact, it was at his own house that he'd learned how to open this type of door even when it was locked. When the security company had convinced him to add extra security, one of their men had shown him how to lift the door off the track, disengaging the lock. It was quick, easy and left no sign of forced entry.

The door was open before he'd made up his mind to do it. It took a moment for him to realize that he'd done it. Even then he hesitated, unwilling to go inside. He couldn't justify breaking into her apartment...could he?

His search was important to him—for the past year the only important thing in his life. Simply by walking through the open door he might stop this woman from jeopardizing what he had already accomplished. Besides, even though he hadn't set foot inside, if he got caught now, he could be charged with breaking and entering. He might as well commit the crime that he was already technically guilty of. He stepped across the threshold.

It took him a few minutes to replace the door on its track; then he closed and locked it and moved into the living room.

The apartment was quiet. A lamp at the end of the sofa cast soft shadows in the living and dining areas and the kitchen. Christopher curiously looked around.

Shelley Evans was neat. There wasn't a thing out of place except a coffee mug and a spoon on the kitchen counter. The flowers on the dining table were wilted and needed to be replaced, but other than that, the place was in order.

He stepped into the hallway. There were doors at either end and one straight ahead. The one in front of him opened into a large bathroom/laundry room. He checked the one to the right and found a neat, clean bedroom. The door at the other end led into the second bedroom: her office. Using the hall light, he made his way across the room to turn on one of the three lamps, then returned to close the door.

Bookcases, loaded with books, awards and a compact stereo system, filled one wall and part of another. There was a brass daybed with a dark green quilted coverlet and matching pillows beneath the room's single window, with lamps on the wooden file cabinets that served as end tables. The only other pieces of furniture in the room were a leather chair and a desk, large and cluttered with the details of Christopher's own life.

He sat down at the desk and turned on the lamp. A folder on top of the pile of papers read "Property." Inside was the tax information on every piece of property he'd owned. He put it down and reached for the other files, gathering them into a neat stack. Searching through the desk drawers, he found additional folders and added them to his pile.

The photograph above the desk caught his attention, drawing a sardonic smile from him. The date was penciled in the margin. He remembered that night. He'd gone to some sort of charity ball at the Hotel del Coronado with a gorgeous blonde. Although he'd since forgotten her name, he remembered that they'd had a hell of a good time—both at the ball and afterward. It had been one of the last good times in his life.

He took the file folders to the daybed, kicked off his shoes, arranged one of the pillows against the brass arm and lay down. Grimly he began reading.

Shelley was surprised and pleased to find her parking space empty when she returned from the grocery store. She dropped her purse inside one of the grocery bags, then picked them up, closed the car door with her foot and hurried to her apartment. She juggled the two bags while she retrieved her keys from her jeans pocket, opening the door just as one bag fell. Muttering a curse, she grabbed it and took them into the kitchen.

She was putting away the groceries when a sound caught her attention. It was soft, hardly noticeable at this distance, but she knew what it was. She'd spent enough hours stretched out on the daybed when she was tired from working to recognize the squeak of its springs.

Someone was in her apartment.

Fear warred with anger, common sense with righteous indignation. She could be hurt—raped or even killed! But at the same time she was furious that someone had dared to break into her house, to go through her belongings, to violate the space that was her own.

Outrage won out over sense and propelled her down the hall to the office. A narrow line of light showed beneath the closed door, confirming her suspicions. She *knew* she had turned off the lights when she'd left the office earlier. She stopped outside the door and listened. A rustle of papers broke the quiet.

Shelley took a deep breath and pushed the door open. She didn't know quite what she expected to find, but the scene before her wasn't it.

Lying on the daybed, with his shoes off, a pillow beneath his head, and reading her notes, was Christopher Morgan.

Chapter 2

Christopher was as surprised as Shelley. For a moment he stared at her, unable or unwilling to believe what his brain was telling him—that the pretty, slender, soft, delicate woman who had drawn a response from him that he hadn't experienced in months was Shelley Evans. It can't be Evans, he thought irrationally. She's a reporter. How can I possibly want to make love to a reporter?

Shelley moved farther into the room, finally stopping to lean one shoulder against a bookcase. Crossing her arms over her chest in a defensive posture, she studied him.

The first thing she noticed were his eyes. Dark. Intense. Compelling. She looked from him to the picture on the wall, then back. It hadn't been the skill of the photographer or a trick of the lighting. It was real. His eyes were dark brown, almost black, the most fascinating eyes she'd ever seen.

He wore jeans, a dark shirt and a black leather jacket. Expensive leather running shoes had been carelessly discarded on the floor. His legs were long and probably muscular; she remembered reading that he jogged daily. His hands were strong, his fingers slender and brown against the manila folder. By the time her gaze returned to his face, the surprise was gone and there was no emotion there at all. Nothing. She felt cheated by the blankness she encountered.

For a moment curiosity had pushed her anger to the back of her mind, but now it returned, hot and simmering. "What do you think you're doing?" she demanded.

Christopher looked at the folders, then flushed a deep bronze, embarrassed that she had caught him snooping. Now she'd think he was not only a spy, but a common crook, as well. It surprised him that he cared what she thought. Raising his chin high, he chose to ignore the embarrassment and guilt and coolly replied, "I'm reading."

"Find anything interesting?"

"Just you." As he gave the flippant response he realized that it was true. There was nothing in her files that he didn't already know, but Shelley herself... Yes, he definitely found her interesting. Interesting enough to cause an unsubtle change in his body that he hoped would go unnoticed.

He had no such luck. Her eyes moved over him again, noticing the slight tightening of his jeans. Blushing hotly, she looked away again.

"Do me a favor," he said coolly.

She looked wary. "What?"

"Tell me you're not Shelley Evans. Tell me you're her neighbor or her roommate or even her sister. Just tell me you're not her."

"I am," she said flatly.

He grimaced and swore softly. He wasn't prepared for this. Gabriel had described her to him—brown hair, brownish eyes and freckles—but that wasn't this woman. Her hair was brown, soft untamed curls that fell to her shoulders and were touched with coppery tints that gleamed like fire. Her eyes were hazel, the color strong enough to identify even from a distance. Her skin was a delicate gold, several shades lighter than his own, and the freckles were just a light sprinkling across her nose and cheeks.

Brown hair, brown eyes and freckles. How had Gabriel managed to leave out the rest? How had Gabriel—a cop, an investigator trained to notice details—overlooked the fact that Shelley Evans was beautiful?

Beautiful. Sensuous. Highly desirable. Christopher bit off a groan. He moved the files, sat up and swung his feet to the floor. He wasn't any more comfortable sitting up, but at least the position made his arousal less noticeable.

"Now you can tell me something," Shelley said stiffly. "What the hell are you doing in my apartment? You have no right—"

He interrupted. "I understand that you want to talk to me."

"You could have called instead of breaking into my home and going through my desk."

He shrugged negligently. "It was more fun this way. What do you want?"

Shelley pulled the desk chair into the center of the room and sat down before grudgingly replying, "I'd like to interview you for an article I'm writing."

"You're out of luck. I don't do interviews. Why do you want to stir all that up again?"

"My editor asked me to do a story to run on the anni—"

"Anniversary of the great Morgan espionage case," he finished cynically. "Nobody cares anymore."

She leaned forward. Her face was pale, her freckles standing out in stark contrast. "*Don't* interrupt me again," she warned in a tightly restrained voice. More calmly, she continued, "The case was never settled."

The blank mask disappeared, replaced by anger. "My brother is dead, and I might as well be. That seems pretty damned settled to me."

Shelley began chewing her bottom lip. "But your innocence was never proven."

He gave a laugh that was short and harsh. "Nobody's interested in my innocence. Come up with proof of my guilt and you'll have your story."

"Were you guilty?"

Christopher stared at her. She appeared to be serious, ready to believe whatever answer he gave her. But appearances, as the saying went, could be deceiving. "What do you think?"

He had intended it as a flippant remark, expecting no answer, but Shelley gave him one anyway. "I thought you were at first. Now...I think that the only thing you were guilty of was giving love and trust to a man who didn't deserve either."

For the second time that day, Christopher flushed a deep bronze. "Gary was my *brother*," he said in a low, furious voice.

She twisted her hands together in her lap to hide their trembling. "And he was a spy. And one of his last acts in life was implicating you in his crime."

"He didn't do it deliberately. It wasn't his fault that he died without clearing me."

"No. But it *was* his fault that you got dragged into it in the first place, wasn't it?"

She was right, Christopher acknowledged, but only to himself. The evidence against him had been found in the private safe in his office at Morgan Industries: a rather cryptic note from him to Gary; a file of top-secret documents; two computer diskettes containing classified data; and a stack of money. One hundred and twenty-five thousand dollars. Cash.

He could have explained the last three items. As president of the company he'd had the security clearance required to gain access to the research materials, even though technically he should never have been allowed to remove them from the labs. As for the money, he was a wealthy man. One hundred twenty-five thousand dollars wasn't an outrageous sum for a man of his net worth.

But the most damning of all had been the note. He had been setting up a dinner engagement with Gary, he had insisted. More likely an information drop, the FBI had countered, and so they had arrested him. And it had all been Gary's fault. Gary had stolen the documents. Gary had placed them in Christopher's safe, apparently planning to retrieve them later. And Gary had died without admitting to any of it.

Shelley watched anger and frustration cross his face and ran her hand through her hair, then sighed. Making him angry wasn't what she wanted to accomplish. "I'm sorry. He was your brother, and you loved him. It's not my place to make judgments on that."

Christopher gave no response to her apology.

Shelley thought of all the questions that she should be asking, notes that she should be making for use in her story. But there would be no mention of Christopher in the story. She had already decided that. No one would know that she'd talked to him. "You have no right to go through my files. They're private."

Her accusation was all the more effective for the quiet voice she'd used. He lashed out at her defensively. "Prahvate?" he repeated, mimicking her drawl. "You're just a regular little Southern belle, aren't you?"

It wasn't the tiresome but friendly teasing that she was accustomed to, but a harsh taunt that made her flinch. She said nothing, however; anger only made her accent more pronounced.

"Those files are about me," Christopher went on. "If anyone in the world has the right to see that information, it's *me*! You think you're entitled to find out everything you can about me, to strip away every shred of my privacy, and that the information you discover suddenly belongs to you." He held up the files. "Well, lady, this is *my* life!"

Leaving the chair, Shelley went to him, holding out her hand. "Give them to me, please."

While she waited he set the folders out of reach behind him and leaned down to get his shoes. He took his time putting them on and lacing them up before he got to his feet. He was going to walk out and take the files with him. It wouldn't stop her, but she would have to take the time to get new copies of everything, and he needed all the time he could get.

But when he stood up, she was only inches away from him, and he forgot the files. He forgot about everything but her. He could feel the heat radiating from her body, and he could smell her perfume. All he had to do was take one step and they would be touching, her breasts against his chest, her thighs against his. He took that step.

Shelley wanted to back away, but her mind wouldn't give her legs the order. Nothing was working properly; her entire system had gone haywire. "You don't want to do this," she said breathlessly.

"Do what?" Christopher spoke very slowly, very carefully. He was no longer in control. His desire had taken over, and he had to be cautious.

He laid his hands on her shoulders, and Shelley gasped, forgetting what she'd meant to say.

Christopher took a deep breath, letting his eyes close, shutting out her face, then lowered his head, stopping when his mouth was almost touching hers. She thought he was going to kiss her—and was afraid that he wouldn't.

"Stay away from me," he whispered, his words a soft rush of air against her lips. "Quit snooping into my life."

"Christopher..."

She said his name almost without a sound, but he heard it. He felt it. His body tensed in response as he issued a warning. "If you don't drop this, someone's going to get hurt. I don't want it to be me."

"Cooperate with me and no one will be hurt," she said breathlessly.

Cooperate. Work with her—closely. If he did that, she would surely destroy him. "Stay out of my way. Stay out of my life."

He closed the tiny distance between them, let his mouth brush across hers in a vaguely unsatisfying kiss, then walked away. He made it as far as the door before muttering "Oh, hell," and turning back. He wasn't going to see her again after tonight, so he knew he could never make love to her, but he wasn't leaving without a real kiss—just one.

He held her face in his hands, tilting it up to meet his. His lips were soft, his mouth hard, his tongue insistent. "Open your mouth," he murmured. "Let me taste you."

Shelley mindlessly obeyed, allowing him entry. He teased, explored, aroused, stirring a hunger that was new to her, a hunger so strong and powerful that it only faintly resembled the desire she'd felt in the past for other men.

Her breasts were swelling, her legs weakening, heat spreading through her body, when suddenly he released her. Her eyes fluttered open, bringing the hard lines of his face into focus.

"No." He shook his head grimly. "No."

She said nothing. She wouldn't plead. She simply stared at him, her hazel eyes round and solemn.

Christopher shook his head again. He'd been a fool to come here. She was far more dangerous than Mike Jennings could ever be. Mike had used their friendship to betray him. Shelley could use herself—her body, her smile, her touch, her lovely soft voice. He wouldn't stand a chance.

Once more he walked away. Once more he returned. "Get your manager to put some kind of security lock on the patio door," he instructed harshly. "It took me less than five seconds to get in here." Then he was gone, this time for good.

Shelley moved the files he'd left on the daybed to one side and sat down, curling her feet beneath her. Although she was alone in the house, she still felt his presence. She still felt his hands on her face, his mouth on her mouth.

So much for not getting involved, she thought morosely. So much for objectivity.

There were more interviews, more visits to county offices, more reviews of her material. Shelley concentrated intensely on her job, but she couldn't shut out the memory of Christopher's visit. She couldn't forget the desire—hers, so new and so strong, and his, so unexpected. Sometimes when she thought she had her memories under control, the heat would suddenly spread through her, the weakness would return. It was driving her mad.

She now knew more about Christopher Morgan than about anyone else she could think of. There was enough information in her files for her to write a book about him without consulting any other source. She could recite his life history from memory. But she didn't know where he was living or whether he was trying to find the man behind his brother's death. She was frustrated and irritable and all the more determined to find out the truth.

That determination took her back to the police station one bright, cool afternoon. She didn't think that going inside would accomplish anything this time; Rodriguez would probably ask for a description before he agreed to talk to any woman about anything.

So she waited in the parking lot at quitting time, her hands inside her pockets, sunglasses hiding her eyes. She saw Gabriel the minute he stepped outside, but she made no move toward him until he was only a hundred feet away.

When he spotted her, he stopped walking. The two men with him glanced curiously at her, then back at their friend. "Trouble?" one of them asked. Shelley recognized his voice as the man she'd talked to on the phone the previous week.

"No. You guys go on. I'll meet you later." Gabriel warily approached Shelley, a scowl darkening his eyes. "What do you want?"

"Where is Christopher Morgan?" she asked bluntly.

"I don't know."

"You're lying."

"What if I am? You can't prove it."

"You told him that I talked to you."

"Who says?"

"He did."

Gabriel looked skeptical. "Yeah, sure. I suppose next you're going to tell me that he called you."

"No." She waited a minute for effect, then continued. "He came to see me. He broke into my apartment."

Gabriel winced. He should have known better than to give Christopher her address. He should have known that he'd do something reckless.

"Where is he living?"

"I told you, I don't know."

"I'm not giving up. I'll find him, either through you or on my own."

"Don't count on it, Miss Evans." Gabriel gave her a sardonic smile. "You're not that smart or that good."

The wind blowing in off the bay was chilly, making Shelley shiver. She huddled deeper into her jacket. "Is he here in San Diego?"

She got his usual response—a silent stare.

"You're helping him hide," she continued confidently. "That's obvious. My uncle the lieutenant says the obvious solution is often the right one. He says the best place to hide something is in plain sight. Where would that be in this case?"

Gabriel's reaction was swift—a flare of anger tinged with fear. It came and went so quickly that Shelley was certain she was mistaken, because an instant later he was smiling. "Then maybe your uncle the lieutenant can come out here and help you look. You need *somebody's* help—and you aren't getting mine." Still smiling, he turned and walked away from her.

She stubbornly followed him. "What's wrong, sergeant? Are you tired of talking to me?"

"You bore me, asking the same questions over and over. Can't you think of any new ones?"

"Nope. Sorry."

"You'd make a lousy cop."

She smiled faintly at the disgust in his voice. "But I'm not a cop. I'm a reporter—a good one. And I keep asking the same questions because you're not answering them."

He whirled then, glaring down at her. "I *have* answered them! *I don't know!* I don't know where Christopher is, where he's living or what he's doing! Now please leave me alone!"

She glared just as fiercely, not the least bit intimidated by him. "You're lying," she accused in a steely voice.

Gabriel bent until he was only inches from her face. "If you don't stay away from me, finding Christopher will be the least of your problems. I'm going to make your life hell. You'll wish to God that you'd never heard of me. Do you understand that?"

Resisting the urge to shrink back, Shelley held her ground, even managed a cool smile. "Your threats don't scare me, Sergeant."

Gabriel smiled, too. It was a truly pleasant smile that made his reply seem all the more ominous. "They're not threats," he disagreed. "They're promises."

She watched him walk to a steel-gray Mazda, a low, sporty RX-7. "Sergeant?" she called.

He fished the keys from his pocket and unlocked the door before looking up at her.

"I'm going to find Christopher."

His eyes narrowed. "Good luck." Under his breath, but loud enough for her to hear, he added, "You'll need it." He gracefully slid his long frame into the car, closed the door, started the engine and roared out of the parking lot.

Shelley watched until he was no longer in sight. *Had* that been anger and fear in his eyes? It had disappeared so quickly, and the smile that had replaced it had been genuine. It was hard to tell. If it had been anger, exactly what had she said to cause it?

She didn't have much time to speculate on it. It took only a few minutes to drive from the police station to the *Chronicle* offices, where she had an appointment with Brad Davis. She went to his office, settling herself into the leather chair in front of his desk while he completed a phone call.

"Thanks for coming, Shelley," he said when he got off the phone. "How's it going?"

"Slowly."

"Problems?"

"The man doesn't want to be found. If he would just cooperate, I'd have it made."

Brad laughed. "Having a tough time?"

"I've checked every place that I can think of. I've talked to just about every single person in the city of San Diego who knew Christopher Morgan. I've talked to Gabriel Rodriguez twice—not that it did any good. I just don't know where to turn."

"You haven't found out anything?"

Shelley hesitated. The words she was about to say seemed, in some odd way that she didn't understand, like a betrayal. It was ridiculous—she hardly knew Christopher. She owed him nothing. She owed Brad, on the other hand, a great deal. "I saw him, Brad. I talked to him."

"You're kidding." He looked both surprised and pleased. "You *are* good, aren't you? What did you find out?"

Briefly she told him about Christopher's visit, leaving out large portions of it. "He doesn't want anyone snooping around. He doesn't want anyone drawing attention to him because..." She paused to remember the correct words. "Someone's going to get hurt, and he doesn't want it to be him."

"That's what he said?" Brad considered the words for a minute. "You're on the right track, Shelley. He's trying to find the guy who got Gary killed."

"But I'm no closer to finding him than I was when I started."

"We still have time, Shelley. Don't get discouraged. In the meantime..." He glanced at his calendar. "I'd like to have a story from you for the Sunday paper. Nothing too elaborate—just something to jog the readers' memories."

"Okay." She rose wearily from the chair.

"Go over all your notes again, Shelley. Sometimes you overlook something that doesn't seem important at the time, and later you find out that it's the key you need."

"Thanks, Brad."

She returned to her apartment to follow Brad's suggestion. The place was quiet. It was always quiet, she thought morosely as she settled on the daybed, the folders in her lap. Unless she turned on the stereo or the television or spoke her thoughts out loud, there was no sound to disturb the silence. No conversation. No laughter. No tears.

Wearily she opened the folder. She had no time for self-pity. She would read over her notes and lose herself, as she'd done so many times before, in the life of Christopher Morgan. Maybe Brad was right. Maybe she had overlooked something.

A detailed study yielded nothing. By supper time Shelley was too tired to read any more. She stopped long enough to eat a frozen dinner, then dragged her typewriter from the closet and began typing a record of her earlier conversation with Gabriel.

What could have made him angry, even for an instant? She studied the transcript, which was accurate as far as she could remember, looking for a clue to his puzzling response. When she found it, she stared at the typed line for several long minutes. Could it be that simple? That obvious?

Her last words to Rodriguez before he'd walked away had been, "...the best place to hide something is in plain sight. Where would that be in this case?" There had been that flicker of emotion in his eyes, then a friendly smile—almost too friendly, she thought now.

What *would* be "in plain sight" in this case? Rodriguez's house? The presence of a reclusive roommate might be hard to explain to friends and lovers, and Shelley didn't doubt that Rodriguez had plenty of both.

Christopher's own house? She discarded that idea, too. The sales of his property had been well documented, and she had talked to the new owners of his La Jolla house, an elderly couple who spent winters in La Jolla and summers in Vancouver. She couldn't imagine them offering refuge to a man with Christopher's problems.

That exhausted her ideas. He certainly wasn't living in the building that had housed his office, or in one of the planes he had owned, or on the yacht that had been sold and moved to Florida, and that was the extent of his property, except for the house he'd sold to Rodriguez.

Shelley groaned aloud. How obvious could it get? She had found out about the sale of that property to Rodriguez at the beginning of her search, and she had written it off as unimportant because Rodriguez was his friend and wasn't going to help her. She hadn't questioned him when she'd questioned the rest of the people who had bought property from Christopher; she hadn't even bothered to copy down all the information available on the mountain house once she'd found out that Rodriguez had been the buyer.

Smiling broadly, she put the files on the floor and lay down on the daybed, folding her hands across her stomach. "Thank you, Uncle Randall," she said aloud. "I owe you one for this."

A trip back to the tax assessor's office the next morning proved her theory. The mountain house and the accompanying acreage had been sold to Gabriel Rodriguez two weeks after Gary Morgan's death for a price far below market value. Shelley's first thought was that maybe the sale was legitimate; Christopher had supposedly lost everything when the company went under. Maybe he'd needed cash right away.

But he'd been a brilliant businessman. He was too smart to lose his personal fortune along with the company. He would have kept his own assets separate. Maybe, for reasons of his own, he wanted people to believe that he was bankrupt, but Shelley didn't believe he was, not for a minute. Besides, if he'd needed money so badly, he could have held out until a real buyer came along and gave him market value for the land. That would have been enough to tide him over for a few years.

With the use of maps and the numbers assigned to the property, Shelley was able to pinpoint exactly where the land was located: a few miles north of the small town of Santa Ysabel. After thanking the clerk with a cheery smile, she returned home, sat at her typewriter and quickly wrote the story that Brad had requested. The words flowed easily, smoothly. She was pleased with the result.

Now she could get on with more important things.

The mountains northeast of San Diego were a beautiful place to take a leisurely Saturday drive, Shelley decided after making her third wrong turn. She really wasn't in any hurry to see Christopher.

It was such a ridiculous lie that she laughed aloud. All she'd thought of since the night he'd broken into her apartment was seeing him again; she'd even had a few dreams about it. Not that she was expecting him to greet her happily. She wasn't hoping for miracles.

At last she found the driveway that she was positive led to the house marked on her map by the obliging clerk in the assessor's office. She'd been this way once before, going in the opposite direction, but she'd driven past the narrow dirt road without even seeing it. After driving ten miles out of her way, she'd finally admitted that she'd missed her turn, backtracked around and had gone straight to it.

The driveway climbed steeply, disappearing into the trees. Shelley drove slowly, listening to the grinding of the engine as the car labored up the hill. She estimated that she'd driven over a quarter of a mile when she came upon a sturdy gate that blocked the road. Bringing the car to a stop, she turned off the engine and climbed out.

Poor Christopher, she thought as she locked the car, then shrugged into her jacket. If he thought that locked gate was going to keep everyone out and guarantee his privacy, he was sadly mistaken—as he would soon find out. Tugging gloves onto her hands, she grasped the top bar of the gate, climbed onto the second bar and lifted herself over, landing lightly on her feet.

The bumpy dirt driveway climbed a steep hill, the gate and the highway disappearing from sight within a few hundred feet. The trees on both sides met overhead, blocking the rays of the sun. It was colder at the higher elevation, making Shelley wish that she'd brought a heavier coat, but the exertion of the walk soon had her warm enough.

She was out of breath when she reached the top of the hill. That made it harder to gasp at the view before her, but she managed anyway.

Below her, a valley dipped low, so that she could look straight across to the other side. A small area in the center had been cleared; though the driveway disappeared in the trees, a blue pickup showed that that was where it ended. The house that sat in the clearing was impressive, blending into its setting with its clean lines and natural materials. The wood exterior was cedar, the fireplace stone. There were lots of windows, large, to admit light, but designed to hold heat in winter and cool air in summer. Decks circled the two-story structure, leading from one level to another and back again with steps, ramps and walkways.

No wonder Christopher had wanted to keep this house, she thought appreciatively. In the middle of her search she'd gone to his multimillion dollar home in La Jolla. As beautiful as it was, it didn't begin to compare to this place.

She started down the hill, moving into the cover of the trees again. It was about the same distance from the crest of the hill to the house below as it had been up to the top from the highway, but going downhill made it seem so much shorter. She was at the house in minutes.

Her knock at the front door brought no response. She went around to the side, where steps led to the first deck. The glass door there was unlocked when she tried it, but she didn't go inside. She noticed a towel draped over the railing, and, remembering that Christopher liked to jog, she sat down on one of the benches to wait. He would be back soon.

Christopher cut his daily run short, walking the last half mile to the house. He was tired. Restless. He had been feeling that way for days, and for days he'd been denying the cause, hoping it would go away if he ignored it. But he wasn't doing a very good job of ignoring it, and it wasn't going away. If anything, it was getting worse. He didn't like that. He didn't like not being in control.

He reached the house and, head down, began climbing the deck stairs. He was almost at the top when he became aware that the towel he'd left on the railing was dangling in front of him. His head jerked up, seeking and finding a serious pair of hazel eyes.

Shelley looked for anger or hostility. She saw neither, just an intensity that made her shiver.

After a moment he reached for the towel, momentarily catching her hand in his grip. He felt the tension in her, even through her heavy knit gloves. She was as disturbed and unsettled as he was.

It hadn't gone away, he realized in dismay—the restlessness, the uneasiness. The need. The simple touch of his fingers on her hand indicated that. The heaviness in his loins confirmed it.

Keeping his face expressionless, he released her hand, pulling the towel through her limp fingers. He dried his face with it before draping it around his neck. Then, after looking at her for another long, silent moment, he spoke.

"What are you doing here?" His voice was as flat and empty of emotion as his face.

Shelley moved safely away, back to the bench where she'd been sitting. She pushed her hands into her coat pockets, leaned against the railing and rested one foot on the bench. She was stalling, using the time to regain control of herself, to carefully pitch her voice so that it wouldn't quaver when she spoke, to empty her eyes of the desire that she knew must be there. At last she looked at him. "I came to talk to you."

Christopher easily lifted himself up to sit on the railing. Like her, he propped one foot on one of the rough cedar benches. The position bent his leg and helped conceal his desire. He could handle conversation. As long as she stayed clear across the deck from him, as long as he couldn't touch her or smell her perfume or feel the heat of her slender body, he could listen to the soft, seductive sounds of her voice without being driven to anything rash—he hoped. "And what do you want to talk about?"

"You."

He smiled faintly. "I thought I made it pretty obvious that I'm not interested in talking to you."

She took a moment to look at him. Even in loose-fitting, black sweatpants and a sweat-stained, gray T-shirt, he looked incredibly appealing. Handsome. Sexy. Slowly she smiled, too. "You made several things pretty obvious," she said coolly, reminding him of the desire he'd been unable to hide—had made no effort to hide.

Christopher flushed, and he silently cursed her. She was giving him nothing but trouble—interfering with his work, with the task he'd set for himself—and pain, the pain of intense, burning, unrelenting, unfulfilled desire. After seeing her, he couldn't forget her. After kissing her, he couldn't stop wanting her. She filled his dreams at night and commanded his thoughts during the day. And, damn her, she had no right!

She was calm and serene and so damned beautiful, and he was aching all the way down to the soles of his feet. He struck out at her in defense, in a merciless attempt to protect himself. "Don't flatter yourself," he said harshly. "It's nothing to do with you. When a man goes without a woman as long as I have, anyone will do. You just happened to be available."

Stung by the sharp words, Shelley bit the inside of her lower lip. His remarks hurt more than they should have—further proof, if she needed it, that she was too deeply involved. She had warned herself for days, but it had obviously done no good. Now the best that she could hope for was to keep him from seeing her pain. "Thank you for setting the record straight," she responded, forcing as much sarcasm into her voice as she could manage. "I could say the same about you. You just happened to be available."

Christopher's smile turned ugly. "Yes, you could, couldn't you?" he agreed. And if she did, he'd kill her, right there on the deck, he decided.

"But I'm not going to lie," she continued. "I liked kissing you. I liked touching you."

It was a powerful stimulus to hear this woman about whom he'd fantasized say that she liked touching him. It sent a surge of desire racing through him that not even the loose-fitting sweatpants could disguise. He pulled the towel from his neck, wiped his face, then dropped it across his thigh for a little added camouflage. "What do you want?" he demanded hoarsely.

She could answer that question so many ways, she thought with a touch of longing. She had the feeling that none of the answers would please him. "To talk. To find out what you're doing."

His dark eyes filled with suspicion, and he looked from her to the door. He had been focused so entirely on his needs and desires that he'd forgotten more important matters, like the records in his office—records that a reporter would probably sell her soul to see. "Did you go inside?" he demanded.

Shelley looked puzzled. "No. I wouldn't just walk in when I didn't even know if I had the right house."

He didn't believe her. Cursing viciously, he sprang to his feet, jerked the door open and disappeared inside. After a moment she followed him through the living room and down the hall to a room that was apparently an office. She stopped in the doorway and watched him gather half a dozen loose sheets of paper from his desk and stuff them into a file folder.

She knew what they were immediately. One part of her cursed her stupidity in not realizing that the records she needed to prove Christopher's activities would be inside. The stronger part knew that she didn't want this story badly enough to sneak into his house while he was away and snoop through his office.

When he saw her standing at the door, he scowled. "Get out of here!" he snarled.

Turning quickly, she returned the way she had come. Although she was cold, she didn't stop in the living room with its fire but went back out to the deck. She walked to the railing and crossed her arms over her chest.

Without seeing one single paper, she knew that Brad had been right. Christopher Morgan was trying to find the man behind Gary's murder.

She stared out at the trees, barely seeing them. Christopher was trying to prove his innocence. He was trying to clear his name. To find the man who had drawn Gary into the world of espionage and had ordered his death. It would be a hell of a story. But what would she have to do to get it?

Christopher opened the drawer where he kept his files and stared. Nothing had been disturbed. Every piece of information that he and Gabriel had dug up on Gary was in this desk—files, statements, records, interviews, photographs—and none of it had been disturbed.

He didn't know what to make of it. Shelley Evans, a bright, ambitious reporter, had tracked him down and come to his house—and had sat on the deck in the cold waiting for him to come home, passing up the perfect chance to search the house and find a gold mine of information. Why? Was she too naive to know that he'd have this lying around? Hadn't she had enough time? Or was she simply not as devious as he'd assumed all reporters were—as he himself was?

Damn her, she had no right coming here. How could he possibly forget how much he wanted her when she was right there with him?

"Who are you kidding?" he asked miserably. He couldn't forget her when she *wasn't* with him. He couldn't forget that he wanted her—wanted to make love to her. Wanted to learn her body intimately, to learn what pleased her, what excited her, what tortured her with pleasure.

He wanted to be her lover—in every sense of the word.

He had to remember that she was a reporter. A reporter, damn it! A female Mike Jennings.

But it was hard when there were other things about her that he preferred to remember. Like her beauty. Her lips. Her breasts. Her hips. Her voice. He remembered the way his name had sounded in her soft, honeyed drawl. Even her voice was erotic.

Taking a deep breath for courage, he left the office, locking the door behind him. He didn't have a key for it, but he'd learned long ago how to open it with a paper clip. Slowly he walked down the hall, expecting to confront Shelley in the living room.

The room was empty. He went to the glass door, swinging it open. Shelley was standing at the railing, staring out.

"Shelley."

He spoke so quietly that for a moment she wasn't sure she'd really heard him. Then she turned and saw him standing there.

"Come inside. It's warmer in here."

Catching her lip between her teeth, she shook her head.

"Stop biting your lip. You're going to make it bleed." He impatiently stepped out onto the deck. "I'm tired and sweaty, and I'll be damned if I'm going to stand out here in the cold. If you're going to talk to me, you're going to do it inside."

Reluctantly she walked across the deck and through the open door. When she passed him, her delicate scent filled his nostrils. The fragrance had haunted him for days, had tantalized him through restless nights. It made him think of heat, of lust and desire. Of long intimate nights and slow, passionate loving.

He reached out to her, his hand resting on her shoulder, trapping strands of her shoulder-length hair beneath it. It was soft. So soft. Her body would be soft, too—soft and yielding, accepting and welcoming the hard strength of his.

Shelley turned her head to look at him. The action tugged at her scalp until he raised his hand enough to free her hair. When her gaze met his, she saw that the emptiness was gone from his eyes. They were dark, almost black, shadowy, glazed. He wanted her. Despite his assertion on the deck that any woman would do, she knew that he wanted *her*. She wondered if he could see the answering desire in her own gaze.

He reached down to unzip her jacket. Beneath it she wore a mint-green shirt that clung to her torso until it disappeared inside her faded jeans. His eyes flickered to her face, then down to her breasts.

Shelley couldn't move, anticipating his next move. Her breathing was rapid and shallow, and her heart was pounding so hard that she imagined she could hear it.

Slowly, deliberately, he put his hands on her waist. Inch by inch he moved them upward, smoothing over the fabric of her shirt, avoiding the buttons, finally stopping when each one was cupped gently over a small, rounded breast.

He rubbed his hands back and forth, swallowing a groan when he felt her nipples grow hard against his palms.

She waited breathlessly, but he did nothing more. Calling upon all his strength, he removed his hands and walked away.

Shelley was bewildered and disappointed by his response. She knew he wanted her, and she'd made it clear that she felt the same desire. So why was he turning away?

He glanced at her face, seeing her confusion. He wondered if it would make her feel any better to know that he was equally confused. "What was it that you wanted?"

"Wh-what?" She wasn't able to shift mental gears as quickly as he could. She was still aroused, still feeling the warmth and strength of his hands on her breasts, still wanting him.

He sat down in a nearby armchair. "You said you wanted to talk to me. About what?"

She stood still for a minute, breathing deeply, wishing that the color that had suffused her cheeks would disappear. When she turned, she saw that Christopher had settled deeper in his chair, his feet propped on the coffee table. His attitude reminded her strongly of Gabriel Rodriguez—relaxed, comfortable and even a little bored—and it angered her. Slowly she walked toward him, taking a seat at the end of the sofa nearest him.

"How nice that I was 'available' for you again," she said, the sweetness in her voice unable to disguise the steely hardness of her anger.

He used one foot to pry off a shoe, then reversed the process. The shoes thudded dully to the floor. "You came here of your own free will," he said with a shrug. "I didn't invite you."

"I didn't invite you to touch me."

He smiled sardonically. "No, but you certainly enjoyed it."

"So did you." Shaking her head, she said softly, "You're an arrogant bastard, Christopher."

"At least we agree on something."

"Are you afraid of me?"

Her question made him smile faintly. She was such a slender, delicate-looking creature. How could he possibly fear her? he wondered, then answered his own question. Because she could control him. She could capture him in her spell and make him love and want and need her, and she could betray him. "I'm not afraid of you, Shelley. I just don't trust you."

"What would it take for you to trust me?"

He could tell by the tone of her voice that the conversation was no longer personal. This wasn't Shelley Evans the woman asking—although he'd bet that she was interested in his answer—but Shelley Evans the reporter. Stubbornly he shook his head. "I can't."

"Why not?"

"You're a reporter."

"I'm not like Mike Jennings."

He had expected to hear that. With all the snooping she'd done into his life, she had to know about Jennings.

"You might *have* to trust me, Christopher." She spoke softly, but he detected the warning in her voice. "I know that you're trying to find the man responsible for Gary's spying."

His mouth thinned into a narrow line. "Do you have proof?"

"No," she admitted. "But I don't need it."

He admitted nothing—but, more importantly, he also denied nothing. "What is it that you want from me?"

"I want to work with you."

The room was quiet as he stared at her. A log in the fireplace crackled and hissed, then fell with a great shudder.

"You want to...work with me." Christopher repeated her words slowly, then smiled. "I hate to tell you this, but my company went out of business a long time ago. I haven't worked since then."

She wasn't amused. "You don't lie as well as Rodriguez does—and he isn't very convincing, either."

"I don't know what you're talking about," he insisted. "I'm not working at anything."

"I'm willing to make a deal with you. If you let me help, I won't write one word about you until it's all finished."

"Until what is all finished?"

Shelley hesitated, studying him. Reaching a decision at last, she stood up, pulled a folded paper from her coat pocket and offered it to him. "Read this."

As she sat back down again, he unfolded it and skimmed the printed words. His eyes grew almost black, and his jaw was tightly clenched by the time he finished. "This is garbage." He wadded the paper in a tight ball, took aim and sent it sailing into the fireplace. He knew she had other copies, but he took pleasure in watching it burn anyway.

"It's going to appear in tomorrow's *Chronicle*. I can stop it if you'll cooperate with me. Give me something to tell my editor and he'll pull it."

His eyes, intense and critical, met hers. "Why are you so interested in what I'm doing? You never met Gary, you don't give a damn about me—what's in this for you?"

Shelley looked at him sadly. She *did* care about him, but he would never believe that—not coming from a reporter. "It's a story," she said tiredly. "The story of your arrest got a lot of attention. If you find the man who was behind it all, if you can prove that you were innocent... It could be a very important story."

"And you say you're not like Jennings." His lip curled in disgust. "I don't give a damn what you do, just stay away from me, all right?"

"Christopher..."

He steeled himself against the soft drawl. How could one word make him want her so damned much?

"If that story runs tomorrow, it's going to stir up the past. You want secrecy so you can accomplish whatever it is that you're doing. Just let me help. That's all I'm asking."

Christopher didn't argue with her, although secrecy wasn't the reason behind his demand for privacy. He knew that most people believed that the combination of his arrest, Gary's death and the bankruptcy of Morgan Industries had left him a broken, defeated man. He preferred to let that image stand. A defeated man posed no threat to anyone—especially Gary's boss.

He stood, moved the few feet to the sofa and pulled her up. Holding tightly to her arm, he dragged her down the hall to the front door. "Go away," he ordered. "Leave me alone. Get out of my life."

"Damn it, Christopher!" Shelley wanted to cry. She'd never met a more stubborn, or more frustrating man. Why couldn't he see that she was being honest, that she only wanted to help? Why couldn't he trust her?

"Like I told you before, if you don't drop this, someone's going to get hurt. If that story runs in tomorrow's paper, that someone is likely to be you." He jerked the door open and literally shoved her onto the porch.

She tried once more. "Christopher, please..."

He yelled then, making her cringe. "Get out, damn it! Just get the hell out of my life!"

Shoving her hands into her pockets, she walked away with a hurried grace that made him ache as he stared after her. Only when she'd been swallowed up by the trees did he turn away and close the door. A moment later he slammed his fist against it.

Chapter 3

Shelley stayed home Sunday, waiting for the visit that she knew would come. She cleaned the apartment, did her laundry and listened for the ring of the doorbell. When it came, she was prepared.

Christopher was leaning against one of the posts that supported her upstairs neighbor's porch. He was calmer than he'd been when she had left his house yesterday. He was staring down at the ground, but he slowly lifted his gaze when she opened the door. "Can I come in?" He sounded subdued. Beaten.

Stepping back, she let him enter. She closed the door, then gestured to the sofa. "Sit down."

He looked around the living room. It was small, with barely enough room for the sofa, upholstered in soft shades of rose and cornflower blue, an oversize rocker of gleaming pine, a couple of small pine tables and a set of low shelves that held a television, a stereo and stacks of tapes. There were baskets filled with flowers, green leafy plants, soft pillows in shades to match the sofa, and a large hand-quilted wall hanging over the fireplace. It was a comfortable room. Cozy, intimate. Graciously, serenely soft. Like Shelley.

He chose to remain standing. "I read the paper."

She crossed to the dining table and moved a flower in the arrangement there. "I didn't think you were here because you wanted to see me." There was an embarrassingly obvious note of longing in her voice. She was grateful that Christopher pretended not to hear it.

"Why did you do it?"

She was puzzled. "Run the story? You left me no choice."

"You could have rewritten it. You could have mentioned the times we've talked. You could have mentioned that I'd broken into your apartment." Slowly he met her eyes. "You could have told them where I live."

She lifted her slim shoulders in a shrug. "What would that have accomplished?"

Christopher's response, before he looked away from her, was also a shrug. Looking into her eyes was difficult. Since he'd seen the story in the *Chronicle* that morning, he'd had the strangest sensation of betrayal. It was ridiculous, he knew. Shelley Evans owed him nothing. She had even gone out of her way to give him a chance to stop the article, and she had deliberately withheld information that her editor would probably consider vital to the story. Still he felt . . . cheated.

Shelley shifted uncomfortably. "If you had agreed to let me work with you, I could have gotten Brad to hold off on printing it," she said softly. "But I had to have something to give him—some concession, some bargain. You gave me nothing."

He didn't respond to her quiet statement. Acknowledging that he'd made a mistake would settle nothing.

"Would you like something to drink?" she hesitantly offered. "I have some coffee on the stove."

He shook his head and started toward the door.

"Christopher?"

He stopped, holding the door open, and looked back at her, still avoiding her eyes.

"I'm sorry." She wasn't certain what she was apologizing for—wasn't even certain that she owed him an apology—but the words had come out of their own accord.

"So am I." He left, closing the door quietly behind him.

Shelley sank down in the rocker. Seeing Christopher like that—quiet and defeated—doubled the feelings of guilt that had plagued her since she'd opened the *Chronicle* and found her story. She had asked him for trust, for cooperation, and then she had, in some way that she didn't even understand, betrayed him.

"You can't betray his trust when you never had it," she scolded herself aloud. Gloomily she added, "And now you'll never get it."

Christopher rarely went to Gabriel's apartment under the best circumstances. Today, with Shelley's article, accompanied by a photograph of him, on every newsstand in the city, he didn't dare visit his friend at home. He called Gabriel instead and they met at a park near Gabriel's Mission Valley apartment.

Gabriel was sitting on a concrete picnic table when Christopher arrived. He stood up, brushing off his jeans, and faced his friend. "It wasn't a bad story."

Christopher looked sourly at him.

"It could have been worse."

Christopher shrugged. "It could have."

It was a bright fall day, with a chilly wind blowing in from the ocean. The park was almost empty, but Gabriel cautiously took note of the few people there as he and Christopher walked along the cracked sidewalk. Christopher was normally as alert and observant as Gabriel, but today Gabriel noticed his friend's mind was elsewhere.

"I got the impression when you called that you weren't too surprised by the story," Gabriel said.

Christopher pulled a pair of dark glasses from his pocket and put them on. For protection from the sun? Or to keep Gabriel from reading his eyes? He didn't want to consider the answer. "She found me."

He said it so quietly that Gabriel wasn't sure he understood. He stopped walking and stared at Christopher's back. After a few paces Christopher also stopped, turning to face Gabriel. He knew then that the glasses were for protection from his friend. He needed to hide the emotional turmoil Shelley Evans had stirred in him.

"*She?* Shelley?" Gabriel's voice cracked with disbelief. "Shelley Evans knows where you're living?"

Christopher nodded glumly.

"When...? How...?"

"She was waiting at the house yesterday when I got back from my run. I don't know how." It seemed strange now that he'd forgotten to ask such an important question. But he'd been too busy looking at her, wanting her. The part of him that needed her had been too grateful that she had found him to wonder how she'd done it. "She gave me a copy of the article."

"Why?" Gabriel was dazed. He felt incapable of speaking more than one word at a time.

"She wanted to make a deal. She said that all she wants is the whole story. That if I would let her work with us, she wouldn't run the article today. I told her no. I lied and pretended not to know what she was talking about." Christopher sighed and ran his hand through his hair.

Privately he had to admit that a story wasn't *all* she wanted. She wanted him, too—for what, or for how long, he didn't know. The desire was easier for her to hide, but he'd recognized it in her eyes. It was the same look he knew was in his own eyes every time he saw her... every time he heard her voice or even thought about her.

"You should have dealt with her." There was no censure in Gabriel's voice, simply a statement of fact. If Christopher had asked Gabriel for advice yesterday, he would have said make the deal. Do whatever is necessary to keep her quiet. "Now you have to anyway."

Christopher's eyes widened. Now he *had* to? He had to cooperate with her? Had to work with her? "But she's already written her story," he protested.

"She's written *a* story—not the one she wants. She knows where you live, Christopher, and she knows what we're trying to do. What's to stop her from writing another story for next Sunday's *Chronicle* talking about that?"

Christopher hated to admit it, but Gabriel was right. He should have dealt with Shelley yesterday, in time to stop the article from being printed but, foolishly, he hadn't. Now he had to go to her, had to offer her anything she wanted. Had to offer his cooperation.

"I don't think I can do it."

Gabriel didn't look at him. "You have to. You don't have much choice. You've got to check out that club on Shelter Island—what's the name?"

"Impressions." Christopher said it with a scowl. A trendy little name for a trendy little club. The kind of place that he hated but had apparently appealed to Gary.

"She can help you with that. You won't have to tell her much—just enough to keep her satisfied. What do you say?"

Christopher considered Gabriel's suggestion. Hours every day in the close confines of a car with Shelley—and worse, long, dark evening hours with her, too. He groaned aloud. She would drive him crazy long before he ever found out who had killed his brother. Crazy with irritation...and crazy with frustration. With longing. With wanting. He'd have to be a fool to agree to anything that meant time spent with her.

To himself, he said no way in hell. He said Gabriel must be insane. Aloud he said, "All right."

In silent accord they turned and started back down the sidewalk to their cars. When they reached them, Gabriel unlocked the RX-7's door while Christopher pulled out his keys to the blue Ford pickup. Before climbing in, Christopher turned to ask Gabriel one last question. It was a revealing one.

"Why didn't you tell me how pretty she is?"

Gabriel grinned. "Is she? I didn't notice. Call me later."

Christopher scowled as Gabriel drove away. He started the engine and pulled out of the parking lot. Delaying the inevitable return visit to Shelley's, he turned toward the interstate and Shelter Island. Toward Impressions.

He'd driven by the club only once before, preferring to avoid the place until it was time for the surveillance. It was sandwiched between two private yacht clubs on the long, narrow island. The parking lot, fortunately for them, was located in front, with plenty of bright lights to aid in their nighttime surveillance.

Them. Their. He was already thinking in terms of a partnership. He supposed that was necessary for success—if Shelley made a deal with him, she would expect him to honor his end completely—but the last person in the world he wanted a partnership with was her. He didn't see any way that he could spend time with her without becoming lovers, and there was no way that being lovers with a reporter could be at all good for him.

After leaving the island he drove toward Shelley's apartment. Following the most circuitous route he could think of, he finally reached it around five o'clock that afternoon.

Just as she had earlier, Shelley found him leaning against the support post when she opened the door. He looked uncomfortable, and his greeting was hesitant.

This time she wasn't so quick to invite him inside. "Hello," she responded, leaning one shoulder against the door. She waited for him to make the next move.

He put his hands in the pockets of his black leather jacket as he moved away from the post. "You look surprised to see me."

"I thought you'd said all you had to say this morning."

"Not quite." He quickly looked away as her neighbor came down the stairs, clumping heavily. The man glanced disinterestedly at them as he walked by. "Do you want to talk business out here where your neighbors can hear?" Christopher asked sharply. "Am I supposed to trust all of them, too?"

Shelley stepped back, making room for him to enter. He looked at the sofa, then the rocker, and chose a wooden chair at the dining table. Shelley pulled out the chair across from him and sat down.

"You don't trust me," she said flatly. "I don't think you trust anyone except Gabriel and yourself."

"Maybe," he admitted. "But Gabriel says I have to work with you." He shrugged out of his jacket and arranged it over the back of the chair. Shelley watched his graceful, muscular movements, thinly veiled by a black pullover sweater. The single button on the placket of the sweater was undone, revealing wisps of curling black hair.

To distract herself from the sight, Shelley left the table and went into the kitchen, taking two glasses from the cabinet. "Do you always do what Gabriel tells you to?"

"In this case, yes. He spent six years with navy intelligence, and he's been with the San Diego PD for nine years. He knows a hell of a lot more about this kind of stuff than I do."

She filled the glasses with ice and carried them and two cans of soda to the table. "What kind of stuff?"

He accepted the glass and can that she offered. "Are you angry with me, or do you conduct all your interviews in this tone of voice?"

Heated blood rushed to her face, hiding her freckles. "I'm sorry. I guess I am a little irritated with you for making me feel so damned guilty when it was *your* fault the story ran."

"Okay, so I screwed up yesterday. Everyone's in agreement on that, so let's drop it. I came to tell you that you can work with us. I'll 'cooperate.'" He gave a sarcastic flavor to the final word, emphasizing the number of times he'd heard it from her. "Do you know where Shelter Island is?"

She shook her head. "But I have a map. I can find it."

"How long have you been in San Diego?" He didn't try to hide the criticism in the comment. Just what he needed— a partner who couldn't find her way around town without a map.

"About six weeks." She flushed again, but less brilliantly. "I've been working since right after I got here. I haven't had much time to get familiar with the city, okay? But I will. Where is this place?"

"Forget it. I'll pick you up in the morning at about ten-thirty."

"What's on Shelter Island?"

He stiffened. Gabriel had said that Christopher only had to tell her what she needed to know, but that was going to be harder than he had expected.

"I'm not asking why we're going there," she said, reading him correctly. "I just wondered what's there. Restaurants? Boat docks? Marinas?"

"All of the above. Look, we need to set up some rules." He cupped his hands around the glass, interlocking his fingers. "First, you can't ask any questions. Gabriel or I will tell you what you need to know. If we don't tell you, you can't ask."

Shelley bit her lip. Telling a reporter not to ask questions was like asking a bird not to fly. How could they possibly expect her to work with them day after day and not ask any questions?

Maybe they didn't. Maybe this was Christopher's way of making sure that she'd fail to keep her end of the deal; then he would have a legitimate excuse for not working with her.

"All right," she agreed. She would stick to the rule if she had to tape her mouth shut to do it.

"Rule number two: you can't tell anyone what we're doing. Not even your editor. If you say anything to anyone, that's it."

Another rule designed to make her fail, Shelley acknowledged. He probably hoped that if she refused to tell Brad anything, the editor would pull her off the assignment. She would just have to find some way to let Brad know that she was doing her job without letting him know exactly *what* she was doing.

"All right."

"Rule number three..." Christopher paused to take a long drink from his glass. He was making the rules up as he went along; he and Gabriel hadn't discussed what kind of "deal" they were willing to make.

Shelley sat back in her chair and quietly watched him.

"Rule number three... Would you quit looking at me that way?" he asked, sounding exasperated. It was hard enough to concentrate on their bargain without her watching him with a gaze that was soft and serious and faintly longing. Hungry.

"What way?"

His fingers tensed, and he carefully set the glass down, then clasped his hands together beneath the table. "The way I usually look at you," he replied in a taut voice. "We have to work together, but surely we aren't stupid enough to get involved with each other."

"What's wrong with friendship?" she asked softly. In her lap, her own hands were twisting tightly together. She knew that he was right—an affair with him *would* be stupid, but that didn't stop her from wanting it.

"Friendship?" he scoffed. "We're not talking about friendship here. I don't take my 'friends' to bed, but that's sure as hell where I'd like to take *you*."

She smiled faintly. "I'm surprised to hear you admit it. You're back in the big city, Christopher. I'm not the only woman available this time."

He should have known better than to lie to her yesterday. Availability had nothing to do with it, and she knew it. He would want her whether she was the only woman around or simply one in a crowd. "I don't want an affair with a reporter.'' There. That much, at least, was true. However much he wanted Shelley, he would never willingly choose a reporter for a lover. ''Willingly'' was the key word. If Shelley decided to seduce him, when his own body was already betraying him with the intensity of its need, he wouldn't have the will to say no.

Shelley nodded once. Considering his past experience with Mike Jennings, she could understand why he didn't want to get involved with a reporter again, especially not intimately. It didn't make her feelings any easier to deal with, but at least she understood. ''Okay, so what's rule number three?''

His mind went blank for a moment. At last he said, ''Rule three is that I can change the rules as I see necessary.''

She smiled at his arrogance. ''All right. But you can't change rule number four.''

''And what is that?'' he asked suspiciously.

''I get the story. When it's over and you've got the guy, I get an exclusive. You have to talk to me before you can talk to any other reporters.''

''All right,'' he agreed grudgingly.

''Do I get that in writing?''

He scowled fiercely. ''You can trust me.''

''Can I? You're a suspected spy.'' She went into the kitchen and began removing food from the refrigerator. ''People who refuse to give trust can't go around demanding it of others. Do you want to stay for dinner? I'm having steak, cheese-stuffed potatoes and sautéed mushrooms.''

Christopher looked at the thin gold watch on his wrist. It was almost six and already dark outside. If he left now, it would be about seven-thirty before he got home, and dinner would be a hamburger and fries from the McDonald's in Ramona.

Shelley waited for his response, hoping her desire for a positive answer didn't show. In the six weeks since she'd moved to San Diego she had eaten every single meal alone.

Company—especially Christopher's company—would be nice, but she wouldn't plead for it.

"Sure," he said with a shrug. "Why not?"

It wasn't the most gracious response he could have given, but Shelley didn't mind. It would be good not to be alone tonight.

He moved into a different chair so he could watch her work. He didn't offer his help in preparing the meal; the kitchen was small and would be crowded with two people. Besides, he had a much better view from the dining table than he would have in the kitchen.

Shelley worked quickly, acutely aware of Christopher's gaze on her. After she'd seasoned the meat and put the potatoes in the microwave, she began washing the mushrooms with a damp cloth.

He left the table then and went into the living room, switching on the lamp at the end of the sofa. A copy of the *Chronicle* lay on the table. Scowling, he picked it up and opened it to Shelley's article, printed on page B1 in the space generally reserved for Brad Davis's editorial.

"What Ever Happened to Christopher Morgan?"

His scowl deepened. Although she'd used the phrase in her article, he would bet that she hadn't chosen it as a heading. It sounded like some low-budget TV special or cheap scandal sheet story.

Remember the days when you couldn't pick up a newspaper without finding some mention of Christopher Morgan? He filled the business section, amazing us all with the phenomenal success of his Morgan Industries. His handsome face graced our society pages as he attended the parties of the social elite, frequently giving spectacular bashes himself, belonging to all the proper and socially acceptable clubs and organizations. We even saw him in the sports pages when the Thoroughbreds he owned were tearing up the racetrack at Del Mar. He was the darling of San Diego's chic set—every man's friend, every woman's dream.

He was the man who had it all: a multimillion-dollar home; a mountain retreat; a garage filled with luxury cars; two planes—one a Lear jet—and a helicopter; a yacht; those above-mentioned Thoroughbreds; a near-priceless art collection. He had expensive tastes paid for by a corporation based in San Diego with interests throughout the Southwest. A corporation that dabbled in a little bit of everything: real estate, computers, construction, mining, defense research—and espionage. Christopher's brother Gary was an accused spy. Christopher himself is a suspected spy.

Was he guilty? The FBI thought so, but couldn't prove it. The business community was convinced of it. His contracts were pulled, relations broken off. Many of his friends were also convinced. Within hours after the story broke, there were few people left in San Diego who would admit to friendship with Christopher Morgan. But was he guilty? Did he sell out his country? The one man who could clear him—his brother Gary—is dead, murdered in jail the day following his arrest. Of course, Gary's KGB contact knows the truth, but we'll never hear from him.

What ever happened to Christopher Morgan? The accusation of espionage cost him his multimillion-dollar company. No charges were brought against him, but his arrest was enough. It took him twelve years to build Morgan Industries into one of the top companies in the southwest. It took doubt, suspicion and distrust only days to destroy it. The companies are defunct; the buildings, the houses, the cars, the planes, the helicopter, the yacht, the horses, the valuable art—all have been sold. He lost it all.

Was he a spy? Did he betray his country? We'll never know. Christopher Morgan dropped out of sight almost a year ago and hasn't been seen in San Diego since. Where has he gone? What is he doing? How does he live?

What ever happened to Christopher Morgan?

Christopher sighed and replaced the paper. Gabriel had been right. The story could have been much worse. She could have written that *she* had seen him since his disappearance, that *she* knew where he was living and what he was doing. Considering that any story was bad, this one wasn't *too* bad.

Shelley opened the drapes and undid the new lock on the patio door. Outside, she lit the gas grill, then stepped back in and closed the door. She noticed that Christopher had laid the paper aside, tilted his head back and closed his eyes. Biting her lip, she went into the living room to sit down at the opposite end of the sofa. "It wasn't so bad, was it?"

He admitted to himself that she probably hadn't done any damage with the article, but he said nothing to her.

Shelley was disappointed. She wanted him to say that it was all right, that he appreciated the fact that she hadn't told everything she knew. She wanted to hear anything that might ease her undeserved guilt.

"I don't want people to realize that I'm still around," he said slowly. "I want to remain forgotten. If anyone thinks of me at all, I want them to think of me as... impotent. Harmless."

"Well, that's too bad," she said hotly. "You should have known that someone would remember that all this happened a year ago this month. You should have worked more quickly so that it could all be finished before now."

Christopher opened his eyes. A grudging smile touched his lips. "Go ahead and say it. I should have 'cooperated' with you yesterday, right?"

Her smile also came unwillingly. "Yes," she agreed. "You should have. And quit making fun of me for using that word. Cooperation is very important to reporters. Otherwise we'd never find out anything."

"Would that be so bad?" he asked dryly.

"You can't deny that there are things people need to know." Her voice was soft and accusing. "Not everyone is one hundred percent trustworthy."

"No, of course not. But *you* can't deny that a lot of stuff gets passed off as news that isn't. A lot of what's printed or broadcast is gossip, and a lot is just garbage. Whose business is it if this senator is sleeping with someone other than his wife, or if that actor died of AIDS, or if this ballplayer uses drugs? Where is the public's right to know that information?"

Shelley shrugged. "All right, so there are times when we go too far. But the good things outweigh the bad."

"Obviously you yourself have never been the victim of the bad," he said bitterly. "You claim to be society's watchdogs, but who's watching you?"

"Do you want to talk about Jennings?" she asked bluntly.

He withdrew from her. Not physically. He made no outward movement, but it was a withdrawal all the same. "We agreed on no questions," he reminded her flatly.

"You resent me because I'm a reporter, and you resent reporters because Mike Jennings was one. Hasn't it ever occurred to you that what he did was unethical?"

"I didn't know you people had ethics."

"Your brother was a businessman. He was also a spy. Therefore, using your reasoning, all businessmen are suspect because they might also be spies. Mike Jennings was unethical and unworthy of your trust, and he was also a reporter, so we're all unethical and can't be trusted."

"You're being ridiculous," Christopher muttered, turning away.

"I'm not the one writing off an entire segment of the population as worthless on the basis of the career they've chosen." She rose gracefully from the sofa and went into the kitchen.

Logically, Christopher knew that she was right. It was unfair to condemn someone simply because of the job he did. But logic had little to do with emotion. Emotion reminded him of how easily Mike Jennings had betrayed him and how deeply it had hurt. Emotion warned him that a betrayal by Shelley could hurt far more.

"How do you like your steak?" Shelley asked, pausing in the open door.

"I'll cook them." He joined her at the door, taking the platter and tongs from her. "How do you like yours?"

"Rare." She watched him go to the grill; then she closed the door and returned to the kitchen. She scooped out the insides of the potatoes, whipped them with grated cheese and milk, then restuffed the skins. After they went into the oven to brown, she melted butter in a skillet, then tossed in the mushroom caps.

They ate at the dining table, sitting across from each other and rarely speaking. Shelley knew that their earlier discussion still bothered him, so she didn't press him for conversation.

Christopher disliked the silence. It gave him too much time to think, too much time to feel. If she were talking, he'd have to concentrate on her words and not on his feelings. "Why did you come to San Diego?" he asked abruptly.

Shelley considered the question. She could give him any number of answers: there was no career advancement for her in Mobile; she'd been restless and had wanted to live in some other part of the country; the situation with Kevin had become intolerable. "When Brad Davis offered me a job, I was ready for a change. I'd lived all my life in the same city. I wanted to go someplace else."

Christopher pushed his plate forward a few inches so he could lean his arms on the table. "You spent... How old are you?"

"Thirty-one."

He looked her over again. He wouldn't have guessed she was anywhere near that. It was the freckles and the smile that made her look younger, he decided. "So you spent thirty-one years in the same place, and out of the blue you decided to move to the other side of the country. I don't believe that."

"People don't ever get restless? From what I remember reading, you were none too settled yourself until a few years ago. You divided your time among the cities where Morgan Industries had offices—San Diego, Phoenix and Albuquerque."

He ignored that. If she knew that he'd traveled a lot, then she knew that most of it was business related. "Do you have any family?"

"My parents still live in Mobile."

"Friends? Lovers?"

"I have friends there."

He noticed that she neglected to answer the second question. "You must have had lovers. At least one or two."

Shelley busied herself with clearing away the dishes. When she reached for Christopher's plate, he caught her wrist and held her still.

"You aren't a virgin." He was positive of that. The response she'd had to his kiss, to his caresses, wasn't that of a woman without experience.

"No, I'm not. Are you?"

He smiled sarcastically when he realized that she was serious. "Is that any of your business?"

"No. And my... sexual experience is none of your business, either."

His thumb moved slowly over her wrist. The bones were delicate and small. His fingers easily encircled them. "Yes, it is."

She pulled, freeing herself from him. "We have to work together," she said sweetly, repeating his earlier words, "but surely we aren't stupid enough to get involved with each other. Would you like something else to drink, or a piece of cheesecake?''

He could have held her, could have made her stand there next to his chair where he could feel her warmth and smell her perfume and feel the contact of his fingers against her skin, but it would have been an incredibly stupid thing to do. So he let her go.

He agreed to a cup of almond-flavored coffee and a slice of cherry-topped cheesecake. While the coffee perked, Shelley cleaned the kitchen, rinsing their dishes and stacking them in the dishwasher, and Christopher watched her.

How many lovers had she had? he speculated. The conversation had made her uncomfortable, making him suspect that a man had been involved in her decision to leave her home and come to a strange city where she knew no one. Had she loved him? Had he loved her? What had he done to make her go so far away? Had he hurt her?

Christopher's expression grew grim. Whatever had happened was none of his business. He had no right to ask. He had no right to care. But when she joined him at the table again he *did* ask, because he *did* care. ''What was his name?''

Shelley was occupied with neatly slicing into her cheesecake with the edge of her fork. When at last she looked up, her face was blank. ''Whose name?''

''The man you ran away from.''

''I didn't run away from anyone.''

''You left home because of him and came here. It looks like running away to me.''

''I didn't ask for your opinion,'' she responded coolly. ''Besides, you shouldn't be making judgments when you don't know the facts.''

''So tell me the facts.''

''Let's talk about you,'' she suggested. ''Let's talk about *your* old lovers.''

''You can't ask me questions,'' he said smugly.

"This is supposed to be a partnership," she reminded him. "Sharing. Giving and taking. If I can't ask you anything, then you certainly can't ask me anything."

That was exactly the way Christopher wanted it. He didn't want to know about her personal life; he might find out that he liked her, that she was nothing like Mike Jennings after all. And he didn't want to share information about his own life with her, for fear that it would end up in another front-page newspaper story. After all, how did he know she wasn't just holding back until she learned more, waiting until she had all the facts before she betrayed him by telling all she knew?

Since this was exactly what he wanted, he should be satisfied. But he wasn't. "What is it you want to know about my old lovers? And I warn you that every one of them would resent being referred to as old."

Shelley sipped her coffee, stalling for time. She didn't want to know about his lovers, about the women with whom he hadn't thought involvement was stupid. She didn't want to know what, besides the fact that they weren't reporters, made them different from her. "It's almost eight o'clock. I don't have time to hear it all tonight."

Christopher smiled. *All?* He'd had lovers, but not many. He'd preferred long-term relationships to brief affairs, so he could count his lovers on one hand. Shelley obviously expected more than that.

"You'll have time tomorrow," he told her, rising from his chair. He set his dishes on the kitchen counter, then slipped into his jacket. "I'll be here at ten-thirty sharp."

"I'll be ready."

At the door he turned to look at her, then grinned. "So will I." Bending down, he kissed her. It was brief, just to see how quickly the heat would come. In an instant he was burning. "Thanks for the dinner," he said; then he disappeared into the darkness outside the pool of light from the bulb above the porch.

Shelley slowly closed and locked the door. She checked the sliding glass door to make sure that it was locked, too. It was. Christopher had secured it when he'd come in from cooking the steaks.

The apartment was empty, its silence broken only by the sound of the dishwasher. Shelley sat on the sofa, her feet drawn beneath her. Tomorrow they would start their partnership. Tomorrow he would tell her at least part of what they were doing. Tomorrow he would ask her once again about Kevin and would expect her to ask about his lovers.

The dread of the last fact canceled the anticipation of the first two. Tomorrow, she felt sure, was going to be a very long day.

True to his word, Christopher arrived at exactly ten-thirty. Shelley was waiting, her dark green corduroy jacket hanging over the arm of the rocker, covering her handbag with the small notebook inside.

As they walked along the sidewalk, Christopher gestured to the Porsche in her parking space. "Reporting must pay pretty well," he commented.

Shelley smiled tautly. "It's okay." Then she pointed. "The red Trans Am over there is mine. The Porsche belongs to the idiot upstairs. He's got two of them, and he's afraid that if he parks one in the visitor spaces, like he's supposed to, someone might dent it."

"So you let him park in your space."

"I don't *let* him," she said defensively. "If he comes home when I'm gone, he parks there. There's not a whole lot I can do about it, besides complain, and that doesn't seem to do much good."

There was something that *he* could do about it, Christopher thought grimly. He didn't like seeing someone take advantage of someone else. One quiet, forceful conversation with the man should solve the problem.

Mentally he pulled in the reins. This wasn't his problem to solve. When Shelley got fed up with being a sucker day after day, she could raise hell with the manager until he took action. Christopher wasn't involved, and he should keep it that way.

He unlocked the passenger door of the truck. Shelley smiled when she saw it. According to the records, he'd owned a Porsche, a Mercedes and, for a short time, a Ferrari. The truck was a poor relation of those fancy sports cars.

As he climbed into the driver's seat, Christopher saw her smile and knew the cause. "You've seen my driveway," he said as explanation. "My cars were okay in good weather, but when it rains or snows, I need this truck."

"When it snows?" Shelley stared at him. "You get snow up there?"

"Occasionally. Not as much as you'll see at the higher elevations, but we get some." His smile was cynical. "You were in such a hurry to get away from Mobile, Alabama, that you didn't bother to find out much about your new home, did you?"

She didn't want to talk about her reasons for leaving Mobile, so she pointedly ignored the question. "Where is Shelter Island?"

"On the bay."

Stubbornly, she waited for more of an answer.

"It's at the north end of San Diego Bay. It's pretty small—long and narrow. You'll see all you could ever want to see of it in the next week or two."

"When do I find out what we're doing?"

Now it was his turn to ignore the question. He pretended to concentrate on his driving, but traffic on the freeway was light, and driving San Diego's freeways was second nature to him, anyway. He could put her off now, but when they reached Shelter Island he would have to give her an answer. He hadn't yet decided what to tell her. He would prefer to say nothing, but she wouldn't be satisfied with that. He would have to give her some answers.

Shelley accepted that he wasn't going to respond, so she turned her gaze out the window. "What are those pink buildings?"

"The Navy hospital. Balboa Park and the San Diego Zoo are over there, too, and downtown San Diego is on the left." He glanced curiously at her. "Have you been to the zoo yet?"

She shook her head. "I haven't had the time to go anywhere. I've been working ever since I got here."

"All work and no play..." He let the words trail off. Old clichés weren't necessarily true. He certainly couldn't find anything the least bit dull about Shelley. Just the opposite—he found her an interesting woman. A *very* interesting woman.

It was ten minutes before eleven when they reached the island. Christopher found a parking space near the end of the lot in front of the club, where shrubs provided a screen of cover for the truck but left them a clear view of the building's doors.

"Impressions." Shelley read the name from the unlit neon sign that spread across the front of the building. Her opinion of it was clear in the softly mocking tone of her voice. "It sounds..."

"Tacky."

She laughed. "Why are we here now? I thought places like this didn't open until evening."

"This one opens in eight minutes. They serve lunch and dinner. Things like hamburgers with avocado and Swiss cheese, or bean sprouts and yogurt, or tofu." His voice was dry with distaste.

"I take it Gary used to hang out here." Shelley shook her head. "You two weren't much alike, were you?"

He stared out the window, seeing his reflection in the glass. "No," he answered softly. "I guess we weren't." They'd been brothers, and Christopher had loved Gary deeply, but they hadn't shared much in common. There had been a side to Gary that he'd never really known.

He reached behind the seat to pull out an aluminum case. Inside were two camera bodies and a variety of lenses, flashes and filters, plus a bag filled with rolls of film of various speeds. "In the glove compartment there are a notebook and a pen and a pair of binoculars. Would you get them, please?"

Shelley did as he asked, laying them on the dash between them.

"I'm going to take pictures of the customers," he explained as he selected a camera and a telephoto lens. "I want you to keep track of them, the time they arrive and the time they leave, what kind of car they're driving and the license plate number, if you can get it."

"Do you want me to number them to match the pictures?"

He nodded without looking up from the film he was loading.

"You've done this before." When he glanced sharply at her, she bit her lip, then went on, "It wasn't a question, just an observation."

Christopher sighed. "Gary spent most of his free time with a woman, or else at a health club, a bar not far from his house, or here. We've already checked out the woman, the health club and the bar."

"If you don't find anything here . . . ?"

"If we don't find anything here, we'll keep looking. He had to meet the man who got him started spying somewhere. Maybe not here, but he's got to be around somewhere. I'm going to find him."

The determination in his voice made her shiver. She would hate to have him coming after her with that much anger. It was all the more dangerous because it was a cold anger, fed by a year of hatred, bitterness and sorrow. Unlike a hot fury that would burn itself out, this anger would endure, growing stronger and colder and harder until it was appeased.

At precisely eleven o'clock a man inside the building unlocked the front doors. A few minutes later the first customers began arriving, and Christopher and Shelley went to work.

The busy hours for lunch were from eleven to one. After that, the flow of new customers slowed to a trickle. Christopher loaded a new roll of film, then separated the exposed rolls from the unexposed ones. That done, he glanced at Shelley. She had removed her shoes, turned sideways in the seat and tucked her feet beneath her as she leaned back against the door, using her jacket as a cushion. She wore navy corduroy slacks and a pale blue sweater, and the look in her eyes was intensely curious.

"You're awfully quiet."

She smile faintly. "I can't ask any questions."

"No, you can't." He settled more comfortably in his seat, depending on her to tell him if any customers arrived while he was looking at her. "But you can answer some."

Immediately on guard, she looked away. "Questions about what?"

"You."

"You don't want to know anything about me."

"Why not?"

"Because you'll find out that I'm just a normal, average person. You'll probably even like me a little, and it's hard to keep accusing me of being like Mike Jennings if you like me."

Her guess was so accurate that Christopher fell silent for a moment, unable to think of a response. At last he said, "I liked Mike, too, but that didn't stop him from being a bastard."

"Some people are just that way."

He silently agreed. Some people were just naturally bastards, and others were just naturally nice. Was it possible that Shelley fell into the nice group, or somewhere in between? He really wanted to know. He needed to know.

He laid the camera on the seat between them and shifted positions, causing the vinyl to crackle. He flexed his fingers and rolled his head, stretching the tight muscles in his neck.

He felt restless. Caged. He needed to move, to take action of some sort. He was familiar with the feeling—he'd experienced it on his other surveillance jobs—but this time he had company. He had Shelley to keep him occupied.

"What was his name?"

She slowly turned the pages of the black leather notebook, pretending that she hadn't heard him. Occasionally she added a note to one of the entries or retraced a line while she tried to find an answer that would stop his questioning once and for all without telling him anything.

Christopher raised his hand from the steering wheel and reached out to lift her chin. "What was his name?" he repeated softly.

"Kevin." She looked up at him, her eyes guarded. "Kevin Hayes."

"Were you in love with him?"

"This is none of your business."

"Yes, it is." Everything about her was his business. "How can I decide whether to trust you if I don't know anything about you?" Without waiting for a response, he asked his question once more. "Were you in love with him?"

"Yes."

He removed his hand from her face, replacing it on the steering wheel. That was the answer he'd expected, but not the one he'd wanted to hear. He glanced back at the club for a moment, then straight ahead. So Shelley Evans was in love. With another man. Lord, he hated that idea.

Shelley sat straighter in the seat. Because Christopher wasn't watching the building, she had to, but to see it she had to look at him. It was difficult to concentrate on a pile of concrete and stucco when his near-perfect profile was in her line of sight.

She had lied to him. She never would have gotten involved with Kevin if she hadn't cared deeply about him, but no matter what she'd thought at the time, she had never loved him. She had never loved any man, she had come to realize, except for the love of a daughter for her father. Kevin had been her coworker, her friend, her lover, but with the newfound clarity of a woman who was at last coming to know her own heart, she knew now that he had never had her love.

"Did he love you?"

She smiled faintly. "Kevin never talked much about his feelings, but I think 'lust' describes them more accurately than 'love.' We had an affair. That's all."

Just an affair—an affair that had driven her two thousand miles away when it had ended, Christopher scoffed skeptically. "What happened?"

"We had a fight, and he began seeing another woman. They got married."

She said it simply, unemotionally, but Christopher was reading between the lines. "You must have loved him deeply if you left town to avoid seeing him."

"That's not why I left," she answered honestly. "It didn't bother me to see him. In fact, we worked together. He was in the office every day."

His brow wrinkling into a frown, he asked, "You didn't leave Mobile because of him?"

"He was one of the reasons, yes, but it wasn't because I was hurt or didn't want to see him."

"Explain."

The simple, terse command irked her, but she obeyed nonetheless. "When I started seeing Kevin, he was just another reporter, like me. Shortly after he married Rhett, he was made editor—my boss. We got along okay, but Rhett knew that we had dated, and she didn't like the idea of us working together, so she started badgering him to fire me. I don't know why she thought I was any sort of threat to her. She's really pretty—slender, with blond hair and blue eyes."

Christopher's eyes were narrowed. She talked about the other woman as if beauty was something that she herself lacked. Was she really unaware of just how pretty she was?

"She's a *real* Southern belle, too fragile and helpless to take care of herself. She needed Kevin," Shelley continued.

"Weak."

She looked at him. "What?"

"Not fragile, not helpless, but weak. Rhett is weak, and if that's the kind of woman Kevin wants, then he must be weak, too," he said derisively. "Rhett. What kind of name is that?"

"A good Southern name. Haven't you read *Gone with the Wind*?" Shelley teased. "I don't know any Scarletts, but I went to school with a couple of Ashleys and Mellies, and then there's Rhett. Anyway, she wanted Kevin to fire me, but he couldn't do it without cause, since I'd been there longer than him and the owner of the paper liked me. So he started a campaign to force me to quit. He began finding fault with the stories I wrote—claimed that he had to re-write too many of them. Then I began missing deadlines. I'd turn my stories in with time to spare, but they would somehow just disappear—it was easy enough for him to lose them. After that, the stories that normally would have been assigned to me started going to other reporters, people with less experience and less talent. I was covering garden club meetings and writing wedding announcements when Brad Davis called and offered me this job."

"And you took it."

She shrugged. "There was no future left for me in Mobile. Eventually I would have been forced to quit. Kevin left me no choice."

"If his wife didn't want you two working together, why didn't *he* quit and find a new job?" It seemed like the sensible approach to him. Why should Shelley have been punished simply because she'd used poor judgment in her choice of lovers?

"Because getting a new job would have meant starting all over—finding a job, moving to a new city, probably going back to being just a reporter instead of an editor. They would have had to leave their families and give up their social status and all the things that are important to Rhett.''

''So instead *you* had to find a new job and move to a new city and start all over.'' Christopher looked at her. ''What about what's important to you? Didn't that matter?''

That was antagonism in his voice, Shelley realized with surprise. She had been afraid that he would be scornfully amused by her tale about Kevin; instead he sounded resentful of the way she'd been treated. ''No,'' she said simply. ''Not to Rhett and not to Kevin. I didn't mind very much. I was ready for a change.''

''Why didn't you fight him?''

''Because I couldn't win. He was setting me up with the rewrites he claimed he had to do and the missing stories. Sooner or later he would have been able to fire me with no questions asked. I didn't want to wait around for that.''

Christopher noticed a car pulling into the parking lot, and he picked up the camera, focusing on the man who got out. Shelley wasn't weak, he thought grimly, but in her own way she needed someone to take care of her as much as Rhett Hayes did. She needed someone to stop people like her selfish neighbor and her obnoxious former boss from taking advantage of her. She needed someone to care for her.

And Christopher needed to be the one to do it.

Chapter 4

"Are you hungry?"

Shelley considered the question briefly. "Yeah," she replied with a faint smile. "I am."

"There are some fast-food places on Rosecrans. Why don't you go and get us something?" He saw the blank expression that crossed her face. "Go back the way we came on Shelter Island Drive. Rosecrans is the main street."

"Okay. What are you going to do?"

"I'll wait across the street." He gestured toward the wide strip of yellow grass growing between the street and the bay.

Shelley nodded, offering the notebook to him. He accepted that, picked up the camera, opened the door and got out. "You do know how to drive a standard."

She slid beneath the steering wheel and grinned wickedly at him. "I'll learn."

Warily he studied her before deciding that she was teasing. Reaching into his front jeans pocket, he pulled out a twenty. "Be careful," he said as he handed it to her. He watched her drive away before he crossed the street and sat down.

He was glad that she was gone, so he could be alone, but he missed her already, before the truck was even out of sight. The realization that he wanted more from her than sex, that he wanted to be more to her than just a lover, was troubling. Having an affair with a reporter would be imprudent. Falling in love with one would be incredibly stupid.

So how did he stop it from happening?

He took a few photographs and made corresponding entries in the notebook. Shelley's notes filled the previous pages. Her handwriting, smooth, flowing strokes, reminded him of her. Neat. Pretty. Delicate. His scrawl looked worse than usual in comparison.

Activity at the club was slow in the afternoon hours, giving Christopher time to consider his problem: how did he stop himself from falling for Shelley? Finally he decided that he didn't really have a problem. His feelings for her were confused and intensified by his desire for her and by the fact that he'd gone so long without a woman. Once he made love to her and satisfied that desire, he would find that he cared no more for her than for any other woman. He had to believe that. He *had* to.

Christopher alternately watched the building, the road that provided access to the island and his watch. When half an hour passed with no sign of Shelley, he swore softly. When another thirty minutes had passed, he seriously considered finding a pay phone and calling Gabriel to see if his friend could take the time to find her. Then he saw the familiar blue truck round the curve and pull into the parking lot.

"Where the hell have you been?" he demanded, pulling the door open.

She looked sheepish. "I—I got lost. I missed the turn and ended up at some navy base, and the guard at the gate had to tell me how to get back here. I'm afraid the food's a little cold. I'm sorry." She moved across the seat, leaving room for Christopher to climb inside.

"Just what I need, a partner who gets lost every time she goes someplace alone," he muttered as he accepted his change, followed by the food that she handed him.

His grumbling made her stiffen. "I will learn my way around," she said defensively. "It just takes time."

They ate in silence. Shelley was used to quiet meals, since she usually ate alone, but even so, she wished Christopher would talk. She wanted to hear the sound of his voice, but he remained silent, seemingly unaware of her presence for long periods of time.

Business at the club picked up in the early evening hours. As darkness settled over the island, Christopher changed to 1000 ASA film, using the faster speed to compensate for the lack of light. Shelley scribbled her notes by the glow of a small flashlight he kept beneath the seat and squinted through the binoculars, using the illumination from the parking lot lights to read the license numbers of the cars driving past.

Its headlights shut off, a car glided to a stop behind them. Its occupant got out and walked around to the passenger side of the truck, pulling the door open. Christopher jerked around at Shelley's startled cry, then smiled as she fell backward into Gabriel's arms.

"You should lock the door when you lean against it like that," Christopher said mildly. To his friend he said, "I didn't expect to see you tonight."

Gabriel grinned. "I thought I'd see how alert you are." He held Shelley until she was able to slide into the center of the seat; then he climbed in next to her and closed the door with a quiet thud. "Seen anyone interesting?"

"No."

"How long have you been here?"

"Since they opened at eleven." Christopher glanced at his watch. It was almost eight o'clock. No wonder he was so tired. "Did you just get off work?"

"Nah. I was on my way home from dinner with Lori. They're raiding a place over in O.B. tonight, so our date got cut short when she got called out."

Shelley sat in the darkness between the two men, listening silently. O.B., she remembered from one of her study sessions with the San Diego map, was Ocean Beach. Lori, she assumed, was also a police officer.

Gabriel slid his arm around Shelley's shoulder. "How are you two getting along? I wasn't really sure you'd be able to stand an entire day with him."

His action didn't go unnoticed by Christopher. Neither did Shelley's response as she edged slightly away from Gabriel and closer to Christopher.

"It's been all right," she replied softly.

Gabriel chuckled. "Well, listen, why don't you guys go on home? I'll take over here for a couple of hours."

"That's all right." Christopher glanced back at the lighted building. The neon sign was on, its combination of pink and aqua and green looking garish in the dark night. "You can take Shelley home, though."

"Do you want to go home now?" Gabriel asked.

Shelley glanced at Christopher. All she could see was his profile. It was too dark in the cab to make out his expression, but his voice had been flat, uninterested. She was reluctant to choose. On the one hand, she was very tired, and her eyes were aching from the strain of trying to see and read and write by too little light. She could think of nothing nicer than her warm, softly lit apartment, some dinner and a cup of hot coffee. On the other hand, she'd come with Christopher, and she was supposed to be working as his partner. She would really prefer to stay until he was ready to leave. But if he wanted her to go...

"I don't think she trusts me," Gabriel said, laughing softly. "Hell, Christopher, Lori's not going to be finished until sometime around midnight. I've got nothing else to do. You guys go on. You must be tired."

"All right." Christopher reached around Shelley to get the aluminum camera case. He handed it, the camera, the binoculars and the notebook to Gabriel. "I'll meet you in the morning to pick this stuff up. Thanks, Gabriel."

"Any time. See you, Shelley." Smiling broadly, he got out of the truck and returned to his car.

As Christopher pulled his keys from his pocket and started the engine, Shelley moved back across the seat, asking wearily, "How can he be so cheerful after working all day?"

"If you'd ever seen Lori, you wouldn't ask that. She's a detective in narcotics. Every man in the department is half in love with her. I imagine the prospect of a night with her could keep a man going for two or three days."

Jealousy made Shelley ache to slap him, just for the pure pleasure of hearing and feeling her hand smack against his face. Grinding her teeth together, she sat rigidly in the seat and stared out the side window.

That morning Christopher had taken the most direct route from Shelley's apartment to the club. Tonight he drove along Harbor Drive instead. Changing routes only served to confuse Shelley, but she liked the view of boats and ships and lights reflected in the shimmering water.

"What made you decide to settle here?" she asked softly, deciding to forgive him for his comments about Lori.

"You mean there's actually something about me that you didn't find out with all your snooping?"

His sarcasm was more than she could stand. When he looked at her in the light of a street lamp, he saw how stiff she'd become again. For a moment he regretted not answering her question, but he made no effort to soothe her ruffled temper.

"You can just let me out," Shelley said when he pulled in to the apartment parking lot.

Ignoring her, Christopher found a parking space and cut the engine. They walked around the building to her apartment, and he waited patiently while she found her keys and unlocked the door. "What time tomorrow?" she asked, standing in the doorway. She was too tired and too hurt to invite him inside.

"You don't need to go tomorrow."

"What time, *partner*?"

"Ten-thirty. Again."

She nodded once and turned to go inside. Briefly she hesitated. "You know something?"

Christopher waited.

"You're not much different from Mike Jennings. You can be a real bastard, too."

Slowly he smiled. "You think I don't know that, honey? I'll see you in the morning." He pushed his hands into his pockets and set off in the darkness for his truck.

It had been an interesting day, he thought as he drove home. He had spent ten hours with Shelley and had touched her only once. He hadn't kissed her or tried to seduce her. He had come to the unwelcome realization that he didn't want sex with her—he wanted *her*—but he was pretty certain now that her desire was for more than just sex, too. She had shied away from Gabriel's embrace in the truck, and she had responded with pure jealousy to his admiring remarks about Lori.

They might not have learned anything about Gary or the man for whom he had worked, but all in all, he thought with a certain grim satisfaction, it had been a very interesting day.

If anyone had told her before this week that she could possibly be bored in Christopher Morgan's company, Shelley would have said they were nuts. From the moment she had first heard his story and seen his picture, she had been captivated by the man and everything about him. But now that she had spent between eight and thirteen hours a day with him for seven days, physically close to him but at arm's length emotionally, she knew that Christopher, like everyone else, could be boring. The difference was that he was boring only when he chose to be. He chose not to talk to her, not to respond to her overtures at friendship, not to even acknowledge her presence most of the time.

He saw her as a nuisance. She had given him the choice between another newspaper article or her company, and he'd chosen her, the lesser evil—but still evil.

Sometimes she considered forcing him to admit that he was aware of her. He had wanted her a week ago—although she'd seen no sign of his desire since then, she admitted dryly. Now that he was spending so much time in the city, there were many more women available, as she had reminded him. She assumed that he'd taken advantage of those other, more suitable, women. Women who weren't reporters.

He had offered to answer any questions she might have about his former lovers, but she'd never gotten the courage to ask them. It would be too difficult to listen to him talk about the women he'd made love to when his lack of interest in *her* was so painfully obvious.

Any other questions she might have asked weren't welcome, so they spent their hours together in almost total silence. It was, she decided, miserable.

"I've been giving the film and license numbers to Gabriel."

Shelley stared at him. His voice was low and hard in the quiet as he offered her the first information since the day they'd started. "What will he do with them?"

Christopher paused. "He'll run the tag numbers through DMV and match them with names, then get photographs from the driver's licenses. The others, the ones we couldn't match with cars, he'll try to identify by other methods."

"Then what?"

He wasn't sure he wanted to tell her this. He had been looking for some way to break the silence, and the information had just popped out. Now he regretted saying anything at all. "Then he'll check with the Department of Defense. He figures that since Gary was selling defense secrets, we're looking for someone with military connections.

He'll send them the names he gets, and they'll run them through their computers."

"Makes sense."

"Have you talked to your editor?"

Shelley met his gaze, her hazel eyes challenging. "Yes, I have."

"What did you tell him?"

"That I'm still working. That I had talked to you again. That I was making progress."

"That's all?"

"That's all. Would you like to call him and see for yourself?"

"Do you think I need to check up on you?" He smiled sardonically.

"Surely you're not saying that you trust me."

"No. But you're an intelligent woman, Shelley. You're not going to jeopardize your story."

She looked at him for a long time, saddened by the brief conversation. "You're wrong, Christopher. I'm not going to jeopardize *you*." Then she looked away from him, directing her gaze once more at the club.

Christopher felt duly chastised for his careless statement. He reached out and touched her denim-clad knee. "Look, I'm sorry. I didn't mean that."

"Yes, you did."

"Shelley..." He pulled his hand back and looked away. "Listen, it's six o'clock. Why don't we call it a night?"

Shelley wasn't quite successful at hiding her surprise. It had been at Christopher's insistence that they had stayed until 1:00 a.m. the three previous nights, and now he was suggesting that they stop at six o'clock? But she agreed anyway.

He put the camera away, closing and locking the case. "I made reservations at a restaurant in Mission Valley for eight o'clock. Think there's enough time?"

That curious sinking sensation was her heart plummeting to her toes, she realized. He had a date. That was the reason he was willing to quit early. He was anxious to see the woman he was meeting.

She told herself that she didn't care. That she would like to spend an entire evening relaxing. She would take a long, hot bath, then catch a movie on TV. She would enjoy herself, and she wouldn't care what he did or who he did it with.

Remembering his question, she responded with a shrug. "Probably. It depends on where you have to go." Where would the kind of woman who appealed to Christopher live? La Jolla? Rancho Santa Fe? Coronado?

Christopher looked blankly at her as he started the engine. "To your apartment. I know you only have one bathroom, but I think we can manage. Married people do it all the time."

Shelley was as slow at understanding as he was. "There are a lot of things that married people do all the time that I'm not sure I want to do. Would you like to be more specific?"

"Get ready. Dress for dinner." Christopher suddenly grimaced. "I don't think I've made myself very clear. I have reservations for dinner at eight. For us—you and me. Okay?"

"Dinner?" Christopher was asking *her* to have dinner with him? The knowledge sent a warm rush of feeling through her. He wasn't eager to leave her so he could be with another woman—he wanted to take *her* out! She smiled slowly. It was lovely and warm and made him ache way down inside with a sweetly intolerable pain. "Are you sure you don't mind being seen with a reporter?"

He smiled, too. "Not if you don't mind being seen with a suspected spy." He pulled out of the parking lot. "I do have one rule for tonight."

His rules made Shelley want to pull her hair out and scream and stomp her feet. People couldn't live their lives by rules—at least, not the ridiculous rules he created. Quietly she asked, "What's that?"

"For tonight the rest of the rules don't apply. We can't have a conversation like two normal people without asking and answering questions. For tonight, all rules are invalid." He was rewarded with another of her smiles. It made the discomfort of the last seven days—and the near-agony of the last seven nights—worthwhile.

When they reached the apartment Shelley showered first, then shut herself in the bedroom to dress. Sitting at the small vanity, she pulled her hair back into a softly feminine chignon, with a few loose wisps curling around her face and neck. After putting on her makeup, she slipped into her dress.

She'd chosen a simply styled dress of royal-blue silk. It had a deep V neckline, long, fitted sleeves, a slim skirt and a narrow matching belt at the waist. With a simple gold chain as her only jewelry, she looked serene and elegant.

Freshly showered and shaved, Christopher changed into his suit in the bathroom, then waited impatiently in the living room. He was anxious to see her, anxious to get the evening started. Tonight was important to him. It might be the only chance he and Shelley would ever have to spend time together like normal people—just a man and a woman.

He was studying the geometric wall hanging above the fireplace when he became aware of her presence. He turned slowly to face her, his dark eyes moving over her. "You look lovely," he said huskily.

"Thank you." Shelley accepted the compliment uneasily. It wasn't that she doubted the truth of his words—she could see it in his eyes. Such a compliment from the Christopher that she'd spent seven days with would have thrilled her, but the man in front of her was a stranger.

Wearing a black, hand-tailored, silk suit, a soft, white shirt, and a burgundy-, black- and white-striped tie, he was the sophisticated, multimillionaire, art-collecting, business tycoon whom she'd never met—suave, self-assured, elegant. He looked out of place in her apartment. He was out of place in her life, she admitted with a forlorn little smile.

What would she think, he wondered, if he canceled the reservation and suggested that they spend the evening at home? After she had spent so much time fixing her hair and her makeup and dressing, all he wanted to do now was spend an equal amount of time undoing what she had done. He wanted to kiss away the rich peach lipstick that she wore and comb his fingers through her hair until the pins fell out and the soft, wild curls returned. He wanted to untie the belt that emphasized her slender waist and find the hidden fastenings that would allow him to open the dress and remove it. He wanted to discover what she wore beneath it, and he wanted to remove that, too.

"Shelley..."

"Yes?" She stifled the urge to add "sir." She couldn't shake the uneasy feeling that he was a stranger. She told herself that the clothes hadn't transformed him into someone else; they were merely a different packaging of the man she knew.

He closed the distance between them and raised his hands to her face. First his fingertips touched her, then his fingers, then his palms. His dark eyes holding her gaze, he murmured softly, "I'm going to kiss you."

"I know," she whispered.

"If you don't want me to, say so now, before it's too late."

It was already too late. Although she had no desire to protest, the instant the last word was completed, his mouth covered hers. He tasted fresh and cool; she was sweet and hot. He caught her lower lip, the one she bit so often, between his teeth and tugged at it with soft, sensuous, painless nips; then his tongue soothed the sensitive flesh before dipping slowly, insistently inside her mouth.

Shelley raised her hands, and they trembled. Inside his jacket, on the fine, expensive fabric of his shirt, she pressed them against his chest. When he groaned, she felt the vibrations in her fingers. The sound, muted and hushed, passed from his mouth into hers and faded away.

Christopher ended the kiss, released her face and covered her hands with his own. His heart was pounding, sending heated blood rushing through his body with a roar. "Oh, Shelley," he whispered. The first on his list of desires was done. Her lips, slightly parted and swollen, were free of any artificial color.

She freed one hand and rubbed her thumb over his lips, wiping away traces of her lipstick. "I think we'd better go now," she said, her voice as unsteady as her smile.

"Yes," he agreed reluctantly. "Do you have a coat?"

She tugged her other hand away and went into the dining room to get the coat she'd left draped over a chair. Christopher held it for her, his hands guiding it along her arms.

"Let's go," he suggested with a faint smile.

The restaurant was quiet and intimate, with subdued lighting and high-backed booths designed to offer complete privacy. It wasn't a place to see and be seen; its patrons, like Christopher, didn't want attention from anyone but their waiters.

Fat candles in the palest pastel shades nestled inside tall, gracefully fluted crystal holders, adding their softness to the artificial light. Their golden glow flickered over Shelley's face. Christopher, leaning back against the comfortable seat, sat mostly in shadow.

"You really are beautiful," he said solemnly. "That's why I was so surprised when you found me in your office. Gabriel had told me that you had brown hair, brown eyes and freckles, but he didn't tell me that you were beautiful."

"That's because he saw me in better light," she said with an embarrassed but faintly pleased smile.

"Don't do that, Shelley. Don't put yourself down. You talked about Rhett Hayes the other day as if you yourself have nothing to offer a man, and you do."

"Oh, yes, of course. Why, there's my breathtaking beauty and my charm and grace and my incredible femininity." With her exaggerated Southern drawl, she had trouble getting the last word out, but she succeeded, drawing out each syllable.

Christopher simply looked at her, unamused by her words or her overdone accent. He seemed almost insulted by her response. After a moment she said in a normal voice, "I'm sorry. You can tell I'm not used to compliments like that."

"No wonder Hayes had no qualms about the way he treated you. You made it easy for him. You let him know that it was perfectly all right for him to dump you for Rhett, because she's pretty and fragile and she needed him. You let him treat you badly both personally and professionally, and you never argued, never put up a fight, never even made him feel guilty about it."

Everything he said was true, which just made it harder for Shelley to acknowledge. It made her sound weak, and she knew from the way he'd said the word when he'd used it to describe Rhett and Kevin that he despised weak people. "I said I'm sorry," she repeated quietly.

An interruption from the waiter delayed Christopher's response. When they were alone again, their wineglasses filled with chilled white wine, he spoke. "Let's start again. I'll tell you that you're beautiful, and you'll say, 'Thank you.'" He sipped the wine, set the glass down and said in a soft, very sincere voice, "You *are* beautiful, Shelley."

"Thank you, Christopher." She smiled.

"You don't do that often enough—smile. When you smile it's like . . . watching the sun rise over the desert, or seeing it set in the ocean. You should smile all the time."

"You don't smile at all," she pointed out.

"Yes, I do."

"No, you don't. Sometimes you pretend, but you never smile real smiles."

Christopher didn't continue the discussion. He knew that most of his smiles were sardonic and mocking. He couldn't help it. His view of life in the last year had become sardonic and mocking. But for Shelley, he wanted to find one "real" smile. "Ask me some questions, Shelley. I want to talk."

"Christopher Morgan, actually inviting an interview?" she teased.

"Not an interview. Forget that I'm Christopher Morgan. Pretend that I'm simply a man who interests you. Ask me the kinds of questions you would ask him."

Shelley didn't need to pretend. He was most certainly a man who interested her. She wanted to know everything about him—all the important things. What was his favorite food? What kind of music and movies and books did he like? Was he an early riser or did he prefer to sleep late? What did he think about when he became so still and silent that she suspected he'd forgotten her presence? Did he have hopes for the future? Did he dream? Had he ever been in love? How did he like to be touched? Kissed? Aroused? Seduced?

Christopher waited patiently, his dark eyes fastened on her face.

Shelley smiled faintly. "You'll answer any of my questions?"

He nodded.

"When you make love," she began softly, "do you prefer to be the aggressor, the dominant one? Or do you prefer to be seduced by your lover?"

It was happening again. He could feel his body changing, growing. It wasn't her words that did it as much as her voice and her cool, measuring gaze. He realized that she wasn't asking the question to pass the time, or to embarrass him, but for future reference, for the day when they made love. She believed that day was inevitable. He was beginning to believe it, too.

He leaned forward, into the light of the candles, resting his hands on the table. When he spoke, his voice was hard but his eyes were soft. "If I were making love to you, I would be the aggressor," he replied. His gaze was compelling, refusing to let her look away, insisting that she see his hunger, his need. "I would take control—of our lovemaking, of you and of your body. I would learn your body so well that my hands would never forget the feel of you. I would do it so well that you would never forget the feel of me. I would fill you with myself, with my body and my soul, and that part of me would stay with you, deep inside you, until the day you died."

Shelley took a sip of cool wine. Her mouth was dry, and her face burned as heat spread through her. It started deep inside and radiated slowly outward, flowing through her veins with her blood, reaching her fingers and her toes and everywhere else. It was a feverish heat, the kind that only a man could quench. Only Christopher.

He leaned back again. "Of course, that's only for the first time," he finished in his normal, slightly sarcastic tone. "The second time I'd let you do whatever you wanted. What's your next question?"

He was smiling, and she was dying. She wished that she had the courage to force him to make love to her, to show her explicitly, exactly what his words meant. She could do it. She didn't doubt her ability to arouse or seduce him, to continue until he was unable to stop, but she wouldn't try. When they made love—*if* they made love—she wanted it to be because Christopher wanted her. Without reservations. Without doubts.

She forced her mind from the intimacy of making love and asked another question. It was nothing important, but it led to still other questions, until they were talking like any other couple in the restaurant. For the evening that was all they were—a couple. Just two normal people.

He told her about growing up in Albuquerque, about his parents and Gary. She learned that he and Gabriel and Mike Jennings had been friends through school and had attended the University of New Mexico together. Gabriel, a year older than the other two, had graduated first, joined the navy and gotten orders to San Diego. Mike had moved there following graduation, and Christopher had gone into business in Albuquerque. The company had grown and expanded, and soon he'd had offices in Phoenix and San Diego. He'd divided his time between the three cities for several years before settling in San Diego with his two closest friends.

Then he had hired Gary.

They had finished their dinner and were drinking a last glass of wine. Shelley reached across to lay her hand over his. "You don't have to say anything else," she said softly. He had been open and honest all through dinner, answering every question she'd asked, volunteering information about himself, but she knew that any mention of Gary would bring his defenses back into place. He would remember that she was a reporter and not to be trusted, and he would grow distant once more.

"Are you ready to go?"

She nodded.

He paid the check and escorted her outside. They'd chosen to leave the truck at her apartment and had driven the Trans Am instead. He helped her inside, walked around and slid behind the wheel and drove to her apartment.

"Come on in. I'll fix some coffee," Shelley offered. Together they had drunk less than a bottle of wine, but they'd both been tired from the week's work. She knew he could use some coffee before he started the long drive home.

While she put the coffee on to brew, he changed back into jeans and a T-shirt in the bathroom. He left the suit carelessly hanging over the back of a chair, then stretched out on the sofa. Only one lamp was on in the living room, and it did little to dispel the darkness. He was tired and sleepily warm, drifting in and out of consciousness.

"Christopher."

How many thousands of times in his thirty-five years had he heard his name spoken in how many hundreds of voices? Yet not once, in not one single voice, had it ever sounded the way it did in Shelley's voice. Velvety, warm, honeyed. Erotic.

He opened his eyes and saw her kneeling beside the sofa, a cup of steaming coffee in her hands. She set the coffee on the floor and reached out one trembling hand to touch his cheek. It was smooth, the skin stretched tautly over finely sculpted bones. Her fingers moved lightly across the face that was burned forever into her memory, stroking across his forehead, down his nose, along his jaw. He was so handsome....

At her touch, his eyelids drifted down again. Her fingertips glided along his skin, leaving a burning trail of sensation that spread through him like fire. When they stopped at his throat, at the neck of his shirt, disappointment stabbed through him, and he struggled not to groan his frustration.

When he'd lain down, his T-shirt had pulled up, exposing a wide strip of darkly tanned skin above his jeans. When he felt her hand, warm and soft and gentle, touch him there, he stiffened as if he'd received an electric shock. He caught her wrist in his hand. "I'm debating," he said softly, "whether to let you go, or to move your hand back to my face where it felt so good, or to move it lower, where it would feel even better."

Shelley swallowed hard. Her fingers were tingling from the contact with his skin and aching to feel more of him, but she didn't dare move a muscle.

"You're the first person who's touched me in over a year." He moved her hand back and forth across his stomach. "I keep reminding myself that you're a reporter and that I can't—" His groan interrupted the words. He looked as if he was in pain—and enjoying every exquisite twinge. "And that I can't trust you. But for this—to feel your hands on my body—for this I can forget everything. Even good sense."

He guided the tips of her fingers onto his bare skin beneath the waistband of his jeans, just a few inches, no more. Then he laid his hand over hers so she couldn't move it any further. "I enjoyed this evening. For one night I got to forget that I'm a suspected spy and you're the reporter who's determined to write my story. For one night I could be a man—just a man—having dinner with a beautiful woman who makes him ache to possess her." He paused for a long moment, savoring the touch of her fingers and her palm pressed flat against his abdomen. "I'm hard, Shelley—from looking at you and wanting you and feeling you touch me. I could make love to you tonight and die a thousand times inside you. But tomorrow will come, and I'll still be suspected of spying, and you'll still be a reporter, and I will be very, very sorry that I made love to you."

With the pressure of his hand, he eased her fingers just a millimeter further. "I'll let you decide. Do you care if I regret making love to you?"

"Why do you have to look ahead? Why can't you just let it happen and enjoy it?" she whispered.

"I just can't. That's not the way I do things." For the first time since he'd opened his eyes, he looked away from her. He was getting ready to lie to her, and he didn't want to do it while looking into her soft hazel eyes. "I want to make love to you, Shelley. You're a beautiful woman, and you've made it obvious that you're willing. But sex is all I want— the use of your body. I don't want *you*."

The coldness started in the pit of her stomach and spread, but not quickly enough to stop the flash of pain caused by his blunt words. She pulled her hand back, her nails scraping over his skin, and he let her go. Moving mechanically, she got to her feet, turned and walked out of the room. A moment later Christopher heard the click of the bedroom door.

He closed his eyes, rubbing them hard with his fingers. He had succeeded. She would never again try to seduce him, never again make the mistake of offering herself to him, never again trust him.

Dear God, what had he done?

* * *

He turned the doorknob. It was locked. Knocking once, he said quietly, "I'm going now, Shelley."

There was no response.

"Shelley, would you please answer me?"

Still nothing.

The guilt that had filled him as he'd told his lies grew even stronger. He'd had no right to tell her such a thing—he didn't know her; he'd had no idea how she would react to it. He knocked at the door once more. "Shelley, damn it—"

The door swung in as his hand touched it. She stood there in a rich, kelly-green robe, her face washed, her hair brushed, her feet bare. "What do you want?" she asked coolly.

He stared helplessly at her. He wanted to take her into his arms and hold her. He wanted to kiss her. He wanted to feel her hands on him again. He wanted to love her, long and hard, all night. He spoke haltingly. "Shelley, I didn't mean..."

"Didn't mean what?" she asked sharply.

"I didn't mean to hurt you."

She smiled. It was a mirror image of his own sardonic smile, and he hated it. "Yes, you did, but it's not your fault. I made it easy for you. I practically begged you to take me without bothering to find out first if you wanted me. Don't worry. It won't happen again."

"Shelley..." He reached out, but she stepped away, avoiding his touch.

"You'd better go now. It's a long drive home, and we've got a long day's work ahead of us."

The idea of spending the next day with her, with the situation he'd gotten them in, was more than Christopher could bear. "Not tomorrow. You can stay home tomorrow."

"Whether you pick me up or not, I'm going to be at the club tomorrow when it opens. I told you, Christopher, it will never happen again. I will never again ask you to touch me or talk to me or even notice that I'm alive. I give you my promise. And I always keep my promises."

He was afraid of that, Christopher thought as he turned away. He was terribly afraid of that.

He picked her up at the usual time the next morning. Sunglasses hid her eyes, but he didn't need to see them to know that they were cold. She was aloof, and so frigid that she made the cool October air seem warm in comparison.

He'd brought coffee and doughnuts. She'd brought a novel and a pad of paper. She ate his doughnuts, drank his coffee, made his notes, but otherwise didn't notice that he existed. When she wasn't making entries for him, she was either reading her book or writing in her exquisitely neat handwriting on the yellow legal pad. She sat facing him, her knees drawn up to support the pad, so he couldn't see what she was writing—a letter maybe, or notes for the story that she would eventually tell.

He couldn't stand it. Gabriel had told him to watch the club for two weeks, so they'd have some idea of which customers were regulars and which had just dropped in. Fourteen days, and this was only the eighth. If Shelley kept this up for six more days, he would be so crazy at the end of the week that he wouldn't know or care if they ever found Gary's murderer.

"We need to talk."

Shelley raised her eyes from the pad and coolly watched him. There was no anger or hurt or disinterest in her eyes, Christopher noticed, but before he put too much meaning in that, he noticed that there was nothing else there, either— no pleasure, no interest, no life.

"About last night, Shelley . . ."

She continued to watch him, giving the appearance of listening while she forced herself to ignore his voice, to hear nothing, to respond to nothing.

"What I did was wrong and unfair and stupid. Like you said before, I can be a real bastard. I want to explain . . ." He slowed his words, looking at her with narrowed eyes. "Shelley." She wasn't listening. She had withdrawn to some private place where he couldn't follow, where he couldn't hurt her. She had shut him out, and he wanted very much to be allowed in. "I'm sorry, Shelley," he said on a sigh. "God, I'm sorry."

The week was the longest that Christopher had ever lived through. Shelley had not only remained cold and unresponsive, she had even gotten worse. The first emotion he'd seen from her came on Sunday evening when Gabriel met them in the club parking lot. After they'd talked for a few minutes and as Gabriel was preparing to leave, Shelley spoke, giving him a slight smile.

"Do you mind giving me a ride home, Gabriel?" she asked, saying his name in that same soft drawling way she'd used to say Christopher's.

Gabriel looked from her to Christopher to see if his friend had any objections. He had plenty, but he said nothing. "Sure, go on and get in the car. I need to talk to Christopher for a minute." He watched her walk to his car, then looked at the other man again. "Anything you want to say?"

Staring straight ahead, Christopher responded. "You lay one hand on her and I'll kill you."

Gabriel grinned. "That message is clear enough. I'll call you tomorrow. Be careful."

Be careful. Christopher scowled in the darkness. He'd been careful all his life, and what had it gotten him? His company had gone bankrupt, his friends were gone, his brother was dead, his life was a miserable cloak-and-dagger spy game, and he was so afraid to get close to the woman who meant more to him than anyone ever had in his life that instead he'd driven her away from him.

Fear. Strong, compelling, nauseating fear. He hated being afraid. He hated looking at Shelley and seeing a beautiful, kind, gentle woman who made him want, need and love, and being afraid of her because she was a reporter. Because her job was exposing his life and all his secrets to the world. Because Mike Jennings had taught him to be wary, and he didn't know how to forget that lesson. He didn't know how to stop being afraid of her.

It didn't matter. Even if he learned to trust her, even if he forgot his fear, it wouldn't matter—not to her. After his clumsy attempt last Sunday to protect himself from her, she would never forgive him for what he'd said. And he wasn't sure that he could ever forgive himself.

"I just got a death threat back there." Gabriel looked at Shelley, watching her expression in the eerie glow of the streetlights while he waited at a red light.

She steadfastly ignored his stare. "The light is green," she said, raising her hand in a careless wave.

Gabriel slowly accelerated, shifting through the gears. "You're no more talkative than Christopher. What happened between you two?"

"Is it really any of your business?"

"Everything that concerns Christopher is my business." The friendly teasing was gone, and his voice was hard. "Christopher has been my best friend since we were in grade school, and I love him more than I ever could have loved a brother, if I'd had one. I stood by him when that mess happened last year and got investigated by the FBI and my own department because of it. I watched his friends forget over a period of days that they'd ever known him. I was there when that article by Mike Jennings appeared on the *Chronicle*'s front page. What you're planning for him *is* my business, because if you do anything to hurt him, lady, *I'm* the one who will make you pay for it—and you will pay dearly."

Shelley stared down at her hands, out the window—anything to avoid Gabriel's piercing black gaze. "As a reporter, I wouldn't do anything to hurt Christopher." She was proud of the smooth, even tone of her voice.

Gabriel, with an intuition developed after years as a cop, knew that she wasn't finished. There was more to her statement of denial, and she'd say it if he didn't push her.

"As a . . ." Shelley clenched her hands into fists, squeezing until her fingertips ached. "As a woman, I *couldn't* do anything to hurt him. He wouldn't give me the chance, for one thing."

He was puzzled by her answer and by the poorly hidden pain that the words caused her. "That doesn't make sense. If he's not interested in you, then why did he say he'd kill me if I touched you?"

She didn't doubt that Christopher had told him that, for reasons of his own, but they had little to do with her, she was sure. He'd made his feelings for her abundantly clear last Sunday. She didn't need any more demonstrations.

When she didn't say anything, he steered the conversation back to business. "It'll probably take a while to run down all the information we need on the people at the club, and there's a chance even then that none of them will be worth further investigation. What will you do in the meantime?"

Shrugging, Shelley shook her head. "Go back to work, I suppose. You know, an awful lot of people came together. You can identify the drivers, but what about the others?"

"I don't know. You may have to go back there," Gabriel said with a shrug. "Does your boss know what you've been doing?"

"No."

"Why is he so tolerant? Why is he willing to pay you a full salary to work on one story? And why does he let you continue this story without a single thing to show for it?"

"He trusts me." She glanced at the familiar scenery outside the car window as he exited the freeway. "How do you know where I live?"

"How do you think Christopher got your address?" He grinned expansively. "By the way, did he really break into your apartment?"

"He really did. I suppose you knew nothing about it."

"I didn't. Look, I'm helping him with this search because there's not much I wouldn't do for him, but I draw the line at breaking and entering. I'm a cop. I can't afford trouble like that."

"This really means a lot to him, doesn't it? I never would have pegged him as the vengeful type."

Gabriel pulled into the parking lot, finding a space in front of Shelley's building. "He isn't," he said as he got out. "I'll walk you to your door. You never know what might be lurking in the shadows. But you're right—it *is* important. *Someone* got Gary to steal defense secrets for him."

"But you're looking for an American. What makes you so sure that his contact or whatever wasn't Russian?"

"Someone had to set it up. Gary wasn't smart enough to arrange it on his own, or stupid enough to deal directly with the KGB." Gabriel waited while she unlocked the door of her apartment, then followed her inside. "Look, if you ever repeat this, I'll deny it, but . . . I couldn't stand Gary Morgan. From the time we met in grade school, he was selfish, self-centered, egotistical, lazy, irresponsible, immature and completely unlikable. I tolerated him for Christopher's sake, but I couldn't stand him. Christopher gave him a job at Morgan Industries because Gary was too lazy to hold down any other job. He wanted everything easy."

The conversation reminded Shelley of her theory that jealousy could have been part of Gary's motivation for selling defense secrets. "He was jealous of Christopher, wasn't he?" She removed her jacket and her shoes, then curled up in the rocker, tucking her feet under her, and motioned for Gabriel to sit on the sofa.

"Yeah. I don't know why Christopher ever put up with him. I guess he just felt responsible for him after their parents died."

She shook her head in disagreement. "For some reason that escapes me—and probably you, too—Christopher

loved Gary. Maybe Gary didn't deserve to be loved, but..."
She shrugged.

Gabriel stretched his long legs out in front of him. "You seem to understand him. Has he told you about Mike Jennings?"

"He hasn't said much about the story Mike wrote, but he told me about their friendship up to that point. The only other time he brings him up is to compare me to him."

"The day that Gary was killed and Christopher was arrested, I had gone to El Paso to pick up a prisoner. When the FBI released Christopher, he was upset and distraught, and he didn't want to be alone. He called my apartment, but I wasn't back yet so he called Mike. He told Mike everything that had happened and talked about Gary. A lot of the stuff was obviously personal and private. The next day everything that he'd told Mike in confidence was printed on the front page of the newspaper for everyone to read." Gabriel looked disgusted. "Try to imagine how you'd feel if one of your closest friends for twenty-five years betrayed you like that."

"What Mike Jennings did was unethical," Shelley said quietly. "I understand how that must have hurt Christopher, but... I'm not like Jennings. I would never use somebody like that, friend or stranger."

"I believe you. But I'm not the one who counts here."

Shelley moved one foot to the floor and slowly rocked herself back and forth. "If he finds this guy, this man who enticed Gary into spying and later ordered his death... Christopher will never truly be cleared, will he? Even if this man swears before God and the world that Christopher wasn't involved, there will always be people who will believe that he *was* a spy. Does he realize that?"

Gabriel nodded. "But at least the man who had Gary killed will be punished. I suppose he can live with the rest of it." In one easy, graceful movement he got to his feet. "You'll be hearing from Christopher or me sometime in the future. It might be a few days or a few weeks, so don't panic." At the door, he stopped and grinned at her. "By the way, Lieutenant Jackson says to tell you hello and that your mother wants you to write. She misses you."

Shelley stared at him until the door closed and blocked him from view. He had called the Mobile Police Department to check up on her! That arrogant bas—

He was being careful and cautious and thorough. She couldn't blame him at all. His thoroughness might have been an important part of his and Christopher's decision to trust her. How could she complain about that?

Brad was surprised to see Shelley at her desk Monday morning. "What's up?"

"I have a little free time, and I thought you might have something for me to do here."

Brad gestured to her to accompany him to his office. "Do you have any news on Morgan, or are you giving up?"

"I have some free time in the investigation. Either he or Gabriel Rodriguez will call me when they're ready to work again."

Her editor was practically beaming. "You really got to him? He's really letting you in on the whole thing?"

Shelley smiled uneasily. She wasn't certain exactly how much she could say to Brad and still keep to the agreement she'd made with Christopher. *You can't tell anyone what we're doing.* She wasn't breaking that rule. But he'd gone on to add, "If you tell anyone anything . . ." Well, she'd keep to the first part. She wouldn't tell Brad anything that they'd done—no details at all. "Yes, but I can't say anything else. I made a promise."

"Does this promise include an exclusive for the *Chronicle*?"

That was her own rule; she wasn't hurting anyone by acknowledging it. "Yes, it does."

"That's great. Well . . . you want to work while you wait for the next move, huh? See Sandy. She'll give you an assignment—or three or five." When she reached the door, he added, "You've done good, Shelley. I'm proud of you."

She had to jog Sandy's memory when she went to the other woman's desk requesting an assignment; Shelley had been out of the office so long that the young editor had all but forgotten her. So had most of her fellow employees. When this story was over, Shelley realized, she'd have to start all over again at making friends. It wasn't something that she looked forward to.

As Brad had predicted, Sandy had enough assignments to keep Shelley busy through the next two weeks. In the evenings she relaxed and cleaned house and did her laundry and shopping, and at night she dreamed. Always dreams of Christopher.

But on Friday at the end of the second week she didn't have time to dream. When she walked in the door after work her phone was ringing. Dropping her purse and coat in the rocker, she picked up the receiver. "Hel-lo-o?" Out of breath, she drew the word into three lilting syllables.

There was a long, heavy silence, then her name.

She bit her lip. "Hello, Christopher."

Chapter 5

He hadn't wanted to call, and he knew it was evident in his voice. He had spent the last two weeks telling himself that the last thing he needed—the last thing *she* needed—was to talk. But he hadn't convinced himself. All he'd been able to think of was Shelley. Seeing her. Talking to her. Hearing her laugh. Making her smile. Touching her.

He couldn't even explain it away as lust. If all he felt was lust, he would have made love to her that night after dinner instead of lying and pushing her away. If it was only lust, it would affect only his body; it wouldn't touch his heart or his mind, yet his body was the least affected. Even if he couldn't make love to her, he wanted to see her. He needed to be with her.

The fear was still with him. It would be a part of him for a long time, but it was no longer controlling him. He didn't know when it had begun to lessen, but he knew the cause. Shelley. Somehow, in some tiny way, he had begun trusting her. Along with liking and wanting and needing and desiring, he had started trusting.

"Christopher?"

He closed his eyes. He could see her, so pretty and soft. So lovely. "I want to talk to you, Shelley. Please."

Her lip was beginning to hurt. She released it and stuck the tip of one finger between her teeth. It was hard to forget the last time they had talked. She could repeat his sentences word by word and feel again the pain that had stabbed through her. "About what?"

"About us."

The desire to hang up, to protect herself from him, was strong, but she couldn't do it. After going so many days without seeing him or hearing his voice, she couldn't hang up on him. "There is no 'us,' Christopher. There's just you and me."

"You know that's not true, Shelley." But he could convince her of that more easily in person than over the phone. "I'm at home. I want..." That sounded too strong, too demanding. "Will you come here?"

She swallowed convulsively. What he was asking was impossible. If she agreed and went to him and he pushed her away once more, she knew she wouldn't be able to bear the pain and disappointment. There had been too many disappointments already.

He knew she was going to turn him down. Hoarsely, he spoke again. "That Sunday..." He hated to bring up that night, knowing that even the memory would be painful for her. "That night you said that you would never ask me to touch you or talk to you or notice you again."

"And I've kept my word," she said hotly, her face burning with remembered humiliation.

"I'm asking you to break it. I need to see you, Shelley."

Her hands trembled, and her knees sagged weakly. She pulled a chair out from the dining table and sank into it. "There are other women," she helplessly reminded him.

"I don't need other women. I need *you*." He was silent for a moment; then he added one word and her name, "Please, Shelley."

She didn't know why she did it. Even knowing that Christopher was dangerous—to her sense of well-being, to her ego and to her sanity—she accepted. She told him that she would come to his house. Praying that she wasn't making a serious mistake, she asked, "What about the gate?"

"It's unlocked."

"You were pretty sure I would say yes, weren't you?" she asked, her voice heavy with bitterness.

"No." Then he added softly, "But I was hoping."

She didn't want to hear that. She didn't want to hear anything in that quietly intimate tone of voice. Closing her ears to that sensuous undertone, she asked for directions to his house.

"You've been here before," he reminded her.

"And I had a map then, and it still took me over two hours to find it." Biting her lip, she wrote the concise directions he gave her on a notepad next to the phone. "I'll be there in an hour or so," she said reluctantly. *If I don't come to my senses first.*

"All right. Shelley..." Christopher was too nervous to continue.

She waited.

"I'd like you to stay."

"For how long?" she asked curiously.

"As long as you want."

As long as she wanted. She didn't even want to go in the first place—and she wanted to stay with him for the rest of her life. "All right," she whispered, hanging up the phone.

Shelley parked next to Christopher's pickup, got out of the car, then bent to get her suitcase from the back seat. When she straightened and turned, she saw Christopher standing on the steps, leaning against the cedar railing with his arms folded across his chest. He wore jeans and a gray sweater and, despite the cold, was barefooted. He looked so confident, so assured.

She didn't know that he'd been afraid she would change her mind. That he'd spent the two hours and fifteen minutes since she'd hung up pacing back and forth in the living room, listening for her car, wishing that she'd come and fearing that she wouldn't.

Now that she was here, he simply watched her, waiting for her to come closer. She was so beautiful. Well-worn jeans fit smoothly over the curve of her hips, and her dark green sweater complemented her coppery hair and hazel eyes. Over the sweater she wore the blousy, green corduroy jacket that she'd worn last week, with a creamy ivory scarf around her neck. Damn, she was beautiful.

When she reached him, he came forward and took the suitcase from her. "Thank you for coming," he said solemnly. "I didn't know..."

Had he thought that she might change her mind? she wondered, standing on the step below and looking up at him. He could rest assured, since she was here before him, that she hadn't yet regained her senses.

"Come inside."

She followed him in, closing the door behind her. He left her suitcase at the foot of the steps, then turned to take her coat. His fingers brushed her hand as he took it from her, sending a jolt through both of them.

It was uncomfortable, knowing that she had agreed to come here tonight to make love with him. Neither of them had put it into words, but the meaning had been clear. If it bothered *him* that much, he wondered, how did it make her feel? It seemed so cold-blooded, but there was nothing cold about his feelings for her. Nothing cold about his blood.

"Have you had dinner?" he asked, gesturing for her to enter the living room. A fire in the stone fireplace was blazing, sending out its comforting, potent heat.

"No." She had considered stopping along the way, but her stomach had been too queasy from nerves.

He sat down in the armchair, and she went to stand by the fire. Neither of them knew what to say.

Shelley sat down on the hearth, drawing her knees up, wrapping her arms around them. "Why did you call me?"

He answered honestly. "I was lonely."

"You could have called Gabriel."

"I wasn't lonely to see Gabriel."

"Lonely, need, want. You use a lot of words, Christopher, but you never say what you mean," she said sarcastically.

He smiled faintly. She was acting tough, hard. It just showed how uneasy she was. How scared she was. He left his chair and sat down next to her on the hearth, taking her hand in his. "Don't be afraid of me, Shelley. I won't hurt you. I know that this is awkward, and it's my fault. I should have asked you out first."

"I wouldn't have accepted," she grumbled.

He smiled again. "Yes, you would have. I would have pleaded. I would have begged." Lifting her hand to his mouth, he pressed a kiss to her palm. His lips were cool and dry, his breath warm and moist. His tongue brushed across her skin, making her shiver. "I apologize, Shelley."

She caught her breath. "For what?"

"For the way I treated you that night. For the things I said to you."

She tugged at her hand, but he didn't let it go. "Sometimes the truth hurts, especially if you're not prepared for it."

"What truth? I lied to you, Shelley. I wanted you so badly that I was dying with it, and I lied to you."

Catching him off guard, she pulled hard and freed her hand, then stood up to pace the room. "Don't, okay? Please. I don't want to talk about that night. I'd just like to forget that it happened."

He followed her. When she stopped to stare out the glass door, he was right behind her, not touching, but close enough to feel her heat. "I don't want to forget it. I don't want to forget the way your hand felt on my face. I don't want to forget the way you touched me...the way you looked at me...the way you made me feel."

He could see her face reflected in the glass. Her teeth had a firm grip on her full lower lip, and her eyes were squeezed shut—to stop the tears? He didn't like seeing her so upset.

He'd been unrealistic. Shelley had come here to make love with him, but he couldn't push her or rush her. She needed to be handled carefully, lovingly. She needed to be comforted, aroused and gently, gently seduced.

He laid his hand on her shoulder. She stiffened at his touch. "I'm going to fix us something to eat, all right?"

He waited for an answer, and she gave it, a barely perceptible nod. After squeezing gently first, he released her and went into the kitchen.

Dinner wasn't elaborate—thin slices of tender roast beef, onions and melted cheese on French rolls—but it was delicious, and it gave them a chance to get used to each other. They ate in the living room, seated on the floor on either side of the coffee table, and Christopher talked.

"Have you heard anything from Gabriel?" Shelley asked when he mentioned his friend.

"Nothing about work tonight, all right?" he cautioned.

"It seems like that's all we ever talk about."

"Just that one question?"

She smiled slightly, and Christopher tilted his head back. "All right, all right." Looking at her again, he said, "You can ask all the questions you want if that's the price of your smiles."

Her smile turned shy. "It's all right...."

He reached across the table to touch his fingertip to her lips. "Nobody has a prettier smile than you do," he said softly. "Absolutely nobody. What was your question?"

"Have you heard from Gabriel?"

"He's called. He's still waiting on a lot of the IDs. He said that there are an awful lot he's not going to be able to identify. We may have to go back and go inside this time."

"Except that you can't go inside."

He lifted his shoulders in a shrug. "That's something we'll have to deal with later, all right?"

Shelley emptied her can of soda into her glass, then leaned back against the love seat and sipped it. Christopher watched her, his eyes darker than ever. To avoid his stare, she looked around the room, her gaze settling on the painting over the fireplace. "That's a beautiful painting."

Christopher hardly glanced at it. "Yes, it is."

"Who did it?"

"Caitlin Pierce. She's one of the best Indian artists in the country."

She studied the scene, a ceremonial dance in a small, adobe village. "It really is beautiful. Do you have any other paintings by her?"

"I have seven others. I sold the rest of my art collection last year."

"Why?"

"Because I wasn't in the mood then to be surrounded by beautiful things."

"Yet you kept *her* paintings." Shelley shifted her gaze to him. "Did you ever meet her?"

"Yes."

"Tell me about her."

He slowly smiled. "Why are you interested?"

"You liked her, didn't you? You . . . cared for her."

Christopher moved to sit on the sofa, sliding down and stretching his arms along the back of the cushions. "I met her before she started making many sales. She was young— she's about your age, maybe a year or two older—and very pretty and very talented. Yes, I liked her. I think . . . I think for a while I was as close to being in love as I'd ever been at that time." But not as close as I am now, he silently added.

"And what happened?" Shelley had expected to be jealous of any woman that Christopher had ever loved, but instead she found the tale fascinating.

"Nothing. Caitlin was in love with another man, although they weren't together, so I never tried to see her.

When a few years went by and I didn't forget her, I arranged to meet with her again on the pretext of commissioning four more paintings. The man was back. Since then, she and Jess have gotten married. They have one daughter. Last time I saw her she was pregnant with their second child, and they're very happy.''

"And you have four more Caitlin Pierce originals."

"Four more Caitlin Pierce Trujillo originals," he corrected with a smile. "They were married by the time she finished them."

"Do you regret not trying to get something started with her before Jess returned?"

He shook his head. "I never would have stood a chance. We're talking about the kind of love that people only dream about. They worship each other. Even if Jess had never returned to New Mexico, she never would have stopped loving him, and he never could have stopped loving her."

That was the kind of love that Shelley wanted for herself, but she doubted that she could inspire that kind of devotion in any man. Kevin certainly hadn't been devoted. She suspected that her biggest attraction for him had been her convenience and the fact that she'd made no demands, emotionally or legally. Her attraction for Christopher—well, that was obvious, she thought wryly. He'd spelled it out for her as plainly as possible. Sex. Or, as he'd put it, *the use of your body*.

Well, that was all right. She could live with it. So he didn't want her the way that she wanted him. At least he wanted her.

"What are you thinking?"

Smiling faintly, she shook her head. "Nothing important."

Christopher studied her for a minute. Her eyes had gotten so serious and sad. Had it been his talk about love? Had it reminded her of Kevin Hayes, who had chosen another woman over her?

Even the mere thought of Hayes made him grit his teeth. Without knowing the man, Christopher was positive that he certainly hadn't deserved Shelley. She needed a strong man, one who would love her and cherish her and treat her the way she deserved to be treated—tenderly. Lovingly. Like a beautiful, fragile, precious, beloved gift.

"Shelley." He was hoarse, unable to strengthen his voice.

She didn't make him ask. As he got to his feet, she easily rose from the floor. He took her hand gently in his and led her through the living room, past her suitcase in the hall and up the darkened stairs to the first room at the top.

He left her at the door while he crossed the room to switch on a bedside lamp. Its light was dim, casting a weak glow, but Shelley, in her uncertainty, would have preferred darkness. When she started to protest, Christopher shook his head. "Not in the dark. I want to see you."

She hugged her arms nervously across her chest. This was so much harder than she'd expected. If they had kissed and touched and simply gotten carried away by their emotions, it would be so different, so much easier. But this way they knew exactly what they were doing. There would be no guilt, no regrets, no recriminations, no shame.

He stood on the other side of the room, watching her. When she made no move to come closer, he grasped the bottom of his sweater with both hands and pulled it over his head. It fell to the floor. "Don't be afraid of me, Shelley."

She didn't move toward him or away from him. "I—I could get pregnant."

He opened the drawer of the nightstand behind him, withdrew a small package and tossed it next to the lamp. "I'm arrogant. Not careless."

She glanced at the small, innocent-looking box. "You were so certain that all you had to do was call and I would come running, weren't you?" she asked with a dismayed sigh.

"No. Honestly, I expected you to tell me to go to hell. But in the event that you did say yes, I wanted to be prepared. I don't take chances with myself, Shelley, or with anyone else.'' He undid the button on his jeans and eased the zipper down, then stopped. The jeans rode dangerously low on his hips. "Have you changed your mind?''

Biting her lip, she shook her head.

Christopher smiled. "You're a hard woman, Shelley."

"There are other women. Easy women."

Shaking his head, he moved toward her. "There aren't any other women, Shelley. Not for me. And there are no other men for you. There's just you and me. Just us.'' He emphasized the last two sentences slightly, reminding her that she had denied the existence of "us" on the phone earlier that evening.

Her hazel eyes were soft, confused and pleading, when she looked up at him. "Will you do one thing, Christopher?'' she whispered. "Will you try to pretend that it means something to you?''

He smiled, closed his eyes and reached for her all at the same time. "I'm no good at pretending, Shelley." He drew her to him, fitting her with ease against his body. "I need you. Not just like this—'' he thrust slowly, lazily against her, letting her feel the extent of his arousal "—but in other ways. I need to talk to you. To look at you. To touch you. To kiss you." *To love you.*

His words didn't reassure her. "Christopher..."

He kissed her gently, beginning the sweetly painful task of seducing her. He pulled her arms away from her body and drew her sweater over her head, then let his hands glide across her silken skin, her beautiful, naked breasts. He braced one arm behind her back as his mouth followed the path his hands had taken, scattering soft, teasing, tantalizing kisses over her skin.

Shelley moaned, the sound vibrating through her. Christopher could feel it through his lips. He raised his mouth and moved it to a new target. Her breasts were small and creamy, crested with rosy nubs that swelled as he covered one with his mouth. The flick of his tongue made her cry out breathlessly.

Bending slightly, he lifted her easily. Her body was limp, her legs dangling over his arm. He took two steps and lowered both Shelley and himself to the bed, never breaking the torturing hold of his mouth at her breast.

His breathing was uneven. He lifted his head and glanced at her flushed face with a slight smile. Her eyes were shut, her lips parted. Ducking, he brushed his lips across hers, exerting only enough pressure to get her to open her mouth fully to him. As soon as she did, he ended the kiss.

"Christopher?" She sounded unsure, bewildered by the brief, unsatisfying kiss.

"We have all night," he reminded her, his voice low and steely. Kneeling beside her, he slid her jeans down her legs, letting them fall on the floor next to his sweater. She wore peach-colored silk panties. His hand started at her breast and stroked downward, over her stomach, across her slender hip to her thigh. Over and over he stroked, touching, sometimes caressing lightly over the pale peach fabric, making her shudder.

Shelley's doubts were gone, replaced by a desire that made her ache. She whispered his name again, trying vainly to avoid the pleasingly painful touch of his hand.

"If you're not enjoying this, then I'm doing something wrong," he said with a wry smile.

"I want more."

His smile turned into a lascivious grin. "You'll get more, sweetheart. You'll get all that you can handle. Just give me time." His eyes grew darker as they swept over her again. "You're so beautiful," he whispered. "You look so delicate." His hand spanned her abdomen. "Like I'll crush you under my weight." Sliding down the bed, he pressed a kiss to the skin covering her jutting hipbone, then stood up and removed the rest of his clothes. Moving onto the bed again, he rubbed her through the soft cover of her panties, his fingers tickling erotically.

Shelley caught his wrists in her hands. He could break free if he wanted, but she held him so tight that it would take an effort to loosen her grip. "Don't play with me." The flush that had colored her face was gone; now she was pale, her freckles standing out across her cheeks in contrast. "Don't toy with me, Christopher. I need you."

He pulled away, then lowered himself until his weight was pushing down on her. His forehead rested against hers, his nose touched her nose, and his breath when he spoke was warm and sweet against her mouth. "I'm not toying with you," he denied, his voice harder than ever. "Looking at you and touching you gives me pleasure—more pleasure than I've had in a year. Later, when there's time, I want you to look at me. I want you to touch me. I want to know your body, and I want you to know mine. I'm not playing, sweetheart. This isn't a game."

Shelley ran her fingers into his hair, holding his head still. "Tomorrow will come," she said softly, quoting him from that still-painful night. "Will you be sorry?"

He solemnly shook his head, their noses bumping. "You're the only thing in my life that's good and warm and real," he said in a low whisper. "I won't have any regrets, honey. I promise." He kissed her then, his tongue gliding into her mouth, encouraging her to forget her doubts, stoking her desire until it matched his own. At the same time his hands moved over her, grazing, kneading, exciting. When he broke off the kiss to finish undressing her, she reached for him with a whimper of frustration at the loss of his warmth.

"Now..."

"Not yet." He sounded as needy as she did. He rolled away from her, but Shelley caught his hand.

She knew that he was reaching for the package that he'd left on the nightstand, but the agony of waiting was too much for her. "No, Christopher. Now."

He looked at her, then at the box. He would love to lie down again and forget precautions, to make love to her without any barriers, but the risk was too great. If she got pregnant... He found the idea of a child appealing, but not now. Not yet. It was too soon.

He bent over her, planting his hands on either side of her head, and kissed her hard. "One second." That was all he needed.

Shelley watched him through slitted eyes. He was so handsome, so beautifully formed. Hard and muscular, yet with a perfection of bone and skin and muscle that seemed almost delicate. He was perfect and, for a time, he was hers.

He returned to her, and she reached for him. Slowly, with infinite care, he eased himself inside her, filling her, feeling her warm, moist welcome. For a moment he did nothing but kiss her—her forehead, her eyes, her cheeks, her jaw—then he urged her to open her eyes and look at him. In her eyes he saw the haze of intense emotion, a need that matched his own, and he shuddered at the edge of fulfillment.

They had all night, he'd told her, but suddenly he could wait no longer. He moved within her, slow and deep, driving her and himself wild with frustration and longing. He tried to control his passion, to make it last forever, but found that he was beyond control, beyond thinking. He could only feel, and he felt everything—every tremor, every moan, every plea, every convulsive shudder that racked their bodies. He felt Shelley's cry, felt her tighten around him, and felt himself fill her; then he could feel no more. Nothing but peace. Quiet, still, blissful peace.

Christopher dozed for a few minutes, then jerked awake. For an instant he felt panic at finding a woman in his arms; then he realized that it was Shelley and everything was all right again. Commanding his muscles to relax, he shifted positions, propping both pillows behind his back. Before she could protest, he pulled her back into his arms and let her rest her head on his chest. "Are you okay?" he asked drowsily.

She raised her head to stare at him. Her eyes were remarkably clear. "I'm okay. You're perfect."

SILHOUETTE DELIVERS FIRST-CLASS ROMANCE— DIRECT TO YOUR DOOR

Mail the Heart sticker on the postpaid order card today and you'll receive:

— **4 new Silhouette Intimate Moments novels—FREE**
— **an elegant pen & watch set—FREE**
— **and a surprise mystery bonus—FREE**

But that's not all. You'll also get:

Money-Saving Home Delivery

When you subscribe to Silhouette Intimate Moments, the excitement, romance and faraway adventures of these novels can be yours for previewing in the convenience of your own home at less than retail prices. Every month we'll deliver 4 new books right to your door. If you decide to keep them, they'll be yours for only $2.49 each. That's 26¢ less per book than what you pay in stores. And there is no extra charge for shipping and handling!

Free Monthly Newsletter

It's the indispensable insider's look at our most popular writers and their upcoming novels. Now you can have a behind-the-scenes look at the fascinating world of Silhouette! It's an added bonus you'll look forward to every month!

Special Extras—FREE

Because our home subscribers are our most valued readers, we'll be sending you additional free gifts from time to time as a token of our appreciation.

OPEN YOUR MAILBOX TO A WORLD OF LOVE AND ROMANCE EACH MONTH. JUST COMPLETE, DETACH AND MAIL YOUR FREE OFFER CARD TODAY!

FREE—digital watch and matching pen

You'll love your new LCD quartz digital watch with its genuine leather strap. And the slim matching pen is perfect for writing that special person. Both are yours FREE as our gift of love.

◐ Silhouette Intimate Moments®

FREE OFFER CARD

4 FREE BOOKS

FREE PEN AND WATCH SET

FREE MYSTERY BONUS

PLACE
HEART
STICKER
HERE

MONEY-SAVING HOME DELIVERY

FREE FACT-FILLED NEWSLETTER

MORE SURPRISES THROUGHOUT THE YEAR—FREE

✓ **YES!** Please send me four Silhouette Intimate Moments novels, **free**, along with my free pen & watch set and my free mystery gift as explained on the opposite page.

240 CIL YABH

NAME _____

ADDRESS _____ APT. ____

CITY _____ STATE _____

ZIP CODE _____

Terms and prices subject to change.
Your enrollment is subject to acceptance
by Silhouette Books.

SILHOUETTE "NO-RISK" GUARANTEE
• There is no obligation to buy—the free books and gifts remain yours to keep.
• You pay the lowest price possible—and receive books before they're available in stores.
• You may end your subscription anytime—just let us know.

MAIL THE POSTPAID CARD TODAY!

PRINTED IN U.S.A.

Remember! To receive your free books, pen and watch set and mystery gift, return the postpaid card below. But don't delay!

DETACH AND MAIL CARD TODAY.

MAIL THE POSTPAID CARD TODAY!

BUSINESS REPLY CARD

First Class   Permit No. 717   Buffalo, NY

Postage will be paid by addressee

Silhouette Books®
901 Fuhrmann Blvd.
P.O. Box 1867
Buffalo, NY 14240-9952

NO POSTAGE
NECESSARY
IF MAILED
IN THE
UNITED STATES

He laughed, but stopped abruptly, unaccustomed to the sound. "Only with you, honey." He tugged, and she moved over on top of him. "You're very special, Shelley."

"Only with you, honey," she mimicked him. She rose over him, her breasts rubbing sensuously across his chest. Bending slightly, she covered his mouth with hers.

He was hard and aching again. Without breaking the kiss, he rolled out from under her. Blindly he reached for the nightstand and found what he needed. A moment later, with his hands at her narrow waist, he lifted her and settled her down again, arching his hips to thrust inside her.

"I need you, Shelley." His words were little more than a hoarse groan, harsh with emotion and effort.

Her face glistened with sweat, and her heart was pounding, visible in the veins of her slender throat. "I'm here," she whispered with the bittersweet wish that his words meant more and the acceptance that they didn't. "I'm here, Christopher."

Christopher awoke early Saturday morning. For a moment he kept his eyes closed, savoring the feel of the soft, warm body cradled next to his. His arm curved over her, keeping her at his side. It was the first time in over a year that he'd shared a bed with a woman, but there had been no discomfort or uneasiness to bother him through the night. Waking with Shelley in his bed seemed the most natural and most pleasant thing in the world.

Slowly he opened his eyes to look at her. She was beautiful. Undeniably, unforgettably beautiful. Simply looking at her was a pleasure. With no more than that long look for encouragement, his desire was revived, evidenced by an uncomfortable fullness in his lower body.

"Shelley."

His whisper was almost soundless. She had to be tired after the long night, so he didn't try to wake her. He could wait.

He kissed her, a simple brush of his lips across hers, and stood up, sliding from beneath the covers. As he left the bed, she moved, giving a whimper of protest at his leaving. He bent and tucked the covers snugly around her, then hurriedly stepped into a pair of sweatpants.

After turning on the heat and building a fire in the living room, he went back upstairs to shower and dress, using the guest bathroom so he wouldn't disturb Shelley. That out of the way, he returned downstairs again to start breakfast.

The phone rang as he opened the refrigerator door. Swiftly he reached for the extension on the wall, hoping to get it before it woke Shelley. "Hello?" he answered softly, guardedly.

"Did I wake you?"

It was Gabriel. Christopher propped the receiver between his ear and shoulder and began taking items from the refrigerator. "No, I'm up. What do you need?"

"I've got some great news. Are you ready to hear it?"

Christopher set the bacon and eggs on the counter. His grip on the receiver was painfully tight, like the tightness in his chest, but he couldn't force himself to relax. For the first time in months they had found something promising. He had waited so long for this day that he was half afraid to hear the details.

Gabriel didn't wait for a response from his friend but went on talking. "I ran the names that I'd gotten so far through the computers at the Defense Department. Of the bunch, there are eleven on active duty with the navy and marines, six with prior service and one retired."

Christopher called a picture that had to be the retired man to mind. He was a frequent customer at Impressions, and Shelley had commented once on his age—early fifties, they had guessed, when most of the other customers were in their twenties and early thirties.

"The retired guy caught my attention because of his age," Gabriel continued, "so I've been running a check on him."

He paused briefly for effect, then said, "I think we've got our man."

"I won't ask her to do it."

Gabriel sighed wearily. He had given Christopher all the information on their prime suspect, then had made what seemed to him to be a perfectly reasonable suggestion. For the last ten minutes Christopher had been stubbornly insisting that Gabriel's reasonable suggestion was out of the question. "She's perfect for it, Christopher. She's fairly new in town. She has no friends here, so she's not going to run into anyone she knows. No one would ever connect her to you, since you disappeared before she moved here. And she's observant—she notices things. She's perfect."

That was true, Christopher thought grimly. Shelley was perfect in ways that Gabriel didn't even begin to suspect. Too perfect. He couldn't let Gabriel involve her in this plan. "No," he said flatly. "I don't want Shelley going in there."

"Why not? You've got to learn to trust her, Christopher," Gabriel said in exasperation. "She can help."

"It's not a question of trust." Christopher paced the length of the kitchen, stretching the phone cord behind him. "We're talking about the man who had my brother killed. He's dangerous. He could kill Shelley just as easily. I won't do it. I won't let her risk her life like that."

"We've got no other choice. I can't do it because of my job, and you can't do it because he'll probably recognize you. She's our only choice."

"I don't want anyone else to get hurt." Christopher squeezed his eyes shut. God, he didn't want Shelley hurt!

"Then we'll hire someone. A stranger."

Hire a stranger. Pay someone for his loyalty, his trust and his silence. Hope that someone else wouldn't offer him more money. Pray that he wouldn't betray them. "I'll talk to her," Christopher said stiffly, his lips barely moving. "Why don't you come up this morning and we'll tell her... everything."

"All right." Gabriel didn't push for anything more. He knew that he'd given Christopher a hard decision to make. "I can bring her with me, unless she'd rather drive."

"I'll tell her." Christopher hung up and went outside onto the deck. The sun was shining, but it added only brilliance, not warmth. His breath formed little clouds that slowly dissipated. The dampness penetrated his jeans and his T-shirt, making him shiver. After a few minutes he was thoroughly chilled, but he kept standing there.

Cold. That was how he felt all the way through. His heart, his soul—both were frozen. He needed help—Shelley's help. He was going to ask her to put her life in danger for him. To ask her to risk death. For him. And if anything happened to her, if this man Gabriel had told him about did one thing to hurt her, Christopher knew that this coldness would stay with him forever. He would never be warm again.

He sighed, a weary, defeated sound, and went back to the kitchen. Mechanically he started coffee brewing in the coffee-maker, cracked eggs into a bowl, put bacon in the skillet. He acted without thought, without conscious effort. He wasn't capable of either.

When Shelley came downstairs, she found him standing at the stove, turning slices of bacon with a fork as they browned. His eyes were almost black, staring at something that only he could see, something that she couldn't share with him.

She had expected to wake up with Christopher next to her, his body hard, yet soft and warm. Instead she'd been alone, and the sheets where he had lain were cold. That wasn't how she'd wanted to start the day.

Now he stared at the skillet, oblivious to everything around him, including her. It wasn't until she seated herself on a bar stool at the counter, only a few feet in front of him, that he noticed her. He smiled, his lips compressed in a tight line. "Good morning."

Shelley stared at him. The smile was as phony as the greeting. It wasn't a good morning. He looked like hell, as if he couldn't remember how in the world he'd gotten himself into this situation. She wanted to shake him, to scream at him that he'd promised he wouldn't be sorry. He'd promised no regrets.

"Scrambled eggs okay, or would you rather have them fried?"

She shook her head. "It doesn't matter."

It didn't matter to him, either. He removed the last slice of bacon, drained the grease from the skillet and poured the eggs in. "Did you sleep well?"

"Yes."

When he risked looking at her, he saw that she was chewing her lower lip. The desire to make her stop, to bathe the reddened skin with his tongue, hit him like a blow. Quickly he looked away again, turning to put bread in the toaster next to the stove.

Awkwardly they set the table, putting platters of bacon and eggs and toast between containers of honey, butter and jellies. Christopher poured the coffee into a thermal carafe, then sat down across from Shelley to eat in silence.

He couldn't do it. He'd told Gabriel that he would talk to her, but now he couldn't find the words, or the courage to say them. He couldn't ask the woman he'd made love to most of the night to jeopardize her life for him.

But if he didn't ask her, he'd have to follow Gabriel's other suggestion: hire a stranger. A private detective, most likely. There was no one else in his life whom he could trust.

"Shelley."

She swallowed the food in her mouth and took a long drink of coffee. She didn't like the way he'd said her name. Was this where he told her that he'd been wrong, that he *did* regret making love to her? If so, she didn't want to hear it. She couldn't bear to hear him say again that he didn't want her.

"I need a favor from you. Gabriel thinks we have a likely suspect at the club—that older man that we talked about." Leaning back in his chair, Christopher cleared his throat.

"He thinks we need someone inside to see what the man does when he's there—who he talks to, if he's meeting someone. We know the days and times that he goes there, so . . . Gabriel thinks it would be best if . . . if you're there at the same times . . . to keep an eye on him."

Shelley stared down at the food on her plate. If she tried to eat anything else, she knew she would be ill. She might be anyway.

Now she knew why Christopher had called her yesterday. Now she knew why he'd made love to her last night after making it clear so many times before that he didn't want her. How difficult it must have been for him to touch her so tenderly, to say those soft, sweet words. How he must have hated the intimacy and the lies.

She had taken a shower before she'd gotten dressed, but now she wanted another one. She wanted to wash away the memory of his lovemaking, to scrub away the feel of his body against her, inside her, but all the soap and water in the world wouldn't make her feel clean again.

He was waiting for her response. When she was certain that the tears stinging her eyes wouldn't fall, she looked at him. "You pay a high price for favors, don't you?" she asked softly. He must have wanted her help badly if he'd been willing to make love to her to get it. God, why hadn't he simply asked? Hadn't he known that she would do anything she could to help him? It hadn't been necessary to take her to bed.

"I don't understand. . . ."

She shook her head as if the question were unimportant, then reached for her coffee. Her hand trembled, though, sloshing the liquid close to the rim of the cup. Biting her lip, she put the cup down again. "I'll do it."

"Think about it first. Shelley, this man—if he's the right one—had my brother killed. He's a dangerous man. He could hurt you."

She was already hurting. What could a little more pain matter? "You don't have any other choice, do you?"

The words were so similar to Gabriel's—and so right. He shook his head miserably. "No. there's no one else."

She smiled, a tight-lipped gesture like his own. "It's nice to know I'm the last person you'd turn to for help."

"In this situation, you're damned right." He welcomed the anger as a way to release the tension that was twisting inside him, filling him with fear. "We're talking about a man who had the power to get Gary killed in jail! He works for the KGB, for God's sake! This isn't a game anymore, Shelley! It's real, and you could get hurt. You could be the one to die this time!"

She stood up from the table. "It's my life and my decision. It doesn't concern you."

Christopher shoved his chair back so hard when he stood that it fell over. Neither of them noticed. "It *does* concern me! We're partners, remember? A pair, a couple—you and me. Damn it, Shelley, you don't even have the sense to be scared!"

"I'm not a coward," she replied stiffly.

"Neither am I," he denied, dragging his hand through his hair. "But this whole thing scares the hell out of me. I don't want you involved."

She stood in front of him and answered in a soft voice that contrasted sharply with the loud harshness of his. "But I *am* involved, Christopher. I know you don't like it, and you don't want it, but it's too late to change it. *I am involved.*"

Christopher raised his hand. He was going to touch her face, and once he'd done that, he knew that he would keep touching her until their clothes were off and he had buried himself inside her. He was moving closer when a sharp knock sounded at the front door.

Shelley jumped back, startled by the sound. "I didn't realize that you were expecting company." She was relieved by the interruption that had stopped him from making a fool of her yet again.

Christopher swore silently. "Gabriel is supposed to stop by. He wants to go over everything he found out about this man." He let his hand, only inches from its destination, fall away. "I'll let him in."

By the time he'd led Gabriel into the living room, Shelley was sitting on the sofa, her feet tucked beneath her. They were bare, and her shoes and socks were nowhere in sight, silent testimony to the fact that hers was no casual visit.

Gabriel was only faintly surprised to see her, although he wondered how she'd gotten there so quickly, unless... Remembering the way Shelley and Christopher had behaved the last time he'd seen them together, he assumed that she had been at the house when he called, that she'd been there at least since the previous night. But it was really none of his business, so he ignored it, shrugged out of his jacket, said hello and sat down at the other end of the couch.

"Do you want some coffee?" Christopher asked. He was cool, wary.

"Yeah, please."

When Christopher glanced at her, Shelley shook her head.

"Did he talk to you?" Gabriel asked while Christopher got the coffee.

"Yes."

"Do you want to do it?"

"Yes." She really had no choice, she thought bitterly. Christopher had already paid for her help. It served him right for not realizing that she would have done it without payment, simply because she cared.

"Anything for a story, huh?" Gabriel teased.

"You've got part of that right," she replied flippantly as Christopher returned with two mugs of coffee. To hell with the story—foolish as it was, she'd do anything for Christopher.

When Christopher was sitting on the love seat opposite them, Gabriel asked, "Where do you want us to start, Shelley?"

"The usual place. Begin at the beginning."

"Christopher?" Gabriel invited. "It's your story."

Christopher wrapped his hands around his coffee cup. He had planned to tell Shelley all this, probably sometime tomorrow. He wished he didn't have to do it now, when she was angry and he was confused. He wished he could tell it to her man to woman, lover to lover, instead of partner to partner, or worse, subject to reporter.

"After Gary died I moved up here to get away from everyone. The press was hounding me, the FBI was watching me, I got some threats from people...." He shrugged carelessly. "I just wanted to be left alone. I had considered trying to clear my name, but I didn't really think it was possible. If the FBI couldn't find the man Gary worked for, how could I? But after a couple of months up here with nothing to do, no place to go, no friends but Gabriel, I started thinking seriously about doing it—about finding the man and seeing that he paid for Gary's death. About proving my innocence. About justice." Despite his mocking tone, he liked the sound of that word. Justice. It tied right in with truth, freedom and a new life.

"Gabriel's been the brains behind all of it," he admitted with a nod toward his friend. "He told me what to do, and I did it. We got Gary's bank records, telephone records, credit card transactions—everything we could get our hands on—so we could track his movements over the last eighteen months of his life. According to the FBI, that was about how long he'd been selling secrets from M.I."

"It was the bank records that did you in," Shelley said. "One of my editor's sources works at the bank. She saw Gabriel when he came to get them." She turned to the other man. "What did you have to promise the woman to get her to turn them over?"

He grinned, raising his brows in a lascivious leer. "You don't want to know."

He was right. Under the circumstances, she *didn't* want to know. She turned back to Christopher. "Then what?"

"We found out that he'd made quite a few phone calls to the club, and there were a lot of credit card charges there. It went on our list of places to check."

"But didn't Gary live in San Diego? How can you get records of local calls?" she asked.

"You can't always do it. It depends on the kind of equipment the phone company uses. San Diego's is sophisticated enough that it's possible."

"Go on," she requested. She wanted to hear more—although she would prefer to hear it from Gabriel. Concentrating on business helped her keep her mind off the events of last night and this morning, but it would be a lot easier to concentrate if "business" weren't being conducted in Christopher's quiet, sometimes sarcastic, incredibly dear voice.

"We've been checking the places where Gary spent a lot of time, along with the women he spent a lot of time with. The club just happened to be next on the list of places to go."

"You've found nothing before this?"

He shook his head. "Nothing—just a lot of dead ends."

"So now you think this man at the club is somehow involved." She turned sideways on the sofa so that she was facing Gabriel. It was a more comfortable position for her since Christopher was only visible from the corner of her eye.

Gabriel finished his coffee in one swallow and leaned forward to set the cup on the table. "It seems likely. To start with, the guy's at the club four times a week. We're talking about a man who's fifty-four years old hanging out in a place geared toward people in their twenties. Except for this guy, Gary was probably the oldest regular customer at thirty-six."

"Tell us about him." The tone of Christopher's voice made the command a polite request. He knew far too little about this man he was asking Shelley to confront.

Gabriel began reciting the facts he'd learned. The man's name was Charles Miller. He had retired after twenty-two years in the navy and had since been unemployed, supposedly living on his military pension. However his life-style was far too lavish to be supported by a pension alone. Miller traveled a lot, rented a luxurious condominium, drove a new car that he'd paid cash for, owned a small yacht, liked expensive gold jewelry.

"No legitimate second income?" Christopher asked.

"None."

"Could be drugs."

Gabriel shrugged. "Could be. Could also be espionage."

Christopher nodded. The search that he'd started so long ago had often seemed so hopeless that now he was afraid to expect too much. He'd been disappointed too many times before. "What else did you find out?"

"He was enlisted—made it to senior chief before he retired." That was the second-highest level an enlisted man could achieve. "He was a cryptologic technician. He had a top-secret security clearance and access to some of the most sensitive information in existence."

Miller was divorced and had no children. He was rather secretive about his private life; none of his neighbors knew anything about him. He was quiet, seldom had visitors, never created any problems. As far as any of them knew, he had no friends or relatives in San Diego.

"One curious little piece of information..." Gabriel turned his attention from Shelley to Christopher. "Miller travels to San Francisco once every couple of months."

Shelley was puzzled by the interest that lit Christopher's dark eyes. "Why is that important?" she asked.

"The Soviets have two embassies in the United States," Christopher explained. "One in Washington, D.C., and one..." He let her finish.

"And one in San Francisco." Her brows drawn together in a frown, she asked, "But doesn't the FBI or someone watch places like that?"

"You bet," Gabriel replied. "You visit the Soviet Embassy, and you can be sure that the FBI will know who you are and what your business with the Russians is within days."

"So if this man is visiting the embassy, why hasn't the FBI found out about him? If he's spying, why haven't they caught him?"

"I doubt that he's actually going to the embassy. Remember, the guy's background is in intelligence. He's going to know that the embassy is under surveillance. No, I think his contact is probably assigned to the embassy, and Miller occasionally meets with him there in the city."

Christopher was shaking his head. "It doesn't fit, Gabriel. The FBI did the same stuff we've done—they checked the club before we did. If that was where Gary and this Miller met, why didn't they find him?"

"Because he wasn't there." Gabriel reached for his jacket, drawing a small notebook from the pocket. He flipped through it until he found the information he wanted. "Gary was arrested last October fourteenth and killed on the fifteenth. Phone calls were made daily from Charles Miller's home phone until October fourteenth. After four calls that day, there were no more until January sixteenth. The phone service wasn't disconnected, he simply wasn't there to use it."

"That's not very convincing proof," Shelley said.

"Not by itself, no," Gabriel agreed. "Miller doesn't seem to have much use for cash. He charges everything—meals, gas, clothes. His credit card accounts are the most active I've run across. From October fifteenth until January sixteenth he didn't make a single charge in San Diego. He left a trail leading from San Diego to Los Angeles, Seattle, Salt Lake City, Phoenix to Albuquerque to Tucson and, eventually, back to San Diego."

"So he was out of town," Shelley said. "You said he travels a lot."

Gabriel ignored her and watched Christopher instead as he stood up to walk around the room. He touched the frame of the painting above the fireplace, ran his fingers over the edge of a shelf full of books, wiped a narrow strip of dust from the television cabinet, switched on the stereo to a low volume, and came to a stop in front of the glass door.

Christopher stared unseeingly outside. Gabriel was right. This was the man. Charles Miller was the man who had killed his brother. Oh, he understood that another man by the name of Garcia was the one who had actually wielded the knife, but Miller had ordered it. Miller had been responsible.

Charles Miller. Age fifty-four. Retired from the United States Navy. Average-looking man. Spy. Traitor. Murderer. And Christopher was asking Shelley to get close to him. He was asking her to risk her life.

Dear God, he loved her too much to let her do it, but he knew with a sickening certainty that she *would* do it, and he *would* let her.

If anything happened to her, how could he live with it?

How could he live without her?

Chapter 6

Christopher clenched his hands into fists. He wanted to hit something, anything, to release his fury and despair. The glass door was a tempting target, and he drew his hand back. But when his curled fingers came into contact with the cold glass, there was no force, no momentum. They soundlessly touched the glass, then flattened against it.

"Charles Miller is a spy," he said tonelessly in response to Shelley's last statement. "One of his boys had just gotten arrested for espionage. He had to drop out of sight."

He turned then, his gaze meeting and holding Shelley's. "My brother was a weak man." It hurt him to make that admission. He'd spent most of his life looking out for Gary, making excuses for Gary, and he had never said one bad thing about his older brother. "Gary never answered any questions when he was arrested. He was waiting for a chance to make a deal. When the FBI offered what he wanted, he would have told them everything. Miller knew that—he knew Gary better than I did. He knew that Gary would give them Miller in exchange for his freedom. So Miller had him killed.''

He went back to the love seat and sat down directly across from Shelley. Leaning forward, his arms resting on his thighs, he continued talking. ''Miller has an intelligence background. He knew that the FBI would conduct a thorough investigation into Gary's life—where he went, who he saw, what he did. Everything and everyone would be suspect. He knew that if he stayed at the club, they would question and investigate him, and they would find a few things out of place in his life, just as Gabriel did. He also knew that the club was the only thing that connected him to Gary. If he left and stayed away long enough for them to complete their investigation, they would never find anything to link him to Gary. So he took a three-month vacation. When the investigation was over, he came back and resumed his life and his spying.''

Shelley drew her knees to her chest, wrapping her arms around them and pushing her feet between the sofa cushions. ''If Gary worked for this man, then chances are pretty good that other people also work for him, right?''

It was Gabriel who answered. ''Exactly. Men in the military lose their access to information when they get out. They have to recruit other sources to continue.''

''It seems as if other military people would be his first choices. Why did he approach Gary? How would he know that a civilian would have access to secret data?'' She suspected the answer, but she looked at Christopher anyway.

''Gary liked to talk. He . . . bragged a lot.'' Christopher leaned back against the cushions and pressed the heels of his hands to his eyes. Lord, he was tired. He wished he'd never gotten out of bed this morning, had never answered the phone. He wished that he had stayed there under the covers next to Shelley until she had awakened and then they had made love the rest of the day.

''Are you sure you want to do this?'' Gabriel asked quietly. ''Risking your neck is a high price to pay for a story.''

"I'm sure."

He offered her a piece of paper. "Here are the days and times that he goes to the club. You'll need to be there then. Watch him, find out anything you can about him and about anyone he talks to. I think it would be best, Christopher, if you hung around outside, for the first couple of days at least. Just in case."

Just in case. Shelley and Christopher both stiffened at the grim warning. Just in case Miller somehow connected her to Christopher? Just in case he decided that she was a problem, too? Just in case he decided to get rid of her, the way he'd gotten rid of Gary?

"I think *I* should go in," Christopher said harshly.

"You think this guy isn't going to recognize you?" Shelley asked. She was as sarcastic and mocking as Christopher had ever been. "You got arrested when it should have been him. Your face was on the front page of every newspaper and on the local and network news. He had your brother killed. If you walk into that club when he's there, we'll probably never see him again."

"She's right," Gabriel said. "We may need to use you later, but right now you've got to stay out of sight. We don't want to spook Miller." He stood up and reached for his jacket. "I'm going to head home. I've got to work tonight."

Shelley also got to her feet. "Wait a minute, will you? I'd like to follow you back to make sure I don't get lost."

Christopher stared at her, but she quickly left the room, avoiding his gaze. Without a word to Gabriel, he followed her upstairs to his bedroom. "What are you doing?" he demanded.

She sat down on the bed to put on socks and shoes. "I'm going home."

"You were supposed to stay—"

She interrupted. "I was supposed to stay as long as I wanted," she reminded him coolly. "Well, this is as long as I want." She tied her tennis shoes, pulling the laces far too tight. She decided that she could stand aching feet until she got into the car. "You got what you wanted, Christopher," she said with a mocking smile. "Don't act so displeased."

He was quietly thoughtful. Her words confused him—everything about her confused him. *You got what you wanted.* In one sense, he supposed that was true. He'd wanted to make love to her, to touch her intimately and gently, and he'd done that. But he'd wanted so much more—to make her his. To be important to her. To bind her to him so that she could never leave him.

He didn't even have the decency to lie and deny that he'd slept with her so she would agree to his request, Shelley thought angrily as she shoved the few things she'd unpacked back into the suitcase and slammed it shut.

Christopher took one step toward her before his thoughts completed their course and reached the natural conclusion. He'd gotten what he wanted, and so had Shelley. Not only was she working with him, but now the final plays of the game were hers. Regardless of the outcome, she was guaranteed a story that every reporter in Southern California would sell their souls for... and all it had cost her was her body.

Silently he stepped back and let her pass. He didn't look at her; his gaze was fastened on the hardwood floor beneath his feet. There was a slight disturbance in the air caused by her leaving; then there was nothing. Just a stillness and a subtle, sensual fragrance that filled his nostrils and made him ache.

Shelley tucked her large, flat handbag under her arm, took a deep breath and got out of the car. She didn't glance around the parking lot, but she knew that Christopher, in a nondescript rental car, was parked near the bushes at the edge of the lot. She knew that he would stay there until she left again, and he would follow her home and question her about what she had seen and heard inside. She didn't know

if the dread that filled her was due to the start of her job or
of that interrogation.

She had lied when she'd told Christopher that she wasn't
a coward. She was. There wasn't a story in the world worth
the fear that was pumping through her blood with every beat
of her heart. She was a good reporter—but she was good
with words, good with people. Not with fear and danger and
murderers.

But she wasn't doing this for a story, she reminded herself as she started across the parking lot. She was doing it for
Christopher. That gave her courage.

It was eleven-fifteen. If Miller kept to his routine, he
would come in for lunch in fifteen minutes and would stay
until twelve forty-five. He followed the same routine Monday, Tuesday, Thursday and Friday. To avoid suspicion,
Shelley was going to have to come in on Wednesdays, too.
She wasn't looking forward to spending five days a week in
a club that was as much a bar as a restaurant.

She opened the door and stepped inside. The place was
dim, so she took a moment to remove her sunglasses and
slide them into a case in her purse; then she let her eyes ad-
just to the light. Just as she took a step forward, there was
a crash and a clatter of breaking glass. Her heart rate, already fast, seemed to double.

"Clean up the mess," a hard, male voice commanded.

Shelley reached the end of the entry hall and saw the
source of the commotion: a waitress, hands on her slim hips,
had apparently dropped a tray of glasses and was now at-
tempting to stare down the man who loomed over her.

"I'm not going to. It wasn't my fault."

"It's always your fault, Melissa," the man insisted.
"Clean it up *now*."

"I've had it with these people, Derek, and I've had it with
you."

She started to walk away, but the man caught her arm in
his incredibly big hand. "What the hell do you mean,
you've had it? You show up for work whenever you feel like

it, you're always causing problems with the customers or the other girls—you're damned lucky I don't fire you."

The woman smiled sweetly and used her fingernails to free her hand from his grip. "You can't fire me," she said, delivering the classic comeback in a sugary voice. "I quit." She walked past Shelley, greeting her with a smile. "Good morning. Welcome to Impressions and go to hell."

Shelley heard Derek shout at the waitress, "Get back here now, Melissa! You can't quit during lunch!"

An idea was forming in Shelley's mind, and she acted on it quickly before common sense could stop her. "Are you the boss here?" she asked, exaggerating her drawl just slightly.

He looked down at her, his blue eyes narrowed with anger. "I'm the owner. Who are you?"

"My name is Shelley, and I just happen to be the solution to your problem."

Half an hour later, Shelley walked out of the club and returned to her car. She hadn't had a chance to eavesdrop on Miller today, but she wasn't too worried. She had met one hurdle. Now it was time to face the second, more formidable obstacle: Christopher.

Even at a distance, she could see the consternation on Christopher's face as he started his car to follow her. They had arranged earlier to meet near the carousel at Seaport Village downtown; Gabriel was supposed to be there, too. She decided to stick to that part of the plan at least.

Christopher didn't wait to reach the carousel. He parked a few spaces away from Shelley, caught up with her and grabbed her arm. "What the hell's going on? Why did you leave early?" he demanded.

She pulled away and kept walking. "Wait until we find Gabriel and I'll tell you both at once." She had a feeling that she was going to need Gabriel's support in this.

"Gabriel won't be here until twelve forty-five or one o'clock," Christopher reminded her.

"Then maybe you'd better call him and see if he can come earlier," she suggested sweetly.

They had chosen Seaport village for two reasons: it was easy for Shelley to find, and it was close to the police station. Gabriel arrived less than ten minutes after he received Christopher's phone call. He found them both facing the bay, separated by ten feet and a world of differences. "What's up?" he asked, pushing his hands into his jacket pockets. "What went wrong, Shelley?"

"Nothing."

"Did Miller show up?"

"Yes," Christopher replied.

"Then why are you guys here when he's there?"

"Because Shelley walked out less than fifteen minutes after he arrived," Christopher said hostilely.

Slowly, Shelley turned from the bay. Her gaze skimmed over Christopher before it reached Gabriel. "I had to leave. But I'm going back tomorrow. As a waitress."

Gabriel approved, as she had expected, but Christopher didn't—also as she had expected. Ignoring his friend's smile, Christopher turned on her. "Like hell you are!"

"It makes sense. If I'm going to be there every time Miller comes in, I need to have a reason. Otherwise he's going to be suspicious. This way I'll have a reason. I'll also be able to talk to the other employees—they'll trust the new waitress more than they would a new customer. And—" she held up her hand to stop his protest "—and it'll give me a chance to look at the charge slips. I might be able to identify some of the customers that Gabriel hasn't been able to." Smiling smugly, she lowered her hand and waited for Christopher to speak.

He moved closer to her, until his breath was a warm touch against her forehead. "You're crazy as hell, you know that?" he asked in an outraged but dangerously soft voice. "If you really believe that I'm going to let you go in there and work as a waitress, you're crazy."

Deliberately she rose onto her toes, so that the tip of her nose was level with the tip of his. "Given a choice between going in there as a waitress or going in there as a customer, I would choose waitressing any day." Backing away from him, she planted her hands on her hips. "What kind of woman hangs around a bar for a couple of hours at a time, five days a week? Did you ever consider that? There are the lushes, although I suppose most of them would prefer to drink at home, and there are the hookers. Which would you prefer me to be: a drunk, a prostitute, or a waitress?"

His eyes cold and dark and angry, he stared at her for a long moment before softly answering, "You don't seem to have any problems with selling yourself."

The color fled her face, leaving her as pale as the lifeless clouds overhead. The gold chain around her neck rose and fell with each ragged breath she took. "You bastard," she whispered.

"That's enough," Gabriel said sharply. "I didn't come here to referee a juvenile name-calling match. I think you made a good choice, Shelley. As an employee, you'll be a lot more help to us. But be careful, will you? Don't try to do anything by yourself. Christopher and I are here to help you."

"Thank you, Gabriel." She zipped her jacket as the wind picked up. "I'm going home now. Derek Robinson, the owner, is supposed to give me my schedule tomorrow. I'll let you know what it is." Without a word for Christopher, she walked away.

When she was out of sight, Gabriel turned to Christopher. "You're driving her away."

Christopher looked sharply at his friend. "I don't want your advice."

"I'm giving it anyway. I tried to warn you about Gary, but you chose not to listen. I tried to warn you about Mike Jennings, and you ignored that, too, and look what it got you. Shelley Evans is probably the best thing that ever happened to you. She's risking her life to help you, and how do you thank her? You call her a whore."

"She's not doing a damned thing for me," Christopher disagreed. "She wants the story."

"If you believe that, then you're a fool, Christopher, and you don't deserve her."

Staring out over the water, Christopher heard Gabriel walk away. Once again he was alone, as he'd been so many times in the past. As he feared he would always be in the future.

Despite the claims she'd made to Derek Robinson, Shelley had never worked as a waitress a day in her life. Shortly after her shift started Tuesday, her feet were already hurting. This must be a hell of a way to make a living, she thought wearily. And it was a hell of a favor to do for a man who thought you were a whore.

Christopher Morgan had gall—she'd give him that. After he'd slept with her for the sole purpose of getting her help, he'd had the nerve to accuse *her* of selling herself. It still made her so mad that she wanted to slap him.

She had started work that morning at ten-thirty, when one of the waitresses showed her around. Charles Miller was due in at eleven-thirty. She glanced at her watch, saw that it was almost time, then looked around the dining room. It was busy; most of the tables already filled. There was one table at the back, though, that remained empty. For a regular customer like Miller? she wondered.

She removed one shoe and wiggled her toes, sighing at the sensation. One of the waitresses walked past and laughed. "Believe it or not, you'll get used to it. Will you get this one, Shelley?" She gestured to a customer. "The corner table is his."

Shelley put her shoe on, pasted a smile on her face and looked up. At Charles Miller.

He looked so ordinary, so decent. How could this average, rather attractive man be guilty of the things that she knew he'd done? How could he look so normal when he had cold-bloodedly ordered the death of another human being?

"Good morning," she greeted him in the falsely cheerful voice that all the waitresses used. "My name is Shelley, and I'll be your waitress for today."

He smiled back at her. "You're new here, aren't you?" he asked as he followed her across the room.

"Yes, sir."

He studied her for a moment when they reached his table, then nodded. "You're pretty. You'll fit in nicely."

Catching the inside of her lip between her teeth, she continued smiling and even managed to thank him for the compliment. "Here's your menu."

He waved it away. "I don't need one, honey." He rattled off his order from memory, finishing before Shelley even had a chance to start writing. She scribbled it down, smiled and fled the table.

Yesterday she'd admitted to being frightened. Now she knew the real meaning of the word fear. Her heart was pounding, her blood rushing, and her head ached terribly. Charles Miller wasn't a frightening-looking man, and that, she thought, was what scared her the most. He looked as normal as the rest of the diners, and only she knew he wasn't.

He was joined a few minutes later by a young man about Shelley's age. They were talking quietly when she approached, but as soon as she got close enough to hear, they fell silent. She offered a menu to the man, but he refused it and ordered only coffee.

She made mental notes of the man's description, the time he came and the time he left. As soon as Miller had also left, she jotted the information in the notebook in her purse.

When she got off at six, Christopher followed her home. Traffic on the freeways was heavy, but they got separated so he arrived a few minutes after she did.

He took a seat in the rocker and studied her. She was still wearing her uniform—a tailored white shirt and a slim, black skirt. On any other woman it would have looked plain and unappealing, but not on Shelley. Her natural softness muted the severity of the style and the starkness of the colors.

She looked as tired as he felt, he thought. He hadn't been sleeping well at night. His dreams all centered around her, and they were too vivid, too intense. Too erotic.

Shelley lay back on the sofa, a fat, pink pillow behind her, her legs stretched out in front of her. She considered rubbing her calves and feet, then decided that a hot bath would be better. Bath, dinner, bed. That would be nice.

But first she had to take care of business. "About five minutes after he came in, another man met him. The guy was young—probably in his early thirties—and looked like he'd be in the navy—you know, short hair, clean-cut. He stayed until twelve-thirty. I couldn't hear anything they were saying. Every time I got close, they shut up."

Christopher knew the man she was talking about. He'd made a note of his license number and also of the fact that his car bore a blue, military base sticker. The color signified that he was an officer. But at this moment he wasn't particularly interested in Miller or his friend. He wanted to talk over personal matters, starting with an apology. "Shelley..."

She hated it when he said her name like that. It always meant that he wanted to start a serious conversation, and it always included things she didn't want to hear. Sitting straighter, she swung her feet to the floor. She felt less vulnerable in that position than when she was practically lying down. "Say whatever you're going to say, then go. I'm tired, and I'd really like you to leave as soon as possible," she said quickly.

He stiffened. She wasn't going to make it easy for him, and, like her, he was tired. Too tired to attempt anything hard. "Forget it. I'll see you tomorrow."

"You don't need to. Miller doesn't go to the club on Wednesday."

He stopped at the door and looked down at her. "I'll see you tomorrow," he repeated. The stubborn set of his jaw showed that he meant it.

When the door closed with a final-sounding click, Shelley sagged back against the cushions. Which was harder? she wondered. Facing Charles Miller, who had sold out his country and murdered one of his own employees, or facing Christopher?

It was no contest. Christopher won hands down. Miller might scare the hell out of her, but all he could take was her life. Christopher had already taken the thing that made life worthwhile: her heart. Worst of all, he didn't know or care that he had it.

Shelley settled into the routine at Impressions with ease. The job was tedious, and some of the customers were obnoxious, especially after a few drinks, but other than sore feet, she had no complaints. Even the routine after-work meeting with Christopher and occasionally Gabriel got easier. She recounted everything she saw, everything she heard. She copied names off credit card slips and passed them on.

In her second week at the club Shelley got a day off for Thanksgiving. She had dreaded the holiday since the beginning of the month, and she really would have preferred to work, but Impressions, along with practically every other place in San Diego, was closed. Two thousand miles away her family had their usual celebration, with all her aunts and uncles and cousins, but Shelley was alone in her little apartment. She could have had her own celebration, but if she couldn't celebrate the day with her family, she didn't want to celebrate it at all.

Fifty miles away Christopher was also alone. Gabriel had invited him to dinner with him and Lori, but Christopher had refused. His reasoning was similar to Shelley's: if he couldn't spend the day with her, he preferred to spend it by himself.

Shelley watched parades and did her laundry. Christopher watched football games and went for an extra-long run between games. They went to bed early, both glad to have survived the family-oriented day, both alone, and both incredibly lonely.

In the middle of Shelley's third week at the club, something unusual happened. She wasn't quite sure what to make of it and decided to say nothing to Christopher until she had thought it out. Unfortunately, with each meeting, he seemed to read her expressions better. This time he knew that she was leaving something out. After avoiding his probing questions for ten minutes, Shelley blurted out, "He asked me to have dinner with him."

Christopher stared at her. Careful, he cautioned himself. Don't blow up. Not yet. "Who asked you to have dinner with him?" he asked in a quiet, tautly controlled voice.

They were sitting on opposite sides of the table in her small dining room. She clasped her hands together on the table, her fingers gripped tight. "Charles Miller."

"You told him no." He was so certain he was correct that he didn't bother to phrase it as a question.

"Well...no. I didn't. I didn't tell him anything. Some customers came in, and he was gone by the time I finished."

Christopher ran his hand through his hair and muttered a string of curses—long, low and vicious. "Shelley, for God's sake, you can't be considering it."

She shrugged. "You're the one who suggested that I sell myself. Who knows what he might tell me if I go out with him? He might confess everything if I go to bed with him." She gave a sharp laugh. "Hell, I know I'm not *that* good. But what would it hurt to try?"

Slumping back in the chair, Christopher ran his hand over his face. He looked so worn out, Shelley thought with a twinge of sympathy. Too tired even to fight anymore.

"Why are you doing this?" he asked in a miserably quiet voice. "Damn it, Shelley, why are you doing this to me?"

"I'm not doing anything to you," she denied. "You asked me to help, and that's what I'm trying to do."

"You're not going out with him. I won't allow it."

Whatever sympathy she'd found for him dissipated in the wake of his command. "You don't have any say in it. You don't own me, Christopher. You're my partner, not my boss."

"Partners?" He gave the word an ugly sound. "We're not partners in anything—not on the job, and sure as hell not *off* it."

She went into the kitchen and began pulling vegetables from the refrigerator. "You don't want me for a partner," she quietly accused.

Christopher twisted in the chair to look at her. His mouth was open to argue, but the way she'd worded the statement gave him pause. She hadn't said that he simply didn't want a partner, but that he didn't want *her* for a partner. "Do you believe that, Shelley?" he asked.

She was trying to act tough again. Her chin stubbornly raised, she flippantly replied, "What's the old saying? 'Better the evil you know than the one you don't.'"

He could think of a lot of words to apply to Shelley, but evil wasn't one of them. He preferred words like beautiful. Lovely. Sexy. Delicate. Loving.

He pushed the chair back so that he was facing her. "Ask me to stay for dinner and I'll help you fix that salad."

She scowled at him. "Why?"

"Because I want to stay." For days now he'd been going home to an empty house and he hated it. That house had been his refuge from the world for a year, but after Shelley had spent one night there, the peace was gone. The place was filled with her presence. In the kitchen, he remembered her watching him cook. In the living room, he remembered eating dinner with her, talking to her. In the bedroom... He

didn't have to remember what had happened in the bedroom with her, because he still felt it in every cell in his body.

She offered the invitation grudgingly by extending the
knife and the cutting board to him. "I have some turkey I
can reheat."

"Fine." Anything would be fine, as long as he shared it
with her.

They worked easily in silence, the first comfortable time
they'd spent together since the night they'd made love. The
relaxed mood prevailed through dinner and the cleanup that
followed, but it was broken when Christopher returned to
their earlier conversation.

They had settled on the sofa, one at each end, with the
television turned on. Ignoring the show, he watched her.
"Don't go out with him, Shelley," he said in a low, serious
voice.

She felt the tension return, making her head and neck and
the rest of her body ache. "I haven't decided yet."

"Listen to me. Right now, as far as Miller is concerned,
you're just another waitress—a very pretty one, but still just
a waitress. He's not going to tell you anything useful. It's
not worth the risk you'd be taking."

"You don't think I can take care of myself, do you?"

He thought of Kevin Hayes, and of the man upstairs
whose precious car was parked in Shelley's space right now,
and he smiled. Then he thought of Charles Miller and the
smile disappeared. "I think that sometimes...you don't use
good judgment," he replied with obvious reluctance.

"Well, at least we agree on one thing," she snapped angrily. "I can think of one time a few weeks ago when I must
have thrown my good judgment right out the window."

His face turned a deeper bronze. "It's not just Miller,
okay?" he said hotly. "I don't want you going out with
anyone!"

They stared at each other for a minute; then Shelley stood
up. "I'm going to change clothes," she said, sounding and
feeling strangely disoriented.

In the bedroom she removed her skirt and blouse, then sat down on the bed in her slip. If she had a thousand years to work at it, she would never understand Christopher. The only consolation she found was that she was certain he didn't understand himself very well these days, either. Sometimes he acted as if he couldn't stand her. He'd told her that he didn't want to work with her, didn't want her around, didn't want an affair with her, didn't want anything from her but to be left alone. But at other times... At other times he acted as if he really, truly cared for her. It was all too puzzling.

After stripping off the rest of her clothes, she put on a pair of faded jeans and a red T-shirt emblazoned with the mascot of the college she'd attended. When she left the bedroom she immediately heard Christopher's voice.

He was stretched out on the sofa, the phone cradled close to his ear. "I know. Here she is. You can tell her yourself."

She accepted the receiver as she sank into the rocker. Gabriel was on the other end, and he delivered a long, heated lecture to her for even considering accepting Miller's invitation.

Knowing that his friend was taking his side against Shelley—for once—Christopher folded his hands beneath his head, kicked his shoes off and relaxed.

"All right," she said when Gabriel paused for breath. "I won't go out with him." Grinning impishly, she added, "I'll tell him that my live-in lover is six-foot-three, weighs a hundred and ninety pounds, carries a gun and probably wouldn't approve."

Christopher's smug smile disappeared as she described Gabriel. He didn't want to hear Shelley even jokingly refer to anyone as a lover besides *him*.

"Look, I just thought . . . I thought it might speed things up. Maybe he gets careless once in a while." She listened to the other man for a moment, gave her solemn promise that she wouldn't get too close to Miller, then hung up. She realized that she should be irritated with Christopher for calling Gabriel, but she didn't care. She was too tired to care about anything.

Ignoring Christopher, she turned her attention to the television show. For the next two hours she watched TV and pretended that he wasn't stretched out on the sofa, looking as comfortable and relaxed as if he were in his own house. When the evening news came on at eleven she watched that, too, then switched the television off. "I've got to get to bed," she said flatly.

Christopher didn't answer.

He was asleep. Shelley shook her head in dismay. She'd had a hard enough time falling asleep for the last few weeks. How was she supposed to do it tonight, knowing that Christopher was sleeping on her sofa?

She spoke his name loudly, jarring him awake. First he realized that the television was turned off; then he looked at his watch. "I need to go home," he said through a yawn.

The decent thing to do was ask him to stay. It was after eleven-thirty. By the time he got home it would be almost one o'clock, and he still had to come back in the morning. It wouldn't hurt to offer him the sofa, even if it meant that *she* couldn't sleep. "You can stay here," she said grudgingly.

Christopher looked at her, wishing that he could give her offer a broad interpretation—not "stay here" but "stay with me"—but he knew that she'd said exactly what she'd meant. He could spend the night in her apartment.

He had options. He could go home. Tired as he was, he could make it home without driving off the side of the mountain. Or he could rent a motel room. San Diego was filled with motels where he would never see anyone he knew. But the sofa was too comfortable, the apartment was too warm, and the company was too beautiful to resist.

"Thanks," he said quietly. "Just turn off the lights and leave me here." His eyes closed again, but he could tell when she left the room by the sudden emptiness around him.

Shelley turned down the covers on her bed, took her pillow and alarm clock to her office, then returned to the living room. "You can sleep in my bed," she said, bending to turn off one lamp.

"I can sleep right here," he disagreed.

"The sofa is too short for you."

"The daybed," he suggested. He remembered stretching out on the brass bed while he'd read her files. It hadn't been a particularly comfortable fit, but he could survive it for one night.

"It's too short, too. I'll sleep there." She waited until he stood up before she turned off the other lamp. The hall light lit their way. "The sheets are clean and fresh, and there's an extra blanket at the foot of the bed if you need it."

Christopher looked at the bed from the doorway. "There's room here for both of us," He'd spoken softly, but in the quiet of the hall the words sounded loud, explosive.

Shelley nervously looked away. "No, there's not. If you need anything—"

He interrupted, lifting his hand to her face. "I need you, Shelley."

"No," she whispered. "Not again."

His fingers moved gently over her cheek to her lips. "Was it so bad for you the first time?"

She was trembling, her heart racing. She stepped back so that his hand fell away, then took a half-dozen more steps to be safe. "Not bad," she lied, unable to look into his eyes, "just not worth repeating." She didn't want to spend another long, loving night in his arms, only to be reminded in the morning that it meant nothing to him. To him, she was just a means to an end.

Christopher watched her walk away. When the office door closed behind her, he finally entered the bedroom and began undressing.

Not worth repeating. She'd been brutally honest, and the words had deeply wounded him. How painful it was to be told by the woman he loved that his lovemaking wasn't worth a second try.

But why should it be? he wondered bitterly. Shelley cared nothing for him. She'd wanted the story, and she'd done what she felt was necessary to get it. He had nothing else to offer her now. She was really no different from Mike. Mike had pretended to care about Christopher to get his story; Shelley had pretended to want him to get hers.

Naked, he slid between cool, soft sheets covered in pastel stripes. A thick comforter striped in deeper hues of the same colors added warmth to the bed. He settled in, a pillow tucked beneath his head, took a deep breath—and nearly exploded with longing.

The sheets *were* clean and fresh—he could smell the combined scent of fabric softener and heat. But they were also permeated with Shelley's scent. Each breath he took held the faint, tantalizing fragrance that came from her. Wide awake now, he breathed. Slow, deep, painful breaths. And he wanted. Needed. Hungered.

The apartment was silent, the rooms dark. Christopher stared at the ceiling until his eyes hurt. When he closed them, the images that appeared made other parts of his body ache.

She was only seconds away, only a few feet down the hall. All he had to do was walk down the hall to the office, to the daybed, lift the covers, lie down and slide inside her. He was hard and throbbing, and she was soft and warm. When she saw, when she felt and knew how much he needed her, surely she wouldn't send him away. Surely she owed him the luxury of feeling her body enclose him just once more.

But he didn't want what was owed him. He didn't want anything given as payment of a debt or from a sense of obligation. He wanted her to want him the way he wanted her. He wanted her to dream about him, to wake up in the middle of the night needing him. Damn it, he wanted her to love him.

To distract himself from thoughts of impossible love, he listened to the night sounds. A door slammed nearby, someone laughed, a helicopter flew overhead. Minutes ticked by and still he wanted her.

Slowly he pushed the covers back and stood up. The chilly night air raised goose bumps all over him as he walked down the hall.

The door to the office opened with a faint creak. A street lamp outside lit the room enough for him to see the bolsters neatly stacked on the floor and Shelley snuggled between pale green sheets and a forest-green comforter.

Did she sleep naked, as he did? He longed to raise the comforter to see, but the cold air would probably wake her. He didn't want her to find him standing over her, aroused, hard and throbbing. He didn't know if she would be frightened or angry or merely disgusted, and he didn't want to find out.

She was beautiful, soft and warm, and her interest in him was purely professional. Somehow he had to make himself remember that. Somehow he had to forget their lovemaking, forget his love, and remember that all she wanted from him was a story. Just a story.

"I made a decision last night."

Shelley looked wary. She'd been quiet all morning since she'd awakened on the daybed in her office and remembered that Christopher was sleeping in her bed. That he had wanted her to share that bed with him. "What decision?"

"Until this job at the club is finished, I'm going to stay here." In the middle of the night, when he'd been unable to sleep and unable to think of anything but Shelley, it had seemed logical. He was at her apartment every evening when she came home from work, and when he wasn't there, he was wishing that he was. This way he could keep an eye on her. He could make sure that she didn't do anything foolish, like make a date with Charles Miller—or any other man. This way he could be close to her.

"Stay here?" Shelley repeated. She knew she sounded dim-witted. In truth, she understood exactly what he meant, but she preferred to pretend otherwise. "You mean you're going to find a place to live in San Diego temporarily?"

He smiled warmly enough to chase away the lingering morning chill. "No, Shelley," he said gently. "I mean that I'm going to move into this apartment, here with you, until it's over."

"No, you can't do that." Her hands fluttered nervously until she wrapped them around her coffee cup. "You—you can't stay here. My lease says another person can't move in. The manager wouldn't approve. *I* wouldn't approve." How could she bear going to bed every night with him in the house? Waking up every morning to the knowledge that he was just down the hall? Facing him every single minute that she wasn't working and knowing that he had used her, that he *was* using her, to accomplish his goals?

What if he decided to seduce her again? How could she possibly tell him no and mean it? Yet how could she possibly let him make love to her when *he* didn't mean it?

"It won't be for long. Your manager will never know." He smiled again, and Shelley felt her resistance melting away. For a smile like that she would do almost anything. "You're the one who wanted to be partners, remember? Partners help each other out. They share. Your partner is asking you to share your home with him. You can't tell him no."

"Why?" she asked helplessly.

"It's more than fifty miles to my house. You try driving that twice a day, every day. It gets tiresome very fast." He had chosen that excuse after discarding the others: I want to be close to you. I want to take care of you. I want to make sure that no one hurts you. I want to love you.

Shelley carefully set her cup down and got up from the table. "I have to get ready for work," she said numbly. She walked down the hall without seeing where she was going and closed the bedroom door behind her.

When she emerged from the room half an hour later in her white shirt and black skirt, she was clutching a key in her right hand. "I'll clear some closet and dresser space for you when I get home this evening." She still sounded stunned, unable to accept that this was happening to her.

Christopher took the key and also her hand. "I won't hurt you, Shelley."

The quiet assurance didn't soothe her uneasiness. "It's too late to worry about that. Are you still going to Shelter Island?"

Since Miller never went to the club on Wednesdays, Christopher shook his head. "If you're sure you'll be all right, I'll go home instead and get some clothes."

She nodded. "I'll be all right." *I'll be away from you.* She pulled her hand free, put on a gray, wool blazer, picked up her purse and left.

Shelley had expected some difficulty getting used to her houseguest, and she had some, but not much. Christopher talked when she wanted conversation and was quiet when she wanted silence. He made no move to seduce her or even to kiss or touch her. He willingly helped with the housework and the laundry and did most of the cooking. And he respected the privacy of the office that now served as her bedroom; he never entered the room and never disturbed her when she was there.

Tonight she changed into jeans and a sweater as soon as she got home from Impressions. Christopher had come home early that afternoon, leaving the club immediately after Miller, and he had fixed dinner for her and Gabriel. After dinner they were going to have a strategy session. Things were moving too slowly. Brad had reluctantly told Shelley over the phone yesterday that she could have another couple of weeks, then he was going to have to pull her off the story and back into the office.

Christopher and Gabriel were kneeling on the living room floor, studying the photos spread out on the carpet. These were the people Miller met each week at the club. There were six of them. He met one on Monday, two who came separately on Tuesday, two who came together on Thursday, and one on Friday. With license numbers, occasional charge slips and the help of the Defense Department computers, Gabriel had identified each of them.

Six people, five men and one woman. Five were in the navy, and the sixth was a civilian working on base. One was stationed at the Anti-Submarine Warfare Base; one was assigned to the Naval Air Station North Island. Two, including the civilian, were at the Naval Ocean Systems Command; one was based at the Naval Communications Station in Imperial Beach; and the sixth belonged to the Naval Station Thirty-second Street. Miller had compromised almost half of the military facilities in San Diego by using these people. Shelley had studied their pictures, and she had seen them in person. They were young, attractive, apparently intelligent, normal-seeming people, she thought for the dozenth time as she looked over Christopher's shoulder at the photos. And they were spies.

They had no real proof. She'd never managed to overhear their conversations, although she had occasionally seen them casually exchange envelopes that she assumed contained information and money. All the three of them had were their suspicions, and suspicions weren't good enough. They had to have proof.

The buzzer on the stove went off, and Christopher moved to get up. Unaware that Shelley was behind him, he bumped her, then steadied her as he swiftly rose to his feet. It was the first time he'd touched her in a week, and the sensation burned through him. The desire that was never far away flared in his eyes, then quickly faded as she looked away. She didn't want to see it, he guessed caustically. She didn't want to know that he wanted her. Nothing had changed. Her price was still high, and he still had nothing to give her—only his heart, and she had no use for that.

Shelley breathed a sigh of relief when Christopher released her and went into the kitchen to check on dinner. When her shaking was under control and the color had returned to her face, she took his place on the floor next to Gabriel. "Any suggestions?"

"Not really. Did he ever ask you out again?"

"Yeah. I told him that I was seeing someone else. He hasn't mentioned it since." She looked again at the pictures. "Why do they do it, Gabriel?"

"These three are married, raising families. They're all pretty deeply in debt. Military pay isn't very good for people with kids. For these two—" he pointed at the two friends "—I imagine it's something of a game. They probably do it for the thrill, for the risk."

That left the woman. Shelley didn't care about her reasons for spying. She didn't care about the woman at all. Next to Miller, the woman scared her the most. She was cold. Hard. Dangerous.

"For Janet," Gabriel continued, "it looks like a case of shared ideology. I think she truly embraces their cause."

"Dinner is ready," Christopher called.

They made a careful effort during the meal not to mention business. Gabriel and Christopher talked about old friends and enemies, related tales from their school days in Albuquerque, and questioned Shelley good-naturedly but relentlessly about her younger days. But the friendly conversation ended when the meal did. While the two men drank coffee, Shelley cleared the table and rinsed the dishes. When she was finished, they moved into the living room again.

"I understand that you don't know these people, Shelley," Gabriel began, "but at least you've seen them. You've seen how they act. Do you think it would do any good to talk to any of them?"

Shelley shifted uncomfortably on the hearth. "You mean tell them that I know they're spies and that I want their help?" She shook her head. She could get a job in the club to keep an eye on Miller and his six friends. She could serve their food, settle their bills and accept their tips, but there was no way she was going to talk honestly with any of them. "You talk to them. I don't want to."

"You think one of them might be willing to turn against Miller?" Christopher asked.

Gabriel shrugged. "Anything's possible."

"If they've been around San Diego long, they must know what happened to Gary. They may not know that Miller was responsible, but you can be damned sure that they suspect it." Christopher shook his head. "I think Shelley should stay away from them. All of them."

For once she agreed, giving a vigorous nod. "If I approach one of them, what's to stop him from turning me over to Miller? Gary's death would be a strong motivation not to turn against their boss."

"We've got to do something," Gabriel said wearily. "You've been working there for a month now, Shelley. If your editor drops the story and we lose you, we're going to have to start all over again. We need to do something to shake Miller up, to make him do something."

Christopher picked up the photographs, gathering them into a neat stack. When that was done, he looked first at Gabriel, then Shelley. "*I* could go to the club."

The other two both spoke at once. "No."

"Look, Gabriel, you just said we need to shake him up. And, as Shelley pointed out before, he's sure to know who I am," he said patiently. "I got arrested when he was the guilty one. He killed my brother. Even if he's never seen me, Gary and I looked enough alike that he couldn't miss the resemblance. Seeing the brother of the man he murdered is going to shake him up. Believe me."

He looked again from one to the other. Gabriel was staring into the fireplace. Shelley was biting her lip. They both knew that Christopher was right, and they both wished desperately that there was some other way.

"The whole purpose of this investigation is to clear my name and to catch the man who killed my brother," Christopher continued quietly. "But so far, you two have taken the risks—you, Shelley, by working at the club, and you, Gabriel, by getting the bank and telephone and credit card records."

"Some risk," Gabriel scoffed. "Paperwork will kill you every time."

"The FBI had already warned you to leave the case alone. If you'd gotten caught you could have lost your job, or worse." Christopher knew that for Gabriel, there wasn't much that could be worse than losing the job he loved so much. "Let me go to the club. I'll have a drink, make sure that Miller sees me, that he recognizes me. That's all."

Shelley looked at Gabriel. Like her, his first instinct was to protect Christopher. Like her, he also realized that this might be their only option. Seeing Christopher more than a year after Gary's murder just might make Miller nervous, and nervous people get careless.

"What do you think?" Gabriel asked.

She bit her lip harder. She thought that letting Christopher confront the man responsible for his brother's death was a terrible idea. Miller had already killed at least once to protect himself; what if he made Christopher his next target? But, worries aside, she also thought that they had no other choice.

Christopher fully expected her to argue, if only for the sake of argument. She seemed to make a habit of opposing things he was in favor of. They had disagreed about working together, about her job at the club, about being lovers. He waited to hear her take the other side on this.

"I think he's right. Miller believes that no one can tie him to Gary. The FBI missed him when they investigated the club, so he thinks he's safe. If Christopher shows up at the club and makes it obvious that Miller is the reason he's there, it's going to scare him. It might scare him badly enough to make the kind of mistakes that we need if we're ever going to finish here.''

"All right." Gabriel sat back. "But not until Friday. I want to be there, but I can't get off until then."

Shelley shivered, suddenly cold. "I think I'll build a fire," she said to no one in particular. "I haven't done that since I moved in."

The night he'd broken into the apartment Christopher had noticed a stack of wood on the patio, so he volunteered to get it. He laid a couple of logs on the iron grate, got some matches from the kitchen and lit the gas jet. When the task was finished, he sat down on the hearth, his arm brushing against Shelley's, and forced a smile. "Okay. Friday at noon I'll go to the club. We'll see what kind of impression I make on Miller."

No one was amused by the play on words. "Don't underestimate him," Shelley said softly, staring at her hands. "He's a dangerous man."

His smile became more natural. "I can be dangerous, too, honey."

Don't I know it, she thought dryly.

Gabriel moved fluidly to his feet. "Well, hell, it's eight o'clock, and Lori's coming over at nine. I'd better head home."

"Absolutely," Christopher agreed. "You wouldn't want to miss one minute with Lori, would you?"

Gabriel grinned lazily. "Do I look like a fool? Thanks for the dinner. I'll be in touch with you tomorrow." He put on his jacket and opened the door, then looked back. "Be careful. Both of you."

The door closed, leaving them in silence. Shelley remained where she was for a moment, then started to stand up. Reaching out, Christopher laid his hand on her arm and gently pulled her down again. She looked down at his hand as if it were some foreign object that she didn't recognize.

"You don't have to run off just because Gabriel's gone," he said quietly. "You're safe with me."

Safe? She hadn't been safe since the day she'd sat in Brad Davis's office and listened to him recite the facts of the infamous Morgan spy case. She certainly hadn't been safe since the first time she'd seen a photograph of Christopher Morgan. And, God help her, she hadn't cared about being safe since the night she'd seen him in the flesh in her office.

"Safe isn't a word I would associate with you," she said warily.

He could imagine the words she *did* associate with him: stupid, jerk, bastard. He didn't want to think about that. "Thanks for backing me up tonight, about going to the club. Gabriel thinks that because he's a cop he has to protect me. If it would do any good, *he'd* be the one going in there instead of me."

"It has nothing to do with being a cop," Shelley disagreed. "Everyone wants to protect the people they care about. But sometimes it's just not possible."

His hand moved slightly on her arm, kneading the tight muscles there. He raised his eyes to meet hers as he slid his fingers beneath the sleeve of her sweater to continue the massage on her bare skin. "I suppose that's true. I know it is for me." He had wanted to protect Gary, but it had been impossible. Now he wanted to protect Shelley, to keep her safe from harm, but that wasn't possible, either. "Tell me something, Shelley," he said softly. "Who do you want to protect? Who do *you* care about?"

Chapter 7

Shelley pulled away from him, tugged her sleeve down and went to sit on the sofa. "The movie at nine is supposed to be good tonight," she said, her voice breathy. "Why don't we watch it?"

"I'd rather watch you." He crossed his arms over his drawn-up knees and rested his chin on them. "Why won't you answer me? You have to care about *someone*, Shelley. You're too loving not to. Who is it?"

"I love my parents," she replied, avoiding his eyes. "I care about my friends back home."

"What about Kevin Hayes?"

"What about him?"

"You told me once that you loved him. Do you still care about him?"

She blushed—not due to any deep feelings for her former lover, as Christopher suspected, but because she had lied. She had never loved Kevin. The only man she ever loved was sitting right here with her.

He shifted from the hearth to the sofa, sitting sideways so he could watch her. "Do you still love him?"

"No."

"Did you ever love him?"

Afraid that she would lose what little trust he had granted her, she didn't want to admit that she had lied to him, but she couldn't continue the lie. It was wrong and unfair. "No. I thought I did ... at one time.... But I never loved him."

He felt relieved of a heavy burden. The jealousy and anger that had been directed toward the unknown Hayes vanished, leaving peace in its place. It gave him the courage to ask his next question. "What about me, Shelley?"

She stared at him, her eyes wide and dark with surprise. She opened her mouth, closed it, opened it again. "Y-you?" she squeaked. How could he know her feelings for him? How had he guessed?

"Yes, me." Her surprise was unflattering, but Christopher stubbornly persisted. "Do you care about me?"

She was off balance, unable to think or put words together to answer the question. Her hands were clenched into fists in her lap, her nails gouging into her palms.

What could she say? No? It was such an obvious lie that he would despise her for using it. That left two versions of the truth: that she cared about him as the subject of her story, and that she cared about him as a man.

She looked at him as he waited for her to make a reply. His eyes were as dark, as compelling as ever, looking into her soul, letting her see into his. This was important to him, she realized with an emotion close to awe. *She* was important to him.

"Yes," she whispered. "I care about you, Christopher. I want to protect you."

Although he didn't smile, she could see that her answer pleased him. His pleasure was in the solemnity of his eyes, the softness of his mouth. He leaned toward her, bringing his hand up to her face, but instead of touching her, it remained just slightly out of reach.

"Can I touch you?" he asked hoarsely.

Her voice had stopped working. Gravely, she nodded.

His fingers tenderly stroked across her cheek until they reached her mouth. They traced the line of her lips from corner to corner, then slid down to press against her jaw. "Every day since we made love I've wanted to touch you like this," he said in a low, hard voice. "I've wanted to feel your skin so warm and smooth beneath my hand."

She remembered that voice from their night together. Unlike other men, when he was aroused, his voice didn't get soft and loving, but was hard and demanding. But he knew how to make his touch gentle. He knew how to be gentle with his body.

"That night you asked me to pretend," he continued, "although no pretense was necessary. Tonight I'm asking you to. Pretend that you want me. Pretend that you need me."

She reached for him then, murmuring his name in a soft rush of air. "Christopher..."

Gathering her in his arms, he pulled her hard against his chest. He had sometimes thought that he would never again hear her speak his name like that.

He kissed her, his mouth warm and sweet as it moved over her face. Shelley slid her hands into his hair, holding it tight as she guided his mouth to hers for the kiss that she desperately craved. Holding on to her, he leaned back against the arm of the sofa, carrying her down with him, settling her comfortably across his hips.

"Feel what you do to me?" he whispered, pressing her against his hardness. "When I look at you, when I hear your voice, when I smell your perfume, when I think about you...I want you. Oh, Shelley, I need you."

She reclaimed his mouth, pushing her tongue insistently inside, stroking, tasting. She paused to nibble his lip, to run her tongue over his teeth, to touch and explore all the different textures of his mouth while her hands started their own exploration. They found their way easily between their bodies and beneath the worn fabric of Christopher's T-shirt, grazing over his stomach and chest, gliding through softly curling hair to his flat nipples.

When she raised her mouth from his and sat back to pull his shirt up, he stopped her. Holding her face gently between his palms, he warned softly, "I have nothing to give you, Shelley. All I have is myself. There isn't anything else."

"That's all I want," she replied in a husky whisper. That was all she'd ever wanted from him.

Gratified by her response, he pressed a hard kiss to her mouth. "Let me take you into the bedroom."

Freeing herself, she returned to her task, dragging his shirt over his head with only a little help from him, then combing her fingers through his tousled hair. "This is all right."

"I don't want to hurt you, Shelley. We'll be more comfortable in bed."

She smiled drowsily. "I'll be comfortable wherever you are." But she moved off both Christopher and the couch, extending her hand to him. "Come and make love to me," she invited.

Ever conscious of security, he paused only long enough to lock the front door before following her down the hall. In the dark, quiet, warm bedroom, he gathered her into his arms and kissed her, his tongue entering her mouth. His hands moved gently over her, enticing her, holding her prisoner when she tried to rush him by reaching for the zipper of his jeans. He had waited too long for this night, and he wanted to take his time and enjoy it.

Her sweater was warm against his bare chest. He knew that she was naked beneath it, and the knowledge excited him. Everything about her excited him: the feel of her body pressed against him; the pliancy of her mouth beneath his; the erotic scent of her perfume.

He lifted his mouth from hers and laid a trail of kisses along her jaw to her ear, tracing its delicate outline with the tip of his tongue. "Shelley."

Her name was a whisper of air in her ear, both arousing and tickling. She shivered in response and turned her head, trying to capture his mouth once more with hers. "Let me kiss you, Christopher," she demanded hoarsely.

He willingly returned to her mouth, but she had other goals in mind. After giving him a brief, hard kiss, she pressed her lips to the hollow at the base of his throat, where the rapid throb of his pulse was visible, then flicked her tongue teasingly over the small hard nub of his nipple.

Christopher groaned aloud. He had to have her. He had to make love to her now, had to be inside her now, or he would die from the need. Blindly he reached for her sweater, catching hold of the hem and raising it; then suddenly he froze.

It took a moment for his stiffness to penetrate the sensual fog that had enveloped Shelley. When she became aware of it, she tilted her head back to look up at him. "Christopher?" She spoke with uncertainty. Surely he hadn't changed his mind, she thought with dismay. Not now!

Sliding his hands into the softness of her hair, he held her head still while he placed a single kiss on her forehead. "I'm sorry, Shelley," he muttered, dragging her into a fierce embrace.

"Sorry for what?" she asked. Bewildered by the abrupt end of their lovemaking, she pushed against his chest until he stepped back, so she could see his face in the dim light.

He looked miserable. "I forgot..." Letting the words trail away, he closed his eyes. If he looked at her, if he saw her, he would take her anyway and worry about precautions later.

"You forgot what?" Then she remembered that little box on the nightstand at his house. "It's all right," she whispered.

He shook his head. "I told you I would protect you. I just didn't think . . . Honey, I'm sorry."

She was touched by his concern. "No, really, Christopher, this time it's all right." With her slightly muddled understanding of biology, she was fairly certain that this was the wrong time of the month for her to conceive. And if she was wrong . . . well, she had a lot of love to give—if not to Christopher, then to his child.

"Are you sure?" He opened his eyes in time to see her smile sweetly. Lord, how he loved her, he thought with a rush of emotion.

Taking hold of her sweater, she pulled it over her head and let it fall to the floor. "I'm positive," she replied, wrapping her arms around his neck. She moved slightly, and her naked breasts rubbed his chest. "Please, Christopher."

He couldn't refuse her. He needed her too badly. He guided her to the bed, settling her on the soft comforter. Standing next to the bed, he pulled her socks off with trembling hands, then unfastened her jeans and carefully removed them, too. Briefly he closed his eyes, fighting the urge to rip off her panties and his own clothes and take her quickly, violently. He had to be gentle. He couldn't hurt her, couldn't frighten her.

The touch of his hands on her hips as he removed her last piece of clothing set off a quiver of need that made her moan. "I've dreamed of this," she whispered, reaching out to him.

"Of making love?" he asked in the hard voice that she loved.

"Of you," she corrected. "I've dreamed of you. Please, Christopher. Love me."

The soft, breathy request snapped the restraint that he'd fought so hard to achieve. He finished undressing swiftly and lowered himself to the bed. To Shelley. She was waiting, ready, when he moved between her thighs. With one sure, steady stroke he found his welcome within her.

Cries, ragged breathing, soft voices and whispered pleas broke the stillness of the room. They were driven by passion, by a near-savage need that had gone unsatisfied too long, but the violence, the wildness, was tempered by gentle, secretly given love.

"Christopher!" His name was a frightened cry as the intensity of their lovemaking swept through Shelley, making her gasp, leaving her quaking uncontrollably.

Still shuddering from his own release, he soothed her, stroking his hand over her brow. "It's all right. Darling, it's all right." He dried the tears from her skin, then kissed each cheek, the bridge of her nose, her closed eyelids. He continued to whisper hushed, comforting words, to offer reassuring touches, to shelter her body with the heavy warmth of his own.

With the going of her shivers came sleepiness. She reached up, laid one finger against his lips and smiled faintly. "I've missed you, Christopher."

He smiled, too. "I've missed you, too, honey."

"Stay with me."

"I will." Giving her one last kiss, he withdrew from her warmth and settled on the mattress next to her.

"For how long?" Her voice was growing weaker as sleep claimed her.

"For as long as you want." He kissed her forehead again, then listened to the deep even breaths that meant she was sleeping. "For as long as you want me." Softly, his lips barely moving, his voice barely audible, he added one final statement. It was cowardly to say it like this when she wouldn't hear it, but he vowed that he would tell her again when she was wide-awake and capable of understanding.

"I love you, Shelley."

* * *

Shelley drummed her fingers on the table, producing sharp, clicking rhythmic sounds that she didn't even notice. Although she'd never been prone to anxiety attacks in the past, she felt quite certain that that was what she was experiencing. In less than half an hour she was going to leave for work. At eleven-thirty Charles Miller would come for his usual meeting, and shortly after that, Christopher would arrive.

She took a deep breath and raised her hand to her face. The heat must be turned too high, she thought. Her face was flushed and hot, and her skin felt clammy. Her hand was shaking, too. Maybe she was coming down with something.

She brought her attention back to the conversation when Christopher laid his hand over hers, stilling her nervous movements. He lifted it to his mouth and kissed the palm, then the fingertips. "You're driving me crazy tapping your fingers like that," he said, smiling lazily at her. "If you need something to keep you occupied . . ."

She blushed under his covetous gaze. "I can't help it. I'm nervous."

"No kidding," Gabriel said dryly. "You haven't sat still for more than a minute since I got here." He slid a piece of paper in front of her. "Where are the best places for Christopher to sit?"

She studied the map of the dining room at Impressions, biting her lip thoughtfully. She'd drawn it yesterday, at Gabriel's request, marking every feature of the large room. Now she used her free hand to point at the square that represented Miller's table. "Here's where Miller sits. These tables with Xs are mine. I can try to keep this one open." She pointed to a table in a direct line with Miller's. If Christopher sat there, there was no way the other man could miss him.

"Okay, what about doors?"

"There's the back door for employees and deliveries, a side door that's always locked, and the main doors in front."

"Don't talk to him, Christopher," Gabriel stressed. He'd already told his friend that several times, but he wanted to make certain that Christopher understood. "Just let him see you. Don't worry about him recognizing you. If he doesn't, we'll deal with that later."

"It's time to go." Christopher looked at Gabriel, then at Shelley, and smiled. "Don't look so worried. I'm going into a restaurant to have a drink. I don't think there's too much danger in that."

"Be careful." Gabriel got up from the dining table and stretched. "I'll see you guys there." He knew that Christopher would want a few minutes alone with Shelley before they left. He wasn't quite certain what had happened between them, but he was glad they had finally settled things. He greatly preferred watching them touch and tease each other to the sniping and glares of before.

As soon as the door closed behind Gabriel, Christopher pulled Shelley around the table and into his lap. "Don't be scared," he said quietly. "Nothing's going to happen to me."

She nestled into the hardness of his body, hiding her face in the fragrant softness of his sweater. "I can't help it. He killed your brother. Aren't you scared?"

Christopher wished, for her sake, that he could say no. He liked her worrying about him, but he didn't like adding to her worries. "Just a little nervous." Rubbing his cheek against her sweet-smelling hair, he softly continued, "You know, I never really believed it would happen. I never thought we'd find him. I started looking almost as...I don't know, a way to hold on to my sanity, I guess. I was living up there in the mountains all alone, and I never saw anyone but Gabriel. Those first few months, I couldn't face anyone. Even if the people I saw didn't seem to recognize me, I was

certain that everyone knew who I was and what I had alleg-
edly done. The idea of being in San Diego—of seeing people who knew me, people who believed that I was guilty—
terrified me."

His voice grew softer. He was talking to himself now more
than to Shelley. She remained very still, so she could hear
every word.

"The idea of finding the man—of getting justice—it was
just a pleasant mind game at first. When I was really de-
pressed or sad I'd think about that, about the satisfaction
it would give me. This man was a total stranger, and he'd
had more influence in my life than my family or my friends.
He had destroyed my life, and I didn't even know his name
or what he looked like."

Christopher bent his head to kiss her forehead. Her skin
was soft and warm. She was like that all over. Soft and
warm.

"What made you decide to do it—to actually start looking for him?" she asked quietly.

"After hearing me talk about it a dozen times, Gabriel
finally said I should do it. He told me how—where to start,
what to look for, how to get the information—and he offered to help me. I realized that it was something I had to do,
even though the chances of success were minimal. I felt like
I was taking control of my life again, and I needed that
feeling." Aware of the time, he pushed Shelley to her feet;
then he also stood up. "I *am* nervous, Shelley. I really don't
want to see this man who's done so much to hurt me. But
he's not going to hurt me anymore. I'll be all right. You'll
be there, and Gabriel will be outside. Nothing's going to go
wrong."

She pressed her face against his chest again, but only for
a moment. "God, I hope not."

Christopher held her, knowing that she needed the close-
ness as much as he did. He had learned a lot about her in the
short time since they'd made love again. He knew when to

talk, when to listen, when to argue, when to be silent, when to hold her, when to love her.

Their new intimacy had changed the woman he already loved into one he also adored. She laughed and teased. She made him smile, even made him laugh—something that he hadn't done in far too long. She made love to him passionately, wildly. And she cared for him. She was healing him, body and soul.

"It's time." He kissed her once, then released her.

Shelley put on a jacket and got her purse. Christopher followed her out to her car, parked next to his truck in the visitor spaces. "Remind me to have a talk with that jerk who lives upstairs," he said sourly, casting a frown at the Porsche.

"It's all right. I don't mind."

"*I* mind. I don't like to see people taking advantage of you."

She smiled at him across the hood of the truck. "Like you do every night?" she teased. "Drive carefully. I'll see you in about an hour."

Charles Miller was right on time. He greeted Shelley with a smile and a wave as he made his way to his usual table. She ordered his usual drink from the bar, turning to watch him while she waited.

It would seem so much more real if he didn't look so nice, she thought. Logic told her that it was foolish to judge a man on his looks. If all criminals *looked* like criminals, there would be little crime because apprehension would be so easy.

But human nature wasn't always logical. Even though she knew what Miller had done, what he was capable of, she still found it hard to believe that this nice-looking man could be so evil.

He was an attractive man, reminding her slightly of her father and a few dozen other average, common men. He was slender, muscular, not too tall. Wiry. Yes, the word suited him. His hair had once been brown, but was almost totally gray now, as was his mustache, thin and neatly clipped.

He was polite, handsome, intelligent and stylishly dressed. He was also a spy, a murderer and the target of Christopher's search.

"Here you go, Shelley," the bartender said.

She accepted the glass and carried it to the table across the room. Putting on her best, phoniest smile, she set the glass in front of Miller. "Here's your drink. Have you decided what you want for lunch, Charles?"

He had asked her to call him Charles, though she could rarely bring herself to do so. Not Mr. Miller or Charlie or Chuck, but Charles. It was appropriate.

"How about a Reuben? Are they as good as usual?"

"I can't say, since I've never tried one."

"You ought to try new things once in a while, Shelley. It keeps you from getting dull. How's your boyfriend? Is he treating you right?"

She felt her cheeks grow warm. "He's treating me just fine."

Taking her hand, he held her at the table while he studied her face with sharp blue eyes. "Yes, he is," he agreed, releasing her hand. "I can see it in the sparkle in your eyes. I'll just take a Reuben today, Shelley."

Christopher stood in the doorway staring. Glaring. He had stopped to get his bearings, to find the table Shelley had marked on her diagram as Miller's. What he'd found was Miller holding Shelley's hand in his. A jealous rage surged through him, making him yearn to crush every bone in the other man's body.

Unobtrusively, Shelley wiped her hand on her skirt as she turned. She had a strong desire to go to the bathroom and scrub both hands with soap to wash away his touch. But a pair of intensely angry dark eyes across the room stopped her. Even at a distance she could read the danger in his expression. She crossed the room to him swiftly, cutting off one of the other waitresses. "Hello. I'm Shelley, and I'll be your waitress today," she said for the benefit of the customers around them.

Christopher spoke in a hard, quiet voice. "If he touches you again, Shelley, I'll kill him." It wasn't a threat. Just a promise. One it would give him great pleasure to keep.

She started across the room with Christopher right behind her. "I've been saving a table for you. There's one table between you and Miller, but if you sit in the chair directly facing his table, you'll be able to see him."

"And he'll be able to see me," he said with grim satisfaction.

"Yes," Shelley agreed softly. "He'll see you." She stopped next to a small table and waited while Christopher sat down. "What do you want to drink?"

He glanced up at her, the way he might look at any waitress. She hoped that not every waitress responded the way she did, with her heart pounding, her lungs squeezing tight. "Beer."

"Do you want something to eat?"

His mouth lifted sardonically. "I really don't think I could eat anything right now."

"No. I guess not."

She sent Miller's order to the kitchen before getting a glass of foaming beer from the bar for Christopher. By the time she'd delivered it and gotten a quiet "Thanks" from him, Miller's luncheon companion had arrived.

"Shelley," Miller called, "could we get another Reuben and a glass of iced tea here?"

Looking up from Christopher, she flashed a quick smile. "Sure, Charles. Just one minute."

"Charles?" Christopher snidely repeated.

"Do you want anything else?"

Christopher shook his head. He watched her until she was a few feet from the table, then turned his gaze back to Mil-

ler. He didn't want to show any more interest in Shelley than
any other healthy man with good eyesight and functioning
hormones.

Charles Miller. Here, less than fifteen feet away from
him, was the man responsible for Gary's death. The man
who was responsible for Christopher's arrest. The man who
had been holding on to Shelley and eyeing her the way a
hungry coyote looks at a rabbit.

Doing nothing was the hardest thing he'd ever done. The
months of searching and investigating were coming to an
end, and somehow, someday soon, this man would pay for
what he'd done to Gary and to Christopher. *Vengeance is
mine....* But he didn't want vengeance. Justice. That was
his goal.

Miller smiled at something his friend said, then glanced
around the room. Christopher felt it the instant Miller's gaze
reached him. The older man started to look past him; then
his eyes grew wider, colder, bluer. His leisurely pose became stiff and tense, and his jaw set into a hard line.

He stared at Christopher, and Christopher stared back,
his dark gaze relentless, unflinching. Reaching blindly,
Miller picked up his glass and swallowed down the contents
at once. His companion, a navy officer named King, questioned him, but Miller gave no answer.

From the corner of his eye Christopher saw Shelley approach their table. She smiled warmly, set the glass of tea in
front of King and left again. She seated several more customers and checked on the other diners before returning to
Christopher.

"I'd say he recognizes you," she said softly, keeping her
back to Miller. "If his eyes get any bigger, they're going to
pop out."

"What do you want to bet that he leaves early this time?"
He picked up his glass and finished the drink, then smiled
up at her. It was a relief to be able to look from Miller to
Shelley, to switch from the hatred inspired by the man in

front of him to the love he felt for her. "You wouldn't mind refilling this, would you?"

She accepted the glass. "Take it easy on the booze. You're driving today, remember?"

She didn't take him up on his bet, but he would have won. Less than five minutes later Charles Miller paid for the lunch that he hadn't eaten and walked out. A few minutes after that King also left.

Christopher signaled to Shelley. "I'm going home now," he said, pulling some money from his pocket for the two drinks. "Gabriel's going to follow Miller and see what he does."

She accepted the money. "Are you okay?"

His smile barely qualified as one. His lips were pressed together tautly, and only the corners tilted up. "I only had two beers."

"You know what I mean, Christopher."

Yes, he knew. His smile grew. Once, long ago, he had let himself wonder what it would be like to meet the man responsible for his problems. He'd figured he would either become deathly ill or murderously insane. Well, he had come face-to-face with Charles Miller, and he'd done neither. "Yeah, honey," he said softly. "I'm all right. I'll see you this evening."

"Let me get your change."

Finally he grinned. "Keep it, partner. You're worth it."

She tucked the bill into the pocket of her skirt. "I'll have you know that I'm worth a lot more than fifteen bucks," she teased.

Christopher's gaze moved slowly over her, his eyes darkening with the response that came so quickly, so intensely. "You're worth more than I can ever give you," he said softly. "All I can give is myself."

Shelley started to reach out, remembered where they were and stuck her hand in her pocket. "Have I ever asked for anything more?"

"Not in so many words," he replied. Studying her thoughtfully, he asked, "What if it had just been me, Shelley? What if I came without a story attached? Would you still be satisfied with just me?"

Her smile was a little bit sad. "Sometimes I think I'd prefer it that way. Be careful, Christopher."

Gabriel was at the apartment when Shelley got home, with the news that Miller had driven straight from Impressions to his condo. He'd done nothing.

"So I go back Monday," Christopher said, laying his arm across Shelley's shoulders.

"Give him a day off. If you're not there Monday, he'll start to relax again," Shelley suggested. "Then show up Tuesday. It'll have a much stronger effect."

Gabriel agreed with her, so Christopher grudgingly gave in. After a few minutes of idle conversation Gabriel left again. In order to be at the club, he'd traded his usual day shift for a friend's night shift and now he was on a break— a short one, he groused—for dinner.

"Speaking of dinner," Shelley began, wrapping her arms around Christopher's neck, "what are we having?"

Bending his knees, he braced one arm beneath her and lifted her into his arms. "*I'm* having *you*," he replied. "I'll feed you later."

He laid her on the bed and, instructing her to keep her hands at her sides and out of his way, began the pleasant task of undressing her. In her uniform of white shirt, black skirt and black pumps, she looked so sensible—almost sexless. It was the knowledge of what was beneath those plain and proper clothes that gave him such pleasure in removing them an inch at a time.

First to go were the shoes, tossed unceremoniously in the corner. Next was the blouse. Beneath the plain, unadorned, cotton-blend shirt she wore another white garment, this one a camisole of silk, decorated with lace and ribbons and tiny satin bows. Beneath it she wore nothing at all. Swallowing hard, Christopher decided to leave it alone for the moment.

The side zipper on the skirt usually gave him trouble, but today it glided down without a hitch. "Lift your hips," he commanded in a coolly detached voice. When she obeyed, he pulled the skirt from beneath her and over her legs. It made a soft whooshing sound before it landed on the floor near the shoes.

Shelley had always loved the feel of silks and satins against her skin, but she had always settled for sensible, serviceable garments. Lately, though, her wardrobe had expanded to include the skimpier, sexier items designed not just to cover but to entice, as well. Like the camisole she wore now, which was more lace then silk. Like the items beneath the sensible half-slip that Christopher was sliding away.

He was kneeling on the bed beside her. Now he sat back on his heels, laying his hands flat on his thighs, and simply looked at her.

Shelley stretched languorously, then smiled. The way he was looking at her was sending heat through her until she felt it in every nerve. The way she looked was spreading a reciprocal heat through him. His jeans were old and faded, softly comfortable, and they molded lovingly to the fullness in his loins.

Christopher closed his eyes. "Damn you," he whispered. "Every time I make love with you, I think that you can never be more beautiful, more seductive, more desirable, that I can never want you more than I do at that moment. And the next time..." Even the whisper faded away. He had to swallow, had to take a few deep breaths and try again. "And the next time you prove me wrong. The next time I want you until I think I'll die from it. I... need you. The way I need food to eat and water to drink and air to breathe. *I need you.*"

She raised her hand to touch the place where his jeans were stretched taut, but he sensed her movement. He opened his eyes and held her wrist in a gentle grip. "If you touch me . . . I'll never last. Wait. Please."

He replaced her hand on the bed, rose to his knees and looked at her again. The garter belt she wore was lavishly fashioned from lace, clinging like skin to her waist and hips and belly. With tentative but gentle touches, he searched for and found the clips that would release the fabric of her stockings. His fingers never left her legs as he peeled each silky stocking away. Obeying another harsh command, she arched her back, and he reached beneath her to undo the fastener on the garter belt, and it joined the other clothes on the floor.

He moved to straddle her, then took her hands and pulled her up. The camisole fell away with barely a tug, leaving her small breasts bare. Bending his head, he took one dusky rose nipple into his mouth, settled his hands behind her and slowly lowered her down again. The movement left him bent over her, the heaviness of his manhood warm and solid against her thighs.

Shelley tangled her fingers in his hair and pulled, using sheer force and the painful tug at his scalp to raise his head from her breast. Her face was flushed as deeply as his, her heart beating as painfully. "I can't stand this," she whispered fiercely. "I want you so badly it hurts. *I* hurt. Please, Christopher. Please, darling."

The only clothing she wore were the panties that matched the camisole and garter belt. They were lace, tiny and fragile, and he removed them with the utmost care. At the same time her hands were struggling with his jeans, undoing the buttons, freeing the heated length of him and guiding him to her, inside her.

She was naked. He was fully clothed. Both were on fire. Both were out of control. Both were shattered by the violence, by the savagery.

Both were saved by the love.

Saturday was dreary and gray, with rain falling in a steady, gentle flow. The apartment was cold, but Shelley didn't want to leave the warmth of the bed and Christopher to turn the heat on. Instead she snuggled deeper beneath the covers, closer to Christopher.

She liked waking up next to him. She liked sharing her house and her meals and her bed with him. When he left... Stubbornly she shut that thought out. She wasn't being unrealistic. She knew that sooner or later she would have to return to her job at the *Chronicle*. If Miller hadn't been caught by then, Christopher would find someone else to help him, and he would leave her. She would have no purpose in his life then.

But she could face that later. When it happened, she would be alone, and she would have all the time in the world to deal with it. Until then she was going to enjoy the time she had with him. She wouldn't let dismal thoughts of the future spoil it.

"I like you naked."

The raspy, sleep-roughened voice filtered through her hair. Tilting her head back, she saw that Christopher's eyes were open, but only barely. She laughed softly. "I like you naked, too."

"I'm serious. I like the way your skin feels against mine. You're so soft, like silk or satin, and when you lie next to me, it feels so damned good."

He lay on his back, and Shelley was on her side. With every breath she took she brushed against him, from shoulder to toe. It was an unusually pleasant form of torture. Christopher closed his eyes so he could fully enjoy it.

"Do you have any plans for today?" Shelley asked, gliding her fingers through the silky hair on his chest.

"I'm beginning to think of some."

"I'd like to do something."

He caught her wrist and guided her hand down his body, molding her fingers gently to his growing hardness. "Honey, you're already doing something," he growled. "If this isn't what you meant, you'd better stop it now and get out of this bed."

Shelley bit her lower lip, giving his command thoughtful consideration. After a long night of the most exquisite lovemaking she had ever experienced, she hadn't considered a repeat performance this morning. Despite the gray, wet skies, she wanted to get out of the house, to go someplace with Christopher, to run some errands, to have some fun. She wanted to forget work for just this weekend and pretend that they were two normal people leading normal lives.

Still, the bed was warm and comfortable, and Christopher was so hard and ready. She loved the feel of him cradled in her hand. She loved knowing that he wanted her so much. Regardless of everything else in their lives, he wanted her.

Shifting beneath the covers, she moved so that she was lying on top of him. Errands and fun and normalcy could wait until later.

Much, much later.

The morning was gone by the time they finally got out of bed. "What was it that you wanted to do today?" Christopher asked as he shaved. Shelley was sharing the small bathroom with him, brushing her hair while she watched him.

"I need to go shopping. Christmas is two weeks away, and I haven't bought any gifts yet."

"All right, we'll go to the stores. What else?"

She looked blankly at him. "Obviously you've never been shopping with me, or you wouldn't ask what else. That will probably take the rest of the day."

"I'll make you a deal. I'll go shopping with you. I'll spend the rest of the day and all evening in crowded stores. I'll carry your packages. I'll even drive, so you won't have to worry about traffic or directions. But in exchange, you have to do what I want tomorrow."

Shelley didn't hesitate to agree. There was absolutely nothing in the world that he could ask her to do tomorrow that she would object to, short of asking her to get out of his life. Since the job at the club wasn't finished, she knew he wouldn't ask that of her. Yet.

"Don't you want to know what I want to do?"

"If you want to tell me."

"You shouldn't agree until you know what you're agreeing to. How do you know I won't keep you in bed until Monday morning?"

She moved to stand behind him, wrapping her arms around him. He wore only jeans, and his back was warm, the muscles hard. "How do you know," she began softly, watching their reflection in the mirror as her hands moved playfully across his belt buckle, "that I wouldn't prefer that?"

Christopher knew that he was a strong man—morally, ethically, physically—but she made him weak. She made him vulnerable, made him tremble, made his hands shake. He put the razor down, aware that he was in no condition to have the sharp blade near his throat.

In the mirror, his eyes met hers. His were somber, intense. "My God, Shelley... I never thought any good could come from the nightmare of the last year, but I was wrong. It brought me you."

He wanted to go on, to say the words that he said to her every night and a dozen times every day—the words that were given silently, that she'd never heard. *I love you.* But he held them back. He kept them inside, where they belonged until the time was right. Until he knew that she would be happy to hear them.

* * *

"Where do you want to go?"

They walked leisurely to the parking lot, unmindful of the rain. It trickled slowly off Christopher's leather jacket and rushed more quickly over the pale gray rubber of Shelley's slicker. As they walked, he named half a dozen shopping centers.

"It doesn't matter to me."

"Which one do you like best?"

She shrugged. "I've never been to any of them."

"You've lived in San Diego since September and you've never been to any of the malls?" he asked in disbelief.

"I haven't had a whole lot of time," she reminded him defensively. "Besides, I don't like to shop alone."

He put his arm around her shoulders, hugging her close. "You don't like to do a lot of things alone, do you?" he asked, his voice warm and sympathetic. "Working alone, eating alone, living alone, sleeping alone..."

"It's hard," she admitted. "I've spent all my life in the same city. My entire family is there. I went to school from first grade on with my friends. I worked with almost the same group of people for ten years—no one ever quit or retired. It was all very stable."

"Until Kevin Hayes." He opened the car door for her, closing it when she was settled inside.

"Oh, good, you're leaving."

Christopher turned to face Shelley's upstairs neighbor. The man was smiling. Christopher wasn't. "Yeah, we're leaving."

Shelley fastened her seat belt, then watched Christopher and her neighbor, wondering what they were saying. Christopher made a rather long speech, which caused the man's smile to disappear, and then his face turned various shades of green. He was still standing there staring when Christopher slid into the driver's seat.

"Damn, that felt good. I've been wanting to talk to him since the day you told me that he was always parking in your space."

Shelley stared at him. If she remembered correctly, that was a discussion they'd had the first day they'd gone to the club. Christopher had hardly been able to stand the sight of her then, yet he'd wanted to stand up for her against her neighbor? The knowledge gave her a warm glow. "What did you say to him?"

"We just talked," he said with an innocence befitting an angel. "I think we reached an understanding of what's going to happen to his precious cars if he parks one of them in your space again."

"Christopher, you shouldn't threaten people because of me."

"You can't threaten people yourself," he pointed out. "It just doesn't work. You're too beautiful, too delicate. Nobody can hear your threats because they're looking at your face."

"That's a chauvinist, sexist remark," she accused. "You are probably one of the most handsome men in this entire state, but people still took you seriously. They didn't get so carried away looking at you that they didn't hear what you were saying."

"So it's a chauvinist, sexist society in which we live, which doesn't change the fact that you're beautiful. Do you like Mexican food?"

Shelley sat comfortably back in her seat. "Typical male—change the subject. Yes, I like Mexican food. I suppose you know a good restaurant?"

"Of course. We'll stop and eat, then go to Horton Plaza. You can start your shopping spree there."

Shelley expected a quietly elegant restaurant like the last one—the only other one, she corrected—that he'd taken her to. Instead it was a small, crowded place located in the Golden Hill district, not far from downtown. Only a counter separated the kitchen from the dining room, which held only four tables.

"This place makes the best chimichangas you'll ever eat," Christopher said as they got in line.

"That shouldn't be too hard, since I've never had them before. What are they?"

He described them—shredded beef, tomatoes, lettuce and salsa deep-fried in a tortilla and served with generous helpings of sour cream and guacamole.

"That sounds good," she said. "Order one for me, and I'll grab that table."

While she waited, she listened to the conversations around her. She and Christopher seemed to be the only ones in the place who chose to speak English; the rest of the customers and all three employees were speaking Spanish. That could explain why the food was so good, she thought. For a Mexican restaurant to survive in a Mexican neighborhood, it had to be.

"Did Gabriel recommend this place to you?" she asked when Christopher joined her.

"No, one of the secretaries at the plant did." Knowing why she'd asked the question, he grinned. "I hate to tell you this, but Gabriel isn't Hispanic."

"He isn't? With a name like Gabriel Rodriguez?"

"It's a fair assumption to make in San Diego, but don't forget that he's from Albuquerque. Both the Spaniards and the Mexicans have had a strong influence on the Pueblo Indians, and it's evident in the names. Gabriel is Indian."

Shelley laid her hand over his. "Your life has changed a lot in the past year, hasn't it?" she asked, thinking of his reference to the secretary. "You used to be rich and powerful and re—" She cut off the word.

"Respectable?" he asked with a wry smile.

"Respected. Everyone admired you. You lived in a beautiful house in La Jolla and drove European sports cars and dressed impeccably. You controlled a huge corporation—

you provided jobs for more people than I even know. Your life was very full."

"And now everyone thinks I'm a spy, and I probably couldn't get a decent job in San Diego if my life depended on it." He shrugged. "My life was busy then, Shelley—not full. I worked twelve to fourteen hours a day, and I went to all the right parties and supported all the right charities. But for your life to be full, you need someone to share it with. I had a few lovers—" he broke into a grin "—but not nearly as many as you seem to think. I cared about them, but I didn't want to marry any of them. I didn't love any of them. There was no one really important in my life except Gabriel. He was my only real friend."

He paused long enough to pick up their order from the woman behind the counter, then finished when he sat down again. "My life has changed a lot, Shelley, but . . . I'd have to say that I'm happier now. I'm still rich, Gabriel is still my friend, and I have you to care about. That's all I need."

As Shelley had promised, her shopping took the rest of the day and most of the evening. She loved to browse and had to make certain that each item she bought was the single most perfect gift for its recipient.

"You like Christmas, don't you?" Christopher asked as they carried the packages into the apartment.

Shelley collapsed onto the sofa, and Christopher sprawled next to her. "My parents have always had a really big celebration," she said, smiling in remembrance. "My mom already has the tree up. We do it...*they* do it the first Sunday of December." She looked wistfully around her apartment. Even if she had a tree, she wasn't sure where it would go. There was so little space.

"Are you going home for the holidays?"

She looked hesitantly at him. "I have reservations for the twenty-fourth," she admitted. "I was alone on Thanksgiving, and it was depressing, so I made the reservations then. But...if things aren't settled with Miller, I can cancel them."

He shook his head. "Don't be ridiculous. Being gone a few days won't hurt." It wouldn't hurt anyone but him. He didn't want to let her go for more than a few hours at a time. Knowing that she was two thousand miles away would be almost unbearable.

Shelley quit biting her lip to ask, "What about you, Christopher? Where will you spend Christmas?"

"At home." He tried to make it sound unimportant, but Shelley heard the loneliness. "After Mom and Dad died, Gary and I used to get together for a couple of days. Now that he's dead, too..." He shrugged. "You don't celebrate a family holiday when you haven't got a family."

"You could come to Mobile with me. I've got a big enough family to share," she softly offered.

"Thanks, but..." He shook his head.

"You would be welcomed. My family believes whole-heartedly in that old saying—the more, the merrier."

He pulled her into his arms and held her tight. "I appreciate the invitation, but I can't accept it. Not now." It was tempting, though. Lord, it was tempting. But as much as he wanted to be with Shelley, he couldn't take her up on an invitation offered out of pity. If he went anywhere with her, it would be because she wanted him there.

Gathering his energy, he got to his feet and invited her to a place where he knew without doubt that she wanted him. "Come on, honey. Let's go to bed."

"Okay, we made a deal yesterday," Shelley said Sunday morning. "You kept your end and did everything I wanted. So what do you want to do today?"

They were sitting in the middle of the living-room floor, with cups of coffee, a plate of sweet rolls and the numerous sections of the Sunday *Chronicle* scattered around them.

Christopher tossed the financial section to one side, leaned over Shelley to get the front page and kissed her when he sat back. "I want to go to my house."

"All right. And what will we do when we get there?"

He shrugged. "Nothing special. Take a walk in the woods, then sit in front of the fireplace and talk." He needed to take her to his house. He wanted to see her there, in a place that belonged to him, in the place that was as much a part of him as she was.

"That all sounds wonderful," Shelley said softly. It didn't matter that anything he suggested sounded wonderful to her. Just being with him was a joy.

They each took a change of clothing so they could spend the night if they wanted, plus an ice chest of food since there was none there.

When they reached the house, they did each of the things that Christopher had mentioned. They took a long walk in the woods, oblivious to the wind and the cold, aware only of each other. Afterward they sat in front of the fireplace, watching the fire, occasionally touching. And they talked—about their pasts and about the present, but not about the future. It was too painful to discuss something that held so much uncertainty for them both.

"Shelley..."

"Hmm." She was lying on her side facing the fire, her head pillowed on Christopher's thigh. She was so sleepily comfortable that she couldn't give more of a reply than that soft sound.

"When did you decide that I was innocent?"

"I don't know." She yawned. "I guess it was after I read all the clippings that Brad had given me. It just didn't make sense that you would do what the FBI accused you of."

"You mean before we met?"

"Hmm."

"Do you always give your trust so easily?"

Finally she rolled onto her back so she could look up at him. "I'm a very good judge of character. I decided that you had lots of character."

"What happened to your judgment when it came to Kevin Hayes?"

"What is it about Kevin that bothers you so much?"

He tilted his head back, resting it on the arm of the couch behind him. Everything she'd told him about Hayes bothered him. The fact that she had cared for him. That he had been her lover. That he had taken advantage of her. That he had hurt her. As much as he hated the idea of Shelley involved with another man, making love with another man, it was the last part that disturbed him the most. He hated the idea of her being hurt—by Hayes, by himself, by anyone in the world. He wanted to protect her from anyone who might cause her pain or unhappiness. He wanted to give her a wonderful, beautiful, perfect life, sheltered from everything bad. He wanted to love her, and he wanted to marry her.

What would it take to make Shelley marry him? He didn't even want to consider it. It was obvious that she cared about him, but he didn't think it went beyond that. Love? No way. Only in his dreams.

He could give her everything she needed to be happy—money, security, children and a lifetime of love. But none of that would mean anything if she didn't love him. He couldn't settle for less than love.

Sometimes he looked so distant, Shelley thought. Where did he go in his mind? Was he remembering? Dreaming? She raised her hand to his chin. When his dark eyes dropped to her face she said softly, "Sometimes you forget me."

He shook his head. "I never forget you. Never."

It was true. Whatever happened, Shelley would live with him forever—if not in his life, then in his mind. In his memories. In his soul.

Chapter 8

They'd been right in deciding to keep Christopher away from the club on Monday, Shelley knew. Miller was as nervous as any man she'd ever seen when he came in. He looked around the dining room, his expression cautious. Finding nothing to cause him concern, he went to his table and sat down, giving Shelley only a faint smile when she approached.

As the minutes passed with no sign of Christopher, Miller began to visibly relax. By the time he'd finished lunch he was acting much as he usually did—unconcerned, friendly, but not too warm. He left her a sizable tip when he left.

When Miller came in Tuesday at lunchtime, he walked confidently to the table without giving the other diners a glance. He waved at Shelley, accepted the drink she brought him and gave his order. Everything was normal.

Then Christopher arrived.

Shelley was busy with a customer, and she couldn't leave quickly enough to reach Christopher before another waitress did. From the corner of her eye she saw the woman, named Cassie, gesture to a table on the opposite side of the room. He shook his head and said something, and Cassie turned a curious look on Shelley.

When Shelley finished with the customer, Cassie met her near the bar. "The gorgeous guy at the door wants *you* to seat him," she complained in a frankly envious voice. "Some people have all the luck."

"Thanks, Cassie." She approached Christopher, striving to look at him as just another customer and knowing that she was failing miserably. "Hi. Cassie said you wanted me."

"In every way. Do you have my table?"

"Yeah, it's waiting." She stopped next to the table, waited until he'd sat down, then handed him a menu.

He moved the menu to the side, out of the way. "Just bring me a beer."

"I'm glad you don't drink that stuff at home."

He glanced up at her, his gaze reaching her breasts and going no higher. "At home I have other things to keep myself occupied."

She started to walk away, but he called her back in a severely impersonal voice. "Take him a drink."

"Christopher...Gabriel said not to make any moves."

"Just one drink. From me."

Sighing, she went to the bar and ordered. After delivering the beer to Christopher's table, she carefully carried the scotch to Miller's.

"What's this, Shelley? I didn't order another drink," Miller said in surprise.

"It's from the gentleman over there."

Miller looked up directly into Christopher's cold gaze. "Wh-which one, Shelley?"

She turned and gestured with a wave of her hand. "The man with the black hair and the black jacket."

Miller finished his first drink. His hand trembled slightly when he put the glass down. "Who is he, Shelley? Do you know?"

"No, I don't. He came in . . . Friday, I think. That's the first time he's been here as far as I know. Don't you know him? I assumed since he bought you this drink . . ."

He looked again at Christopher, who was still staring at him, then away. "Find out his name, if you can. He looks familiar. . . ."

She smiled sweetly. "Sure, Charles, no problem." It was quite a while before she was able to return to Christopher's table. When she did, she stood so that her back was to Miller. "He recognizes you, but he wants to be sure. He asked me to find out your name."

"Just give him my last name." Christopher slowly transferred his attention from the man to Shelley. "Unless he sends you back, don't come over here again. I'll just leave the money on the table. The less contact you and I have in front of him, the better." He took a long swallow of beer while looking at her. "Tell me something."

"What?"

"What are you wearing underneath those clothes?"

She smiled and shook her head. "I guess you'll just have to remove them this evening and find out. I'd better go now."

Miller was cross when she finally returned to him. "It took you long enough. What was he doing? Giving you his life history?"

Shelley bristled at his arrogance. He was treating her as if she was . . . precisely what she was: a waitress. Someone there to wait on him. "No," she replied. "He was asking if I'd like to meet him when I get off work tonight." She deliberately made her accent heavier.

"Typical," he said with a frown. "He always did go after whatever he wanted. Did he tell you his name?"

"Morgan. That's all he said."

And that was enough to verify what Miller already knew. Somehow Gary Morgan's brother had connected him to Miller. Somehow he knew. "Are you meeting him?" he asked sharply.

Shelley was surprised. "No. My boyfriend tends to get a little hostile if I go out with other men."

"Too bad." He spoke softly, almost to himself. "Maybe you could tell me what he wants...."

"Sorry, Charles. You'll have to ask him yourself."

"He's gone."

She glanced over her shoulder. Indeed, during her conversation with Miller, Christopher had quietly left. She could see a folded bill wedged beneath the empty beer glass. "Maybe he'll be back."

That was what Miller was afraid of. He was beginning to be very afraid.

Wednesday morning, when Shelley started to dress for work, Christopher pulled the shirt from her hands. "Don't wear your uniform. Take it with you and change there."

Shelley replaced the shirt on the hanger, buttoning the top button to hold it in place. "Do you want to go somewhere?"

"Yeah, to the tide pools. You've been living in San Diego for months, and you still haven't seen anything. We have plenty of time before you have to be at the club."

She took a mint-green sweater from the dresser drawer and put it on, then removed her slip and stepped into a pair of jeans and sneakers. While Christopher dressed, she put everything she needed for work in a small bag and slung it over the hanger that held her uniform. "What are the tide pools?"

"Pools that form when the tide comes in." He grinned when she stuck her tongue out. "You'd better put your hair up or something, or you'll never get the tangles out."

She brushed her hair back into a ponytail, securing it with a big, wide, gold clasp. "Where are they?"

"Out at Point Loma, near the Cabrillo monument. It's not too far from the club. I think you'll like it there. It's...peaceful."

He shrugged into his leather jacket, then held her loose-fitting corduroy jacket while she slid her arms through the sleeves. He pulled the ivory knit scarf from the coat pocket and wrapped it around her neck, arranging it smoothly beneath the collar of the coat. "Are you ready?"

She nodded.

"Follow me. I'll make sure you don't get lost."

The tidal pools were located on the ocean side of a narrow spit of land that formed the western side of San Diego Bay. The road led them through a gate onto government property and past signs identifying the buildings as the Naval Ocean Systems Command. Shelley found them an unpleasant reminder of business, one that was easy to forget as soon as they turned off the street onto the access road that wound steeply down to the Coast Guard lighthouse and the shore. They parked in the lot above the pools, then walked hand-in-hand along the sandy hilltop to the steps that led downward.

Because the wind blowing from the ocean was uncomfortably chilly, few tourists were out that morning, and they kept to the left portion of the rocky area, where trails led down to a sheltered, crescent-shaped beach. Christopher led Shelley to the right, walking along the edge where there was rock to support them. When they finally stopped, they were far enough away from the tourists that they might as well have been alone.

Natural steps, created by the relentless wind and occasional sprays of water, led down to a large, odd-shaped rock formation at the water's edge. "Come on," Christopher urged. He jumped the two feet from the first step to the second, then held his arms up to Shelley.

She went with him until they reached the rock. There she saw the foot-wide fissure that separated it from the shore. Below, through the crack, she could see the water surging and receding with each wave. "That rock's not attached," she pointed out.

"It's safe, believe me."

She stubbornly held back. "If I can see the water all along here, it can't have much of a base to stand on. It's like an inverted triangle."

He stepped back over the crack and put his arms around her. "Don't you trust me?"

She wrapped her own arms tightly around him, hugging him close. "Implicitly."

"Then come out here—just for a minute. I want you to see the water."

"It's a big ocean. I can see it from here." But she walked to the edge anyway, looking down eight feet to the water below. The tide was coming in, each wave crashing a little higher on the rock, occasionally reaching high enough to splash Shelley and Christopher. The force with which the water hit created a dirty-looking foam that swirled and eddied, drifting out and rushing back.

When Christopher had described the place as peaceful, she had envisioned gentle waves, a restful quiet. These waves were anything but gentle, and the noise of the water, the wind and the sea gulls was almost deafening. Still, she understood what he'd meant. It was the feeling of being alone, surrounded by rugged beauty—grotesquely eroded cliffs and eerily shaped rocks, with the pounding sea and the unremitting wind inexorably eating away at both.

Christopher turned her to face him, brushed a strand of hair from her face and grasped the fringed ends of her knitted scarf. "Do you like it?"

She smiled. "Yes. I understand why you're drawn to it. It's a powerful place."

"I feel...comfortable here. Like no one can touch me."

Shelley shivered with a strong gust of wind, and Christopher turned his back to the ocean so that his broad shoulders and chest provided her with a shelter from the wind.

"Do you ever get scared?" she asked curiously. He seemed so strong, so invincible.

Christopher's smile was mirthless. "All the time, honey. I'm scared as hell every time you go into the club, and I stay scared until you come out. I'm scared every time I think of you in the same room with Miller—waiting on him, talking to him, smiling at him.''

"He isn't going to hurt me. I'm just a waitress."

"He killed Gary," he reminded her. "I don't want to lose you, too."

The statement warmed her even more than his body did. It was further proof that he cared for her, and she treasured it. After savoring it for a moment, she asked, "What will you do when this is over?"

Christopher smoothed his hand over the dark green of her jacket, then traced one cold fingertip around the V neck of her mint-green sweater. "I don't know. I don't guess I've ever allowed myself to look that far ahead."

"Will you move back to San Diego?"

"Probably, at least part-time. But I've gotten used to the privacy and quiet of the mountain house. I don't think I could give that up now."

Shelley tried to imagine her life without Christopher, but she found it too grim. He was such an important part of her, but once Miller had been caught, Christopher would be gone. She couldn't imagine a single reason why he would stay with her once she'd served her purpose. Their love-making was exquisite, but there were lots of women in the world, and she was nothing special.

She left his embrace and walked once more to the edge of the rock, staring down at the water. When he was gone and she was back working daily at the *Chronicle*, she knew that she would come here often, but not for the peace that drew Christopher. It would be the memories that brought her back.

"What about you?"

Knowing before she turned that he was watching her, she carefully composed her face. She didn't want him to see all the emotion, all the sadness. "What about me? I guess I'll be working."

He shook his head. "Could you live in the mountains?"

Shelley forgot the damp cold that seemed to have seeped into her bones and the wind that rushed past her ears with enough force to make hearing difficult. What was he asking? Did he want to marry her? To live with her? Or simply to continue their affair?

It didn't matter. The answer to any of the three propositions would be a resounding yes. Like most women, she wanted the commitment and respectability of marriage, along with the legality for the sake of the children that she wanted to have. Also like most women, though, she would settle for the impermanent sharing of a live-in relationship or, failing that, for a prolonged love affair. She would accept anything that Christopher wanted to offer her.

"Yes," she said softly. "I could live in the mountains."

"It wouldn't be easy, because of your job," he warned.

"Nothing worthwhile is easy."

He took a step toward her. She also moved closer. "I can't make any promises, Shelley, because I don't know what's going to happen. We may never get Miller. I may have to live with the stigma of being an accused spy for the rest of my life. But I know that whatever happens with Miller, I don't want to lose you. I can't let you go."

Shelley closed the distance between them, and he welcomed her into the strong circle of his arms. He tilted her head back and pressed a kiss to her forehead. "I love you, Shelley," he said quietly. "I've never said that to any woman, but I want you to know in case…just in case. I love you."

He didn't expect her to respond with her own vow of love, but the sheen of tears in her eyes was enough for him. He would like to hear the words, but he had acknowledged that she might never say them; she might not even feel the feelings. She cared about him, but she'd cared about Kevin Hayes, too. For all he knew, in her mind he might still be nothing but a vital part of an important story. But that didn't diminish his love one bit. Nothing could change the way he felt.

For long minutes he held her. He knew she was crying because he could feel the dampness spread across his chest. At last he bent his head to kiss her again. "Don't cry unless they're good tears," he murmured. "I don't want to make you sad."

She smiled, drying her cheeks with the back of her hand. She wanted to tell him that she loved him, too—had loved him for as long as she'd known him. But fear kept her silent—fear that he would change his mind when his life returned to normal and he was surrounded by friends. His life was so restricted right now—where he could go, what he could do, who he could see. It was natural that his feelings for the two people who shared those restrictions with him—Shelley and Gabriel—would be intense. But after he was exposed once again to other people—to other women—he might find that his love for Shelley was nothing more than fondness. He might find that she was no more than an easy, available solution to his loneliness. The only way she could endure that was to accept his promise of love with a large dose of skepticism and to keep her own love secret. If she lost him, she would need that secret to survive.

"I'm not sad," she assured him truthfully. Even if the worst did happen, she would always have her memories. Then her gaze fell on his chest. His sweater was steel gray and expensive and delicate and bore a large stain right in the center of his chest from her tears. "Oh, Christopher, your sweater..."

He laughed, hugging her with one arm. "It'll dry. Don't worry." He glanced down at his watch. "We're running late. You're not going to make it to work on time."

"That's okay," she said with an impish grin. "With any luck I'll be quitting soon, anyway."

Hand-in-hand, they returned to the parking lot. At the Trans Am, Christopher kissed her once more and reviewed the route that would take her to the club before sending her on her way. When she was out of sight, he walked back onto the path that led to the pools, stopping only a few yards from the parking lot to stare out to sea.

He had told Shelley that he found peace here at the ocean. It was true. But now he had no need to drive out here for peace. Now he could find it anywhere. With her.

Christopher and Shelley met Gabriel for dinner that night at a small Mexican restaurant near her apartment. "I followed Miller when he left the club yesterday," he told them when they were seated. "His only stop was a pay phone on Sports Arena Boulevard. He made one call, talked about five minutes and hung up. He seemed pretty agitated—like he was arguing with whoever was on the other end."

"That doesn't do us a lot of good," Shelley said glumly. "We don't know who he called, or what they argued about."

Gabriel looked haughtily at her. "Speak for yourself. *I* have a fair idea of who he called, which gives me an even fairer idea of what they argued about. You have no understanding of our phone system out here, do you? Don't you even have telephones in Alabama?"

She ignored the gibe. "So what am I missing?"

"I knew all the important things: where the pay phone is; what the pay phone number is; and exactly what time the call was made. So I took that information and my trusty little badge to the phone company. It took their computers about half a second to pick out the one call, from all the thousands of calls made that afternoon, that Charles Miller made. In another half second they found the number for me." He smiled smugly, like a child with a secret.

Christopher and Shelley exchanged tolerant glances, then Christopher spoke. "Okay. I see you're not going to volunteer the information, so I'll ask. Who did Miller call?"

"I don't know—exactly. The number belongs to the Soviet Embassy in San Francisco. As far as who he talked to there, I don't know."

Shelley scooped up the filling that had fallen from her taco with a piece of taco shell then bit into it. "Isn't that awfully careless?" she asked. "I thought they'd have some sort of elaborate system set up for contacting each other—you know, pay phones in parks or bus stations or something."

"Nervous people get careless," Christopher said quietly. "Apparently we've succeeded, at least partially. We've shaken him up. Now what?"

"We wait a couple more days," Gabriel suggested. "If nothing else happens, I vote that we talk to Taylor. See if he's willing to help."

"Who is Taylor?" Shelley asked.

Quietly, Christopher explained that Ron Taylor worked with the local FBI Foreign Counterintelligence Unit. He had also headed the investigation that culminated in Gary's and Christopher's arrests. Shelley was impressed that Christopher was willing to trust the man who had arrested him enough to ask for his help.

After the meal, Shelley and Gabriel waited near the door while Christopher settled the bill. Gabriel commented, "It ought to be over soon. Are you nervous?"

"Some," she admitted. "But not so much for myself."

"Yeah, I know. You take care of yourself, though. Since I'm responsible for your involvement in this mess, I'd hate to see anything happen to you. Christopher would never forgive me."

"You're not responsible," Shelley disagreed. "He's the one who asked me to go to the club, and I'm the one who said yes."

Gabriel shook his head in disagreement. "He asked because I pressured him into it. When I called him that Saturday morning to tell him about Miller, I insisted that you were our only choice. I pushed him hard, and he gave in. But I still think I was right. I don't think we could have turned to anyone but you."

Shelley tilted her head back, staring up at him for a long time. "When you called him... You mean the Saturday that you went to his house when I was there?"

"Yeah. What about it?"

Before she could answer, Christopher joined them. They went to the cars together, then separated, Gabriel going his way, and Shelley and Christopher going home.

"I owe you an apology," she said softly as they got ready for bed.

Christopher was pulling his shirt over his head. He looked puzzled when he emerged from under the garment, unable to think of anything she'd done that merited an apology. "For what?"

One on each side of the bed, they folded down the covers, then Shelley sat down on the edge of the mattress. "That Saturday at your house...I was supposed to stay for a while, but I left early, remember?"

His dark frown was his answer.

She took a deep breath, half wishing that she hadn't started this. Christopher had never asked for explanations; she didn't need to go into it. But because of the misunderstanding she had said some things that had been cruel, and her conscience demanded that she clear them up. "I was...hurt. I thought...I thought that the only reason you'd made love to me was because you needed my help. I thought you knew all about Miller before you asked me to come, and I—I was upset."

Christopher sat down facing her, leaning against the headboard. He clasped her hands in his, his thumbs rubbing back and forth. "You thought I made love to you as a bribe?" he asked. Though his voice was quiet, it rang with disbelief. "That I slept with you so you would watch Miller for me? My God, Shelley... How could you believe that I'd use you that way?"

"I didn't know what else to think. You had made such a point of telling me that you didn't want me. Then suddenly you called and invited me to stay with you. You made love to me as if I was the most important thing in your life. Then, the next morning, you couldn't even look at me. Over breakfast you said, 'I need a favor from you—and by the way, it could get you killed.'" She squeezed his hands tightly. "What was I supposed to think?"

Indeed, what was she supposed to think? he silently agreed. Her experiences with men had been neither varied nor good. "Oh, Shelley..." He turned her hands over and raised them to his mouth, pressing a kiss into each palm. "I didn't even know about Miller until that morning."

"I know. Gabriel mentioned that tonight."

Pulling gently, he gathered her against his chest. "I made love to you as if you were the most important thing in my life because you were," he whispered. "You are. I love you."

I love you. Her face hidden against his chest, she mouthed the sentiment. Christopher felt the movement of her lips and knew what she had said as surely as if she'd said it out loud. He smiled faintly. Someday she *would* say it out loud. He could wait until then.

Business at Impressions, like everything else in life, went in cycles. The flow of customers that Shelley had grown accustomed to at lunchtime was barely a trickle on Thursday; she and the other waitresses spent more time talking behind the bar than waiting on customers.

Charles Miller arrived at exactly eleven-thirty. His face was lined with stress, his movements jerky. Christopher's appearance had disturbed him even more than Shelley had expected. He paused in the doorway and looked furtively around the room before he hurriedly took a seat at his table.

A few moments later one of his informants met him. It was the enlisted man who worked at the Naval Ocean Systems Command. He generally came with his friend, the lone civilian in the group, but this time he was alone. They talked in hushed, solemn tones, but every time Shelley approached, they broke off before she could hear a word. It was so frustrating that she wanted to scream.

Christopher waited until twelve o'clock, then walked in as if he owned the place. He acknowledged Shelley with a nod, as many of her regular customers did, then made his way unescorted to his table. Without waiting for him to order, she got a beer from the bartender and carried it to him, as she did for most of her regulars. But her hands didn't tremble when she served most of her regulars, and her heart didn't pound harder every time she looked at one of them. But that was to be expected, since she wasn't in love with any of them.

"Anything unusual going on?" he ask softly.

"Only half the duo showed up, but other than that, nothing. It's been pretty quiet today."

"It started raining really hard on my way over. Maybe most people decided to be smart and stay inside."

She noticed for the first time that his leather jacket was wet. She had to clench her hand to stop from running it through his hair to see if it was wet, as well.

"I wonder why his pal didn't come. Isn't this the first time one of them has shown up alone?" he asked.

"Yes. Maybe the other guy is sick today. Or maybe he couldn't get away for lunch."

"I don't suppose you've been able to overhear anything."

She looked irritated. "Please, Christopher, don't you think I would have told you if I had?"

He compressed his lips in a thin smile. "Sorry. Thanks for the beer. Bring me another when I finish it, will you?"

"Sure." She returned to the bar and slid onto a stool next to Cassie.

"That guy is gorgeous," the other woman said. "Has he ever come on to you?"

"No." Shelley sighed dramatically. "Just my luck—all he does is drink his beer. But he leaves great tips."

"Honey, he wouldn't even have to tip me. I'd be satisfied with one look from those sexy dark eyes." She arranged her red-lipsticked mouth into a pout. "But he hasn't even noticed me. The only time he's looked at me is to see that I'm not you."

"I don't really think he's noticed me, either," Shelley said as the phone behind the bar rang.

"Hey, Shelley," the bartender called. "That guy with Charles—is his name Montgomery?"

"I don't know," she lied. In fact she knew almost everything there was to know about John Montgomery, courtesy of Gabriel's background investigation. "Is that call for him?"

The man nodded.

"I'll check." She slipped off the bar stool and crossed the room to Miller's table. Both he and his companion were bent over, studying something drawn on a napkin.

"...meeting Petrovich on Saturday at the lighthouse," Miller was saying. "It'll be the last time. With that—"

Shelley's first impulse was to turn away until she could control the excitement that was coursing through her. Only the knowledge that it would make her look suspicious stopped her. She forced herself to take a deep breath, but it didn't stop the trembling, inside and out, as his words sank in. Petrovich was about as Russian-sounding a name as any that she'd ever heard. He must be Miller's contact, the man at the Soviet Embassy. This was it—the break they'd been waiting for! Now if she could just stay calm enough to get through this contact with Miller and Montgomery, then tell Christopher.

She could barely conceal her elation, but she knew that now it was more important than ever that she stay calm. As far as Miller was concerned, she was just a waitress, and the name Petrovich would mean nothing to a waitress. Hoping that her smile was normal, she stepped up to the table. "Excuse me, Charles." She didn't apologize for interrupting him.

Her voice was a little unsteady, but he didn't seem to notice. His expression was grim, but not suspicious. "What do you want, Shelley?"

She turned her smile to the other man. "Is your name Montgomery?" When he nodded, she continued. "You have a phone call at the bar. Can I get you something else, Charles? Another drink?"

"No thanks." He looked past her at Christopher as Montgomery left the table. "Does that man come here at any other times besides lunch?"

She knew before she turned that he was referring to Christopher. "Not that I know of. But, of course, I don't work nights or weekends, so I can't really say."

"Has he ever asked you anything about me?"

"No." She prayed that she sounded convincing. "That one day he *did* ask me to bring you a drink, but other than that . . . he really doesn't talk much. Excuse me, will you?"

A few minutes later, when she took Christopher a refill as he'd instructed, she said quietly, "Finish this drink, then leave. I've got something to tell you. Go out in the hallway and wait there."

He followed her orders without question. His gaze still fixed on Miller, he drank the beer slowly, resisting the urge to gulp it. When the glass was empty, he rose from the table, tossed down some money and walked out. As soon as he reached the long entry hall, he stopped, pacing back and forth while he waited.

He was nervous. His heart was beating faster, and his palms were clammy. What had Shelley learned? He couldn't wait to hear it, yet some part of him didn't want to know. All along he had been apprehensive. Now he was just plain scared. The closer they came to the end, the more frightened he became.

Shelley left the dining room as quickly as she could. The hall was empty, except for Christopher. She laid her hand on his arm. "He's meeting someone named Petrovich on Saturday. At the lighthouse, he said. Christopher, this is going to be the last time. If we don't get them now..."

Christopher stared at her. "You're sure that's what he said?"

She reined in her impatience. She understood how important this was to him; of course he wanted to be positive. "I'm sure. They didn't see me approach, and Miller said he's meeting Petrovich Saturday at the lighthouse, and that this was the last time. He was going to say something else, but I had to interrupt him. I didn't want him to think that I was eavesdropping." Which was exactly what she had been doing.

"Which lighthouse?"

This time her impatience slipped its reins. "Good Lord, how many lighthouses can there be in San Diego?"

"Two." He smiled tightly. "But they're both on Point Loma. The Coast Guard lighthouse is down by the tide pools. Then there's an old one at the top of the hill. It's part of Cabrillo National Monument."

She moved her hand down to grasp his. "This is it, Christopher. This is what you've worked so long for. We're going to see that Miller is punished for everything he's done."

He nodded solemnly. "Shelley..." His voice was soft and husky. He broke off and gave her a quick kiss. "I love you. I'll see you at home."

She watched him until the door swung shut and he was out of sight. Sighing softly, she turned to go back into the dining room to finish what she hoped would be her last day of work. She felt a great sense of relief that this case was almost over, that soon Christopher would be cleared of any wrongdoing, that nobody had been hurt. She turned the corner with a springy step, then came to a sudden stop. The relief fled in a rush of overpowering fear.

Charles Miller was standing before her.

"That was a cozy little scene."

The sound of that frighteningly pleasant voice sent ice rushing through her veins. He was coldly furious. She raised her gaze to meet Miller's eyes. Looking into their chilling blue depths, Shelley felt a fear stronger than any she had ever known. In that moment, for the first time in her life, she knew that she was going to die. She *felt* the fury and the hatred that would allow him to kill her, the same way he'd killed Gary.

"Here I was just checking to make sure that Morgan had gone, and what do I find? Sweet little Shelley telling him everything that she'd found out while spying on me."

"Ch-Charles, wh-what are you t-talking about?" Her pathetic attempt at innocence failed as her voice broke in the middle of the sentence.

"Are you working *for* him? Or *with* him?"

"I—I don't know what you..."

He took a step closer to her. "Don't lie to me, Shelley," he warned. "If you lie, I'll know it. I'd like to keep you alive a while longer, but it wouldn't bother me if I had to kill you now."

She backed up, but the wall was behind her. "You can't be serious," she bluffed. "We're in a room filled with people. You can't do anything to me here."

"No," he agreed. "I can't. But we're not staying here. You're going to leave with me."

"But... my job..."

He smiled kindly. "Don't worry, Shelley." Then he coldly added, "Dead people don't need jobs. Let's go." He grasped her arm and started toward the door.

"No." Shelley pulled back, dragging her feet. "Let me go. Christopher is out there. He won't let you take me with you." It was a lie. She knew that Christopher was already on his way to meet with Gabriel, and probably Ron Taylor. He wouldn't be in the parking lot.

"If he's out there, which I doubt, and if he sees us, then he'll die, too. If you yell at him or do anything to get his attention, he'll die first," Miller warned. "You'll have to watch him die, Shelley, knowing that it was your fault."

His fingers were like steel, cutting into the tender flesh of her arm. She had to bite her lip to keep from crying out at the pain.

She considered screaming, but she had no doubt that Miller would kill her right there. She'd seen no sign of a weapon, but she was certain that he must have one.

The rain was still falling, but Miller paid it no mind. He stalked across the parking lot, pulling Shelley through puddles and over curbs. A frantic glance around verified her suspicions. Christopher was already gone. There was no one around to help her.

After Miller grinned with satisfaction at Christopher's absence, he pushed her into the car on the driver's side, shoving her across the seat. She grabbed for the door handle, but he flung her back against the seat so hard that her ears rang when her head hit the headrest. "Lean forward," he commanded, then pushed her before she had a chance to obey. From the glove compartment he produced a pair of handcuffs and a roll of electrical tape. He put the tape in his pocket, then forced her hands behind her back and fastened the handcuffs brutally tightly around her wrists, making her gasp at the shock of the pain. After shoving her back against the seat again, he reached over her for the seat belt and secured it across her hips.

"If you try to get anyone's attention," he warned, "I'll kill you now. Do you understand that?"

Then she saw the weapon. It was a pistol of some sort, worn beneath his sports coat in a shoulder holster. She wasn't familiar with guns, but she had a healthy respect for them and for the damage they could do to the fragile human body. Numbly, she nodded. She understood.

She watched where he drove, trying to identify street names, to remember landmarks and directions. But her brain never handled directions well under the best of circumstances, and right now fear was short-circuiting everything. No, not fear, she decided. Terror. Stark terror.

Her hands hurt from the lack of circulation. The position in which she sat forced too much of her weight onto her wrists, pushing the steel circlets into her skin. She felt the slow, heavy trickle of blood on one wrist until the tingling in her fingers canceled out all other sensations.

"Are you a cop?"

It was the first time that Miller had spoken since leaving the parking lot. Shelley was startled by the loudness of his voice, by the sharp, staccato words. "N-no, no, I'm not."

"What then? FBI? NIS? DIS? DIA?"

She shook her head. "N-no." She didn't even know what any of those initials, besides FBI, meant.

"Don't tell me you're just a waitress," he snarled. "I told you—if you lie to me, I'll kill you now."

"I'm not a cop or an FBI agent or any of those other things you mentioned," she insisted. "I swear I'm not."

"Then what the hell are you?"

She suspected that, in Miller's eyes, a reporter was as bad as the others. She preferred to risk a lie if it meant staying alive a little longer. "I—I'm just helping Christopher. He needed help, he needed someone to go into the club there, and I—I wanted to do it."

"How long have you known him?"

"A couple of months. We met right after I moved here." Her voice was breathy, feeble. It wouldn't take much, she was afraid, to send her right over the edge into hysteria. It wasn't a comforting fact to face. She had always believed that she was strong, above tears and fits and panic. In a moment, though, she fully expected to dissolve into a flood of tears that nothing short of death could stop.

"I suppose you think you're in love with him." He was mocking, full of disgust for such feelings.

She tasted blood in her mouth where her teeth had broken the delicate skin of her lip. Rain dripped from her hair onto her face, where it ran down to her throat. Her clothes clung uncomfortably to her, making her feel trapped.

Trapped? That wasn't because of her clothes, she thought with a dark humor that frightened her. Try the simple facts that her hands were cuffed behind her back and that the seat belt served as effectively as any rope in keeping her in place.

"Answer me!"

She flinched at his roar. "Yes!" she cried. "Yes!" And with that, the tears came. That was the source of her terror—not dying, but leaving Christopher. Leaving him without ever saying "I love you." That was what she found so painfully frightening.

She ducked her head and cried. Quietly, sadly, her heart breaking. For reasons that she no longer remembered, she had never told Christopher how much she loved him, and now she might not have another chance. She understood now why her mother and father so often told each other—and Shelley herself—that they were loved.

"I hate you," she whispered when the tears dried. "Dear God, I hate you!"

He laughed. He was still laughing when he turned into a parking lot. "I'm going to take the handcuffs off," he said. "We're going to walk inside together, and you're not going to make a sound, because I'm going to have this gun pointed at your back. Okay?"

He removed the steel cuffs, tucking them into his pocket. Shelley pulled her hands from behind her and looked at them. Her fingers were swollen and purplish blue, and there was a streak of drying blood on one hand.

Miller got out of the car and walked around to her side. They were at a motel, she noticed, when he pulled her out. A cheap one judging by the look. A sign outside the office advertised hourly rates, along with triple X-rated movies shown right in the rooms. She thought she was going to be sick.

Inside the dingy office he gave the clerk a thick stack of money in exchange for a room key. They went to the room, where he pulled the handcuffs out once again. He forced her wrists between the metal bars of the bed's headboard and fastened the cuffs securely. From another pocket, he extracted the roll of electrical tape. A few strips of it across her mouth wouldn't keep her quiet, but they would certainly muffle any noise she made. Besides, she thought bleakly, in a place like this, who would listen to her frantic cries?

Ron Taylor was an intelligent, distinguished man who looked every inch the lawyer that he was. He was also unfailingly polite when Christopher was escorted into his office. He had been polite before, Christopher remembered. He had thought at the time of his arrest that, under better circumstances, he would have liked the man.

Circumstances weren't necessarily better for this meeting, just different. Being in the building where he had spent the single worst day of his life wasn't pleasant, but at least his reason for being there was a better one.

"How have you been, Mr. Morgan?" Taylor asked. He could tell that Christopher had something on his mind but wasn't ready to say it yet. Taylor wouldn't rush him. Christopher would state his business at the proper time.

"Okay." Christopher shifted in the chair. So far, this meeting hadn't gone too differently from the last. He was nervous as hell, and Taylor was calm and composed; Taylor was asking questions, and he was answering them.

He opened the manila envelope he'd brought with him and pulled out the first picture. "Do you know this man? His name is Charles Miller."

Taylor accepted the photograph and studied it for a minute. "No," he said at last. "I don't know him."

"I think he's the man...the man who Gary worked for."

Taylor looked at the picture again with new interest. "Why do you think that?"

Christopher explained about their investigation. He left out nothing, even admitting that "a friend" had gotten around the FBI's flag on Gary's bank records. When he mentioned the club, Taylor broke in.

"We checked out everyone at the club. Other than the waitresses who served him, there was no one we could connect to your brother."

"Charles Miller left San Diego the day that Gary was killed, and he stayed away for about three months." Christopher continued his narrative, telling Taylor of Shelley's involvement, about her job at the club, about the six people who met Miller regularly. He pulled out the remaining photographs, turning them over to the gray-haired man, then fell silent, waiting to hear what Taylor had to say.

"We'll investigate this, of course, but I can't make any promises. You, Miss Evans and your 'friend' will have to stop your own investigation. We'll take over."

Christopher studied him for a minute. He had once been pretty good at judging people, until Gary and Mike Jennings had taught him that no one could tell what another person was really like; you only saw what they wanted you to see. Fortunately, Shelley had undone that lesson. She had taught him to trust his instincts once more. His instincts told him that Taylor wasn't particularly impressed with what he'd heard so far. That was all right. He still had one piece of information to give the man.

"Does the name Petrovich mean anything to you?"

Taylor's interest doubled. His eyes were sharp and clear, focused on Christopher's face. "Where did you hear it?"

"He's a KGB agent, isn't he?"

"Is he connected to Miller?"

They could keep asking questions with neither of them giving any answers for the rest of the day. Christopher decided to give in first. "Yes. Today, Shelley overheard Miller talking about a meeting with Petrovich."

"Where?" Taylor demanded.

"At the lighthouse."

"Which lighthouse?"

"He didn't say," Christopher said dryly. "I assume that the man he was talking to already knew which one."

"When is this meeting?"

"Saturday. Petrovich is at the embassy in San Francisco, isn't he?"

Taylor hesitated only a moment, then nodded.

"And he *is* a KGB agent, isn't he?"

"Yes," Taylor admitted. "Who was Miller talking to when Miss Evans heard this?"

Christopher leaned forward and fished Montgomery's photo from the pile. "Him. John Montgomery. He's stationed out at N.O.S.C."

Taylor blanched. Christopher didn't know what sort of research was done at the Naval Ocean Systems Command, but judging from the FBI agent's reaction, it was obviously very sensitive.

"Where is Shelley Evans right now?"

Christopher looked at his watch. "She's still at the club. She usually gets home around six-thirty."

"I want to talk to her—tonight. Can you call and ask her to come here as soon as she gets off?"

"No."

The flat refusal brought Taylor's gaze back from the photograph to Christopher. "No?" he repeated.

"You can talk to her, but I'm not going to call her. As soon as she comes home, I'll bring her in. I'm not going to do anything to jeopardize her safety." He rose from the chair. "Will you still be here between six-thirty and seven?"

"Yes." He had a lot of work to do in very little time. He would be staying very late.

"We'll be back then."

Christopher drove to Shelley's apartment. In the afternoon, with all her neighbors at work, the building was quiet. He'd been keeping the apartment clean while she was at the club, so there was little to keep him occupied. He wandered from room to room, restless, excited, nervous, scared. It was

almost over. Just two more days, and the FBI would take
care of those. He and Shelley and Gabriel were safely out of
it. He would have been overwhelmed by relief if Shelley
hadn't still been at the club. Once she left Impressions this
evening, she would never have to go back. Then she would
really be safe.

He had finally settled on the sofa, preparing to watch the
late-afternoon news, when the phone rang. Expecting to
hear Gabriel's voice, Christopher reached over to pick it up.
"Hello?"

There was a long pause, then, "Morgan?"

The hairs on the back of his neck stood on end. "Yes."

"Christopher Morgan?"

"Yes."

"We haven't had the pleasure of meeting...yet. My name
is Charles Miller."

Instantly, Christopher understood the reason behind the
call. There was only one way that Miller could have learned
where Christopher was staying, only one way that he could
have known to call Christopher at this number. Shelley.
Miller had Shelley.

His knuckles turned white from holding the receiver too
tightly. Nausea swept over him, leaving him weak and unable to think or speak.

"Morgan?" Miller didn't wait for a response. "Shelley is
all right...for now. I want you to meet me Saturday. If you
come to the meeting, if you come alone, if you say nothing
to anyone, I'll give her back to you unharmed. If I see even
one cop, I'll kill her. Do you understand that?"

"Yes." It was a hoarse croak. "Wh-where...? Wh-
when...?"

"I'll call you again Saturday morning at this number and
tell you. Remember—if you go to the police or the FBI or
anyone else, Shelley will die."

Christopher was numb. He sat for long moments after
Miller had hung up, still holding the receiver. *I'll kill her.
Shelley will die.*

He forced himself to breathe slowly, painfully expanding his lungs with fresh air. His heart began beating at a near normal rate, his blood kept flowing, his brain began functioning.

Gabriel. The first thing he had to do was call Gabriel. As he'd done so many times in the past, his friend would help him. He would help him save Shelley.

He dialed the nonemergency number for the police department and asked that a message be passed along to Gabriel, who was out. The message was simple and short: "Call Christopher. Urgent." The cold, empty voice in which he gave it added its own sense of urgency.

Gabriel was completing a report when the dispatcher passed the message along. Instead of heading for a pay phone, he drove to the apartment and rapped sharply at the door. Once inside, he stared at his friend.

He'd never seen Christopher looking this terrible—not after his arrest or Jennings's betrayal, not even after Gary's death. He knew there was only one thing that could put such anguish on his friend's face. "What's happened to her?" he demanded.

"Miller has her."

Ron Taylor hung up the phone and sat back in his chair, rubbing his hand over his eyes. At what should have been the end of a routine day, his work was just starting. If Morgan was right, the next forty-eight hours were going to be hectic.

In the three hours since Morgan had left the office, Taylor had gotten an extensive investigation under way. There were agents double-checking Morgan's information on Charles Miller and the other six subjects. In San Francisco, other agents were watching Yuri Petrovich, a KGB agent assigned to the Soviet Embassy. Still others would keep watch on the San Francisco and Oakland airports. If Morgan's information was correct, chances were very good that Petrovich would catch a Friday flight to San Diego. If he did, they didn't want to miss him. They had known for some time that he was spying, but they'd never been able to catch him in the act. This might be their golden opportunity.

Yet another team of agents was investigating their informants. Taylor was already familiar with Morgan; he'd been their prime suspect a year ago, and he still hadn't been cleared of suspicion. Taylor also wanted to know everything there was to know about Gabriel Rodriguez, who he'd quickly pinpointed as Morgan's mysterious "friend," and Shelley Evans. Where and how had they gotten their information? Could they be trusted? Were they right?

"Ron?"

He looked up. One of his agents was waiting at the door. "Christopher Morgan is back. Sergeant Rodriguez is with him."

Taylor frowned. "I told him to bring Evans."

The agent shrugged. "They want to see you. Want me to bring them in?"

"Yeah, go ahead."

Taylor could see by their expressions that something was wrong. He rose from his desk, asked them to take a seat, then sat down again. "Where is Miss Evans?"

Christopher was staring at the floor. Since explaining everything that had happened to Gabriel, he'd been doing nothing but staring silently. Coldly.

"Christopher got a call from Charles Miller about an hour ago. He's kidnapped Shelley," Gabriel said. "I called the club and one of the waitresses confirmed that Shelley left a couple of hours ago with Miller."

"What did he say?" Taylor asked, directing the question to Christopher.

He repeated the brief conversation word for word in an emotionless monotone until he got to the last three words. "Shelley will die." He looked up at Taylor then, his eyes icy and filled with hatred. "I want her back. If he hurts her . . . if anything happens to her . . ." He stopped. There was no need to complete the threat to a detective and an FBI agent. They understood.

Taylor picked up a pencil from the desk and twisted it in his hands. This was all he needed. Here was his chance to arrest eight spies—one of them a KGB agent. As if that weren't complicated enough, now he had the kidnapping of a presumably innocent citizen thrown in. "He said he'd call you Saturday?"

"Yes."

"His meeting with Petrovich is scheduled for Saturday at the lighthouse. We're assuming that they'll meet at the old lighthouse at Cabrillo monument. The Coast Guard lighthouse is too isolated. It's hard to be inconspicuous there. Still, unless we find out for sure that it's up above, we'll have agents at both." He rolled the pencil between his palms; it made a clicking sound each time it rolled over his wedding band. "This is supposed to be his last meeting with Petrovich?"

Christopher nodded.

"He might be planning to leave town. If he thinks that you can somehow connect him to your brother... I think he'll have you meet him at the same place, after his meeting with Petrovich. It'll save time, be less complicated for him. He's using her to ensure that you cooperate, so nothing goes wrong with Petrovich, but he'll want her nearby in case something *does* go wrong."

"But nothing will, right?" Christopher stared across the desk at Taylor. "You're not going to do anything to endanger her life, are you?"

Taylor was silent for a moment. Obviously the relationship between Morgan and Evans was more than just business. He wondered if the younger man had realized yet that Shelley's life was already in danger. Had he considered the odds against Miller letting her walk away, with everything that she knew about everything that he'd done? "Of course not, Mr. Morgan. We don't want anyone hurt."

"But you want the spies. You want the Russian. Where does Shelley rank in your priorities?"

Taylor smiled thinly. "I think we can work it out so we can get them all—Shelley, Petrovich and the others."

"You *think*?" Christopher started to rise from his chair, but Gabriel's hand on his arm held him down.

"Calm down, Christopher," he commanded in a quiet, authoritative voice. "They're going to need your help, and if you go off the deep end, it's going to make things a hell of a lot harder."

Christopher looked at Gabriel for a moment, then sank back in the chair. He knew that his friend was right but it didn't ease his anguish.

Taylor came around the desk then leaned back against the front edge. "We're going to need to put a tap on your phone. Did the call come to your house in Santa Ysabel?"

Christopher shook his head. "Shelley's apartment."

"Rodriguez is right. If Miller insists on meeting with you, you'll have to work with us. When you meet him, you'll have to follow our instructions. And I'd like you to wear a wire. Anything that he says to you will help."

Christopher agreed with a shrug. He didn't care about Miller anymore. He didn't care about anything but getting Shelley back alive.

Damn it, it was all his fault! All he'd wanted to do was protect her and instead he'd gotten her involved in this mess. He had known that it was dangerous, yet he had still asked for her help, and she had willingly given it.

Now it might cost her her life.

Chapter 9

Christopher lay on his back, his hands folded beneath his head, and stared at the ceiling. The ceiling was the only safe place to look. It was the only place in the entire apartment that didn't remind him of Shelley.

Was she all right? Was she frightened? Stupid questions—of course she was frightened! A man who was guilty of murder and God knows what other crimes was holding her prisoner. Christopher was terrified himself, and he wasn't the one whose life was in danger. She must be scared out of her wits.

He had thought he could feel nothing but love so intensely, but the terror that clawed through him and made him shake and gasp for air was the most powerful thing he'd ever known. It was ripping him apart inside, filling him with fury and rage, but there was nothing he could do. He was helpless.

His eyes were gritty and fatigued. His entire body was tired, but his mind was working at a frantic pace and it wouldn't let him rest. Images of Shelley raced through his brain: the last time he'd seen her, smiling triumphantly; beneath him in bed, loving him gently; laughing; talking; touching. Dead.

"*No!* Damn it, no!" He ground his knuckles into his eyes until the images gave way to bursts of rich, dark color.

Shelley wasn't dead. She wasn't going to die—not now, not for years to come. They were going to spend the rest of their lives together, and they were both going to live to be old and white-haired. He had to believe that. He had to, or the terror would destroy him.

Gabriel took Friday off from work and spent the day at the apartment. It was he who insisted that Christopher eat lunch and dinner. It was he who kept Christopher from giving in to the fear. He didn't make any attempts at conversation. He understood that, until Shelley was free and back home, normal conversation would be impossible for Christopher. But he stayed with him and offered his support and his concern and his love. That was what Christopher needed.

An FBI agent came to the apartment Friday morning and set up the recording system on the telephone. He changed the receiver on the phone for one from the case he'd brought with him, which was designed with an additional jack for use with recording equipment. They'd gotten a court order so that a tape of the conversation between Christopher and Miller could be used as evidence in court. Christopher didn't care now if it ever got that far. He would, he decided, rather see Miller dead. Death was a fitting punishment for what he'd done.

Shelley tried to find a more comfortable position on the bed, but it was impossible. The way her hands were secured she had to sit sideways, with nothing to lean back against. She had slept little through the night, just brief snatches before the pain or the fear jerked her awake again. Her body ached from holding the same cramped position for hours, and her fingers were swollen and numb. She hadn't eaten for more than twenty-four hours, and her stomach rumbled occasionally, even though the thought of food made her feel sick.

Miller had left her alone last night. Shortly after they'd arrived at the motel, he had questioned her about Christopher; then he'd gone to call him. He had been in an almost jovial mood when he'd returned. He'd said little about their conversation, just that he was certain Christopher would cooperate. He had freed her then, removing the handcuffs and the tape from her mouth long enough for her to go to the bathroom and get a drink of water. When she'd returned, he had retaped her mouth, fastened her to the bed again and left. She had been alone ever since.

She was so tired that she had little energy to expend on fear. If he was going to kill her, she thought wearily, she wished that he would get it over with. The terror of yesterday had given way to apathy. Dying might not be so bad, if it got her out of this filthy room, made the pain in her hands and wrists go away, and removed Charles Miller from her mind.

But it would also take Christopher away. She would never get to see him or hear him say once more, "I love you." She would never get to tell him that she loved him.

The desire to live was still inside her, hidden somewhere. Thinking about Christopher strengthened it, helped it grow. Miller would only hold her another day; his meeting was scheduled for the next day, and somehow Christopher would find a way to free her then. She could live through twenty-four more hours of this. She could be strong for twenty-four more hours.

A key turned in the lock and the door swung open. Miller was carrying bags from a fast-food restaurant. He set them on the bed, yanked the tape from Shelley's mouth and unlocked her wrists. "We're going to talk," he said brusquely.

She rose awkwardly from the bed. Her legs were unsteady, but they carried her into the tiny bathroom. Before she left the room again she curiously studied her reflection in the cracked mirror. She didn't look too bad, she noticed with surprise. She had expected to see some evidence of her ordeal in her face, but there wasn't much. There were dark circles beneath her eyes from the restless night, and her lips were chapped and red from the tape, but she didn't look as if she'd been scared senseless for the last day.

The queasiness she had expected when faced with food didn't appear, either. She was too hungry, she decided, to waste time throwing up. She sat down on the bed and started to eat. Miller was sitting in the only chair in the room. He didn't bother to restrain her again. His pistol was prominently displayed on the table beside him.

"Who else was helping Morgan?"

She chewed slowly, taking her time before answering. "Me."

He glared at her with disgust. "You wouldn't even know how to begin this kind of job. Who's giving the orders?"

Shelley debated the wisdom of lying, weighing the risks of admitting that a policeman had been involved from the beginning against sticking with an obvious lie. Miller was right in thinking that neither she nor Christopher could have done it alone. She chose an edited version of the truth. "Gabriel. He's a friend of Christopher's."

"And how does he know what to do?"

"He used to be in the navy. In intelligence."

Miller seemed to accept that response. "Anyone else?"

She shook her head.

"What are the chances that Morgan will go to the cops?"

"About me?" She shook her head again, hoping her pretense of confidence was convincing. "He won't. He wants me back."

"What about the FBI?"

"What about them?"

"Will he talk to them?"

She wiped her mouth with a napkin and reached for the soft drink balanced against her leg. "Are you kidding? After what they did to him last year? For God's sake, as far as they're concerned, *he's* their spy. They believe he's as guilty as sin. He's not going to trust them with anything."

Miller fell silent then, watching her while she finished her meal. As soon as she was done, he taped her mouth and cuffed her to the bed, then left her alone once more.

The FBI offices downtown were a flurry of activity. Everything that Morgan had given them had been backed up by their own investigation. Ron Taylor was confident that, with Morgan's help, they could pull off the operation with complete success, unless... unless Miller killed Shelley before the meeting. Taylor didn't think that would happen— if Christopher didn't see Shelley when he arrived, it would lessen Miller's chances of getting him, too—but he had to consider the possibility.

He was in the middle of a meeting when the phone rang. The conversation was brief, the information encouraging. Very encouraging. "That was Phillips in San Francisco," he announced to the agents around him. "Yuri Petrovich just caught a flight to San Diego." He handed the notepaper with the airline and flight number to one of the men. "Romano is also on the flight," he said, referring to one of the agents assigned to San Francisco, "to make sure he doesn't get off in L.A. You know Romano?"

The man nodded solemnly.

"Take your people to the airport. Stay with Petrovich. As soon as he checks into a hotel, get a tap on his phone."

The agent left the room, and Taylor turned back to the photographs they'd been studying. As soon as Morgan had told them that the meeting would be at one of the lighthouses, Taylor had ordered aerial photographs of both locations. The pictures were very detailed, allowing them to precisely formulate a plan of action.

Precision was important. At the same time that they picked up Charles Miller and Yuri Petrovich, teams of two agents each would arrest the remaining six suspects. There would be little room for mistakes.

And Christopher Morgan showed a great deal of potential for mistakes, Taylor thought somberly. He hated having a citizen play such an important role in such an important case—particularly a citizen who had no fondness for the FBI and who was emotionally involved to boot. Between his own arrest, his brother's death and his girlfriend's kidnapping, Morgan had good reason to want Charles Miller dead. But because of his girlfriend, he had an even better reason for cooperating with Taylor.

He looked again at the photos. Miller was supposed to tell Morgan where to meet him the next morning, presumably with just enough time for Morgan to get there. Working on the assumption that both meetings would be at the lighthouse, Taylor planned to have his people in place early Saturday morning. In case he was wrong, though, he would keep a team of agents in reserve at a different location, for backup.

They were going to get them—Miller, Petrovich, all the others. He sighed grimly. He just hoped that Shelley Evans, alive and well, was included in the "others."

"If you don't try to get some sleep, you're going to be exhausted tomorrow," Gabriel warned.

Christopher moved slowly back and forth in the rocker. "I'm already exhausted." He was existing on pure nervous energy. There was no chance that he was going to relax enough to sleep tonight. Until the meeting with Miller ended tomorrow, he wasn't going to relax. "You don't have to stay here. You can go on home."

Gabriel didn't look at him. "I know." But he made no move to rise from the sofa.

Christopher was glad that his friend was staying. If he had to be alone tonight... He preferred not to think about what he would do. "Do you think he'll call?"

"He'll call."

There was a deep silence, then Christopher's next question. It was one that he'd wanted to ask all day—of Gabriel or Taylor or one of the agents who'd come to the apartment—but he hadn't found the courage. Now, in the late-night darkness, he found it. "Do you think she's alive?"

Gabriel stared at the wall hanging above the fireplace. Shelley had quilted it herself, she'd told him, when she'd gone through a crafts phase. It was the only piece she'd ever completed. When he answered, his words were carefully chosen. "Miller knows that he needs Shelley to get to you. I think...I think he plans to kill her—to kill both of you—but I don't think he's done it yet."

That was what Christopher thought. That was what Taylor thought, too. During their brief meeting this afternoon the older man had carefully avoided any unnecessary mention of Shelley, but Christopher had been able to read his expressions, his actions.

He rocked in silence for a few more minutes, then asked curiously, "Have you ever been in love?" Gabriel had been his best friend for most of his life, but Christopher didn't know that one fact about him. He had never asked, and Gabriel had never volunteered the information.

Gabriel had never volunteered the information because it was painful, but he could stand the pain for a few minutes if it helped Christopher deal with his own despair.

He closed his eyes. It had been years since he'd seen her, but he remembered her face so clearly. She was both the person he loved most and the one he hated most in the world. "Yeah," he answered grimly. "I was in love once." He smiled, but there was no pleasure in it. "I might even have a kid out there somewhere. She was pregnant when she left me."

Christopher stopped rocking to stare at his friend. He wasn't sure what kind of an answer he'd expected, but this wasn't it. "When did it happen?"

"A couple of years after I joined the navy. It was before you moved here permanently. You were still spending a lot of time in Albuquerque and Phoenix." He exhaled softly. "I tried for a couple of years to find her. At first I wanted her back. Then I just wanted to know about the baby—if she'd had it or gotten an abortion, if I had a son or a daughter. But I couldn't find her, so eventually I just gave up."

Out of respect for the sorrow that shadowed Gabriel's face, Christopher let the conversation drop. He'd never known that his friend had lost the woman he loved. But he had to ask one last question, although he already knew the answer. "Do you think of her often?"

Gabriel rubbed his fingers over his eyes, then let his hands fall away. He answered in an empty voice. "Every day."

The call came at precisely ten-thirty Saturday morning. "Morgan?"

He recognized Miller's voice immediately. "Yes."

"Be at the lighthouse at Cabrillo monument at eleven-fifteen. You know where it is?"

"Yes."

"Shelley's still all right, but whether she stays that way depends on you. Come alone. Don't tell anyone."

"I'll be there."

The line went dead, and Christopher slowly hung up. He looked up at the men waiting expectantly. The agent who'd been introduced as Matthews, a specialist in electronic surveillance, continued the work he'd started before the phone rang. The small radio transmitter was already in place, taped to Christopher's chest; now Matthews positioned the slender antenna along his spine, between his shoulder blades, and taped it securely.

"The lighthouse is right here," Taylor said, pointing it out on the large photograph. "Since it's so warm today, you can count on having quite a few tourists around, so we want you to lead him down this way if you can. We have people all along the trail down there." He indicated a broad path that led from the lighthouse toward the point, then angled down the steep hillside. The trail had originally been a road, part of the coastal defense system during World Wars I and II; now it was used primarily by visitors for long, private walks.

Christopher looked at the picture and nodded, then glanced out the patio door. It was about seventy-eight degrees outside, thanks to the Santa Anas, the desert winds. A week before Christmas and seventy-eight degrees. He shook his head in dismay, then pulled his sweater on, careful not to disturb the transmitter or the antenna. The sweater was going to be warm, but with the sleeves pushed up it wouldn't arouse suspicion, and it was bulky enough to hide any sign of the electronic gear.

"Get him to talk," Taylor instructed. "He's planning on killing both of you, so there's a good chance that he'll answer your questions. Find out anything you can—about your brother's death, the spying, Petrovich." Taylor glanced at his watch. They had very little time left. "Don't do anything rash, Morgan. Any mistakes, and you or Shelley could get killed."

Christopher smiled thinly. "I won't make any mistakes." He picked up the keys to his truck, then looked back at the silent agents. "I want Gabriel there."

Taylor glanced at the other man, who was sitting quietly in the rocker. "We don't want any extra people around," he hedged.

"With weather like this, the place is going to be crawling with tourists, in addition to your fifty or so agents. One more man isn't going to be noticed," Christopher said coldly. "Besides, he's a cop. He isn't going to get in your way."

It wasn't worth arguing. Taylor nodded. "You can ride with me," he said to Gabriel.

Christopher didn't allow himself to think as he drove to the park. Cabrillo National Monument. Leave it to Miller to carry out his dirty work in a national park, he thought with disgust.

True to Taylor's prediction, the park was busy. The parking lot held dozens of cars, and several tour buses were parked at the curb. Christopher had asked why they didn't put the place off-limits for a while, and Taylor had explained that Petrovich probably had at least one associate along to keep an eye out for him. If the watcher saw them barricading the only road into the area or ordering people out, he would warn Petrovich to call off the meeting. Then their only charge against the Russian would be for being in San Diego without the required State Department permission.

He left his truck and began walking toward the lighthouse. He passed a bronze conversion van with tinted windows, where Matthews and a fellow electronics specialist had set up shop. The range on the wire was good, Matthews had assured him. There was no way he could get out of range without leaving the park.

The sidewalk that led past the lighthouse to the trail was crowded. Christopher saw Miller standing right in front of the building at the far edge of the sidewalk. He was talking to a tall, blond man who Christopher guessed must be the Russian. Petrovich held a thick packet in his hands, and a brown leather briefcase was sitting on the ground between the two men.

A further examination of the site led his gaze to Shelley, who was standing a few yards away, and his fear eased slightly. Thank God she was alive. She was staring out over the city, facing away from the two men, her back turned to their business deal. She appeared to be all right, but at this distance he couldn't really tell.

Five more minutes. Christopher's impatience was growing hard to control; he alternately watched the time and the passersby. He saw Gabriel walk past, followed an instant later by Taylor and the dark man who had been present at Christopher's arrest. They were the only two agents he recognized, although he knew there were others whom he'd seen before. When he'd seen them at M.I. last year, they had all worn blue windbreakers. At the FBI offices they'd worn suits, mostly dark blue or gray. Today they were all dressed casually in jeans and T-shirts or running clothes. Today they looked like all the other tourists.

The blond man handed the brown packet he held to Miller, then bent and picked up the briefcase. He walked away then, coming toward Christopher, almost causing him to panic. Had Petrovich ever met Gary? he wondered. Was it possible that the Russian would recognize him? Would it even matter? Maybe Petrovich knew all about Miller's next appointment.

He still had three minutes. He started walking toward the Visitor Center before the Russian could see him. He forced himself to walk slowly for half that time, then turned and retraced his steps.

Miller pulled Shelley over to stand next to him. "You're going to stand here and not make a sound, aren't you?" he asked silkily. "Because if you create any problems, I'll kill him right here. Do you understand?"

She freed her arm, raised her chin and turned away without answering. That was when she saw Christopher walking toward her. Knowing that Miller would carry out his threat, she bit her lip to keep from calling out a warning. But Christopher wasn't stupid. He hadn't come here alone. She'd seen Gabriel a moment earlier, and she was certain that some of the many people around them must be with the FBI.

Christopher came to a stop a few feet away. He pushed his hands into his pockets to stop himself from reaching out for Shelley. "Are you all right?" he asked in a low, hard voice.

She nodded.

His dark eyes searched her for some sign of mistreatment. She was a bit paler than usual, and there were dark circles under her eyes, to match those under his own. She seemed tired, her skirt and shirt were wrinkled, and her hair was limp, but she looked fine. She looked beautiful.

Then he turned his gaze to Miller. By now the agents in the parking lot would have picked up Petrovich, and his briefcase filled with top-secret data. Now they were waiting for Christopher to give them Miller.

Christopher had never before felt the urge to kill someone, but he felt it now. The strength of the hatred that surged through him was overpowering. Now he understood why Taylor had warned him against doing anything rash. Taylor must have suspected that Christopher would feel this outrage, this violence.

"Let's take a walk," Miller suggested.

It sounded like a friendly invitation, but it was an invitation to die, Christopher knew. "Where?" he asked.

His voice was harder and colder than Shelley had ever heard it. The emptiness frightened her more than anything else that had happened. She watched him with worried eyes, biting her lip in concern.

"Down there."

Miller gestured in the direction that Taylor had told Christopher to go. Down the hill and onto the trail. Out of sight of nosy tourists with cameras. A good place to arrest someone, in Taylor's view. A good place for a double murder, from Miller's viewpoint.

"And don't do anything stupid," Miller said pleasantly. Removing his hand from his jacket pocket, he showed Christopher the revolver that he held.

Christopher extended his hand to Shelley. "Come on. Let's go." He slid his arm around her shoulders, holding her so tightly that his fingers bruised her tender skin.

She sagged against him, resting her head against the solid warmth of his shoulder. When she leaned into him, she felt the tension that left his entire body hard and strained. When she put her arm around him and rested her hand on his chest, she also felt the slight bump made by the transmitter above his ribs and raised fearful eyes to him. Whatever he wore beneath his sweater was small—but was it too small to be a gun? she wondered. Had he come here planning not only to rescue her but also to kill Miller? He was capable of it; she could see it in his eyes, in his coolly detached manner. He would find it easy to kill the man who had caused him such pain. The knowledge terrified her, and she looked up at him, silently pleading.

He simply smiled down at her, bent his head and kissed her forehead. "I love you." His mouth formed the words, but there was no sound.

"Turn here," Miller commanded from behind them.

Christopher obediently did so, guiding Shelley onto the path that led downward. "Why are you taking us down here?" he asked over his shoulder.

"Don't pretend to be stupid," Miller replied nastily. "You surely don't think I can let you live. I like my freedom, and I intend to hang on to it. I'm not giving it up—not for you or anyone else. No one's sending me to prison." The farther they got from the crowds, the more talkative he became. His voice held equal parts derision and surprise. "I never expected any trouble from you, not after what happened to Gary. I thought you were smart enough to learn a lesson from that. Gary would have given me to the FBI on a silver platter if they had offered a deal soon enough. That's why he had to die."

Christopher stiffened even more. "You paid Garcia to kill him, didn't you?"

"No. Actually, I did hire him to do the job, but I never had to pay. He was killed immediately afterward. It was convenient that the deputy killed him. It saved me from having to do it myself." There was a moment's silence, then he continued. "Gary was a nuisance. If the information from your research projects hadn't been so valuable to the Soviets, I never would have done business with a man like him."

"How did you get together with him?" Christopher asked. "How did you know that he had access to that research?"

Shelley was bewildered by Christopher's questions. She was curious, too—as a reporter, she had more than her share of curiosity—but she couldn't understand Christopher's desire for answers to questions that no longer mattered. Was he delaying, distracting Miller, waiting for the right time to turn on him? Or, after so many months of searching, did he feel that he *had* to have the answers, no matter what happened next?

"You look like Gary, you know that?" Miller shook his head as he remembered. "When I first saw you at the club...for just an instant I thought you *were* Gary. I almost panicked. Then I remembered the younger brother." He paused to consider the question. "How did I find out about Gary? Your brother liked to talk. He was always trying to impress the women at the club—the waitresses, the customers. You know how he was about women."

Yes, Christopher acknowledged silently. That sounded like Gary.

"Anyway, he was bragging to one of the waitresses about how important his job at Morgan Industries was. He told her that he worked on all these top-secret defense contracts, and I overheard him. After I got to know him, he admitted that he didn't actually work on the contracts, but he did have access to them. We made a deal." Miller glanced around, then commanded, "Stop here and turn around."

Christopher and Shelley both obeyed.

"You know, I don't think your brother liked you very much," Miller said thoughtfully. "I think he resented the fact that you had everything he wanted—success, power, wealth. But he was too weak to work for things the way you did."

Somewhere deep inside, beneath the ice-hard shell that surrounded Christopher, he was stung by Miller's assessment, although he knew now that it was true. Gary hadn't been much of a brother. He hadn't been much of a person. "You're a real bastard," he said in a low, frigid voice.

"We all have our faults," Miller agreed mildly. "Move away from her, would you? You stand over there, and you—" he removed the gun from his pocket and carelessly waved it at Shelley "—you stand over on that side."

"How did you get involved with the Russians?" Christopher asked as he moved to the edge of the path.

"That's a long story that you don't have time to hear." Miller smiled. It was ugly and evil. "Are you afraid to die, Morgan? Is that why you're asking so many questions? To delay the inevitable? I can kill you first, if you'd like. But then Shelley would have to watch you die. I don't think you're that much of a coward."

Christopher *was* stalling, Shelley realized, and suddenly she knew why. She had thought that the bump underneath his sweater, small as it was, might be a gun; now she knew that it was some sort of radio transmitter. The conversation was being recorded, and when whoever was listening in had heard enough, they would move in and arrest Miller, hopefully without incident.

"No," Christopher agreed. "I'm not a coward. But what would it hurt to answer my questions? Are you in such a hurry to get out of here? Are you afraid of being seen with us? Are *you* a coward?"

"Not at all. What was your question? Oh, yes, how I started working for the Soviets. That's really the proper word to use—not Russians. I started years ago, when I discovered that the Soviets paid far better than the American military. I suppose my tastes were expensive, but I just couldn't get by on what the navy paid. I was stationed in San Francisco at the time, and I was recruited by a KGB agent there. It became a lifelong career. But I'm getting out now. Once your bodies are discovered, the cops will be coming around the club, asking lots of questions about Shelley, and I'm afraid everyone there Thursday saw her leave with me. It will be too dangerous for me to stay here any longer.''

"Why did you recruit Gary and the others to work for you?"

"As you probably know, I lost my access to classified data when I retired. I had to find others to work for me, to provide the material that my Soviet friends wanted. It worked out really well, until Gary. He was the only problem."

"Until now," Christopher dryly reminded him.

"Yes," Miller agreed. "But this problem will be taken care of just as easily." He looked pointedly at the gun.

"Doesn't this bother you?" Shelley asked. She hated the fact that her voice trembled, but she couldn't control it.

Miller looked genuinely confused when he turned to her. "What? You mean killing you two? No, not at all. Self-preservation is important in this business. If you get in trouble, the Soviets will pretend that they never heard of you. You have to take care of yourself. I killed Gary to protect myself. Now I'm going to kill you two for the same reason."

Up above, in the bronze-colored van, Matthews made a quiet statement over the radios that each of the agents carried. "We've got it. Move in." The agents chosen to take part in the actual arrest obeyed. The others, following orders, held their positions.

Taylor led the group of six agents onto the path. Gabriel followed but stayed behind, out of the way. When Taylor stopped twenty yards from the three people on the trail, he commanded, "FBI, Miller. Drop your weapon!"

Miller saw several men, guns in hand, step onto the path ahead as soon as the command came from behind him. Jerking around, he saw Taylor, Gabriel and the others. The agents all had their weapons drawn.

"You son of a bitch!" Miller spat out, looking back at Christopher. "You lied to me! I told you to come alone! I thought you cared enough about her life to cooperate!"

"I *do* care," Christopher replied with a chilling smile. "But I'm not stupid enough to trust you." He reached for Shelley's hand, pulling her over next to him.

"Miller, drop your weapon now!" Taylor ordered, slowly moving closer.

Miller stared at Christopher for a moment with pure hatred, then glanced once more at the group of agents. There was no way out, but that didn't mean he had to give in without a fight. He could still punish Christopher for disobeying his orders. He *would* punish him, in the most unbearable way possible, for calling in the FBI. He raised his right hand, the one holding the gun, only a fraction of an inch and turned it toward Shelley.

She barely had time to realize what Miller was planning; then Christopher moved. His foot connected with Miller's wrist, knocking it up and back. Miller fell backward, and the pistol landed on the trail near Christopher.

The agents started to move in, but the movement stopped as suddenly as it began when Christopher bent down and picked up the gun. He looked at it with vague curiosity, hefting it, checking its weight and feel. The grip was still warm from Miller's palm.

He raised the gun, pointing it at Charles Miller. "Get up," he ordered, his voice little more than a whisper.

Watching him warily, the other man slowly got to his feet, then backed a few steps away.

"Don't do this, Morgan," Ron Taylor warned. "Put the gun on the ground and move away from it."

Christopher gave no sign of hearing the command. His eyes left Miller for an instant to sweep around him. It was a beautiful day, he thought, mentally detached from the situation. One of those winter days that made everyone in San Diego glad they lived there. The sun was shining, warm and pleasant. There were birds singing in the trees around them. The bay was filled with boats, their sails ranging in color from white to black and every shade in between. A ship was pulling into the bay, and a helicopter from the naval air station flew overhead.

When this was all over, he would like to take a walk with Shelley along this path. Although the city and the bay with all their activity were in view, it seemed isolated on the trail. They could walk without meeting anyone else, with no purpose other than to talk and to touch.

His eyes settled on Miller again. The gun was an unfamiliar weight in his hand, but it didn't waver from his target. He knew how to use it—Gabriel had taught him years ago—but he hadn't held a gun for at least five years. He had never pointed one at another person, and he had never considered using one to take another person's life. Until now.

Miller was a coward. An immoral, unethical coward who had planned to kill Shelley because Christopher hadn't followed his instructions. For that alone he deserved to die. For everything else that he'd done, he *had* to die.

"Put the gun down, Morgan," Taylor repeated, his voice sharper. If Christopher didn't obey in the next moment, Taylor would have to take action that he didn't want to take. Failure to put the pistol down after repeated orders to do so would result in shots being fired and almost certain death for Christopher.

"Wait."

Christopher recognized the soft voice as Gabriel's. He had noticed his friend with the squad of agents, but he didn't turn to look at him.

"Let Shelley talk to him," Gabriel advised. "If anyone can get through to him, she can."

Taylor looked from Gabriel to Shelley, who was standing a few yards from Christopher and Charles Miller. Tilting his head, he silently asked a question.

Nodding, she silently replied. She took a step forward. "Christopher."

God, he loved the sound of his name in her voice. He loved everything about her—and Charles Miller had tried to take her from him. He had used her to get to Christopher; then he'd planned to kill her.

From the corner of his eye he saw her. There was fear in her face—fear for him. She knew what he wanted to do, knew that he was capable of doing it. He was calm, quiet, controlled. It would be so easy for him to pull the trigger. He'd never been an especially good shot, but at this range "close" would be good enough. "Close" would kill Miller, and Christopher wanted to kill him. Dear God, he wanted him dead.

Shelley began speaking softly. She didn't attempt to go to him. She was too smart to get in the way of a man with a desire to kill and a loaded pistol. "If you do this, Christopher, they'll send you to prison and I'll lose you forever. I love you. I can't let you go."

His eyes never left Miller. "He murdered my brother. He kidnapped you. He was going to *kill* you, Shelley. He was going to *kill* you."

"I know, but let them take care of him." She gestured toward Taylor and his men. "They'll put him in prison, Christopher—*in prison*. He'll never be free again. He'll never hurt anyone again."

He turned his head slightly so he could see her better without letting Miller out of his sight. "He was going to kill you," he repeated in a hard, emotionless voice. "Just like he killed Gary."

"Yes," she agreed. "I'm not asking you to show him any mercy. I don't care if he dies, but *not at your hands*. I don't want to see him die at the cost of your life." She was shaking—her voice, her hands, her body. She was so afraid that she could barely talk, yet the words she was saying were the most important of her life. "My God, Christopher, don't you realize what you've done? You've got the man who killed Gary. You've proven your innocence. Don't throw it all away now, just for the chance to kill him. He isn't worth it."

He considered her words. He could kill Miller and Gary's death would be avenged. Shelley's kidnapping would be paid for. The betrayal of the United States would be settled. He would have justice.

And he would be alone, alone in the prison where Miller belonged. He would never get to be with Shelley again, never get to hold her, touch her, kiss her, love her. Without her, he would die.

He took a step back from Miller and glanced at Shelley again. Slowly he smiled, bent and laid the gun on the ground.

Taylor's men moved in, taking the pistol, handcuffing and searching Miller, reading him his rights.

Christopher tilted his head back, his eyes closed. The sun was still shining, warm on his face, bright against his eyelids. The birds were still singing, oblivious to the drama that had unfolded on the trail. He was alive and he was free, and he was in love.

Knowing that Shelley was standing only a few feet away and watching him, he opened his eyes and extended his hand. With a soft laugh, she crossed the distance that separated them and placed her hand in his. "Did you mean what you said?" he asked, pulling her against him.

"I love you," she whispered. "Oh, Christopher, I love you."

One of the agents stepped forward. "Excuse me, Mr. Morgan," he said. "If you'll let me remove that transmitter, we can give you a little more privacy."

Shelley moved away, and Christopher raised his sweater. The antenna came off easily, the sticky tape pulling slightly at his skin. The transmitter was a different matter. It pulled off easily, too, but removed a large patch of hair from his chest with it, making him wince.

Shelley tugged his sweater back down and wrapped her arms around him. "I love you," she whispered before his mouth covered hers for a sweetly gentle kiss.

Christopher finally raised his head. "Let's go home," he suggested. Shelley was only too happy to agree.

They walked past the agents holding Miller, stopping only briefly when they reached Gabriel. Christopher extended his hand to his friend. "Thanks."

Gabriel didn't hesitate to hug both of them. "You guys take care."

"We will," Christopher responded as they started off again. He was anxious to get Shelley home.

"We'll need to talk to both of you later," Taylor called.

Christopher raised his free hand in acknowledgment, but he didn't stop walking. They could talk later. Now he and Shelley needed to be alone.

The flight to Mobile took more than four hours. When the pilot announced that they would be landing soon, Christopher reached across to wake Shelley, then turned back to the window.

"That's the airport?" he asked skeptically, looking down at the terminal and runways as they flew overhead. Two of the three runways looked too short to even consider landing on.

Shelley didn't bother to look out. "Uh-huh."

"We're going to land there?"

"Unless the pilot's decided to try the street out front." She smiled, patting his hand reassuringly. "Relax, Christopher. Big jetliners land there every day. This is a small plane."

He scowled at her. "This is a Lear jet. For the price of this charter, I could probably have *bought* a small plane."

"I told you it cost too much. It would have been a lot more sensible if we'd waited until tomorrow. You could have bribed someone on the flight I was supposed to take to give you their seat."

He felt the plane start to descend, and his stomach sank, too. "Maybe," he agreed, "but with my luck, I couldn't have gotten a seat, and you would have come without me. I'm not letting you out of my sight again." It had been five days since Miller's arrest at Cabrillo National Monument, but the terror of that day still haunted him every night. It would be a long time before he felt safe again with Shelley out of sight.

Understanding his fear, she squeezed his hand, softly reassuring him. "It's all right."

"Did you call your parents?"

"No."

"You didn't tell them anything?" Christopher looked faintly green. He had been nervous about meeting Paul and Lois Evans ever since they had arranged this trip. Under the circumstances, he would have felt better if Shelley had given them some advance warning.

"They aren't expecting me until tomorrow evening, so I'll call them in the morning." She undid her seat belt when the plane came to a stop, then reached for Christopher's belt. He laid his hand over hers, holding it in place for a minute. The sun shining through the window glinted off the gold and diamond ring on her finger and the solid gold band that he wore.

He lifted her hand to his mouth for a kiss. "I love you."

Shelley smiled sweetly. "I know."

"Will they mind?"

"That we got married without telling them?" She considered it for a moment. "Yes," she finally replied. "They'll be a little hurt, but once we explain everything to them, they'll understand."

Christopher had offered to wait if she'd wanted, but she'd been as eager as he was to have the ceremony right away. After coming so close to losing him, she'd been unwilling to wait any longer.

"They can blame me," Christopher offered as they descended from the plane.

"They won't blame anyone. When they see how much you love me, they'll be too thrilled to blame anyone," she teased.

A rental car was waiting for them near the terminal. Christopher accepted the keys from the driver while their luggage was stowed in the trunk.

It was a short drive to the hotel. There they settled into their suite, Shelley unpacking while Christopher ordered dinner from room service. At the bottom of the suitcase she found the newspapers she had packed. Her parents, proud of their only daughter, kept copies of every story she'd ever written. In the past five days she'd had four long articles in the *Chronicle*. But before she gave the papers to her mother and father, she wanted them to meet Christopher. She wanted her parents to know what a wonderful man he was before they read about the last year of his life.

"Are you sure your parents are going to accept me?" he asked as they finished their meal.

"They have to."

"Why do they have to?"

Shelley gave him the smile that he'd fallen in love with. "Because you're my husband, and because you make me very happy, and because you're a kind, honest, loving man. Don't be nervous, Christopher." Pushing her chair back, she rose from the table. "Why don't you get rid of these dishes while I take a bath?"

Christopher leaned back in the chair and watched her cross the room. His lips were turned up in a faint smile, and his eyes were darker than ever with emotion. He would stop worrying about Paul and Lois Evans. If they were like most parents, all they wanted for their daughter was a husband who would love her and be good to her. He knew that nobody could possibly love Shelley more than he did, and he intended to spend the rest of his life proving it.

* * *

Shelley filled the bathtub with warm water scented with
an oil that matched her cologne while she pinned her hair
up. She would have liked time to relax, to linger, but that
would come later. She bathed quickly, dried off, applied
powder and lotion, and slid a nightgown over her head. It
was white silk and lace, with only the faintest hint of peach
in the ribbons that decorated it.

When she stepped out of the bathroom, Christopher was
standing next to the bed, turning back the covers. The delicate scent of her cologne reached him before she did. It was
an expensive but popular brand, one that many women
wore, but whenever he smelled it, he thought of Shelley.

She stopped a few feet from the bed. "Take your clothes
off, Christopher," she softly requested. "I want to see you.
I want to touch you."

His eyes never leaving her face, he undid the single button on the placket of his sweater and peeled it over his head.
The button on his well-worn jeans slipped easily from its
hole, and the zipper glided silently down. Leaning back
against the nightstand, he removed first one shoe, then the
other; then he straightened again, slid his jeans and briefs
down, and stepped out of them.

She stared at him, her eyes moving caressingly over his
chest, his lean hips, his runner's hard-muscled legs. She
swallowed at the sudden swell of emotion. "Did I tell you,"
she began in a voice that trembled, "that you're beautiful?"

He shook his head solemnly. "Take off your gown, Shelley."

Her hands shook as she lifted one thin strap and let it
drop. The other strap followed. Its support gone, the gown
slithered slowly over her small breasts and past her hips,
landing in a tangle around her feet. She stepped out of it and
raised her arms over her head to remove the pins that held
her hair up. It tumbled around her shoulders, swinging and

swaying against her bare skin. Slowly she moved toward him, reaching out her hands until they touched him.

He let her touch and explore. Her fingertips and palms were gentle, hesitant. They glided over his face, along his throat, over his chest and his stomach. "Do you want me?" she whispered breathlessly. It was an unnecessary question. She held the proof of his desire cradled gently within her palm.

"Always." He held himself rigid, struggling to retain control over his body, its wants and needs. He wanted her to look at him, to touch him. He wanted her to enjoy him.

She rose onto her toes and kissed his mouth. "Then make love to me, Christopher," she invited huskily. "Now." She kissed him again, the tips of her breasts brushing against his chest. With a groan, he pulled her into his arms and onto the bed.

For a long moment he simply looked down at her, his eyes almost black with emotion. She was so beautiful, so precious, and she was *his*—his wife, his lover, his friend.

"Christopher?"

"I love you," he whispered, lowering his body to hers. "Dear God, I love you."

Their joining was slow, long and easy. The passion was there, but it was restrained, forced back for the sheer pleasure of taking it slowly. They moved together, each knowing what the other wanted, offering what the other needed. They were like old lovers, old friends, content with the release that was gentle and soft, but no less satisfying for all that. There would be time for wild passion later, but tonight . . . tonight they enjoyed sweet loving and the knowledge that the future was theirs.

*   *   *   *   *

COMING NEXT MONTH

#237 AFTER MIDNIGHT—Lucy Hamilton

Luke Adams knew that Thea Stevens didn't want a man in her life, especially not a movie star whose every action was public property. But he was determined to show her that actors had a life offscreen, and that happy endings weren't only in the movies.

#238 THE ECHO OF THUNDER—Linda Turner

Streetwise Alex Trent could take care of himself in any urban situation, but communing with nature was a new experience for him—and so was Jessica Rawlings. Their quest for stolen money hidden in the mountains was fraught with danger—not the least of which was falling in love.

#239 WILLING ACCOMPLICE—Doreen Roberts

Ross Madigan had been framed for murder, and he was determined to get the man responsible. But Bernard Damon had disappeared, and the only clue to his whereabouts was Eve Andrews. Ross had had his eye on her for years, but there was one problem—could he really trust the woman he loved?

#240 ROGUE'S VALLEY—Kathleen Creighton

For Sandy Stewart the Idaho wilderness was a beautiful refuge from the outside world, and she was determined that no hotshot geologist was going to develop it. But she hadn't reckoned on Jason Rivers, who was strong, tough—and a match for her in every way that counted.

AVAILABLE THIS MONTH:

Silhouette Romance™

Legendary Lovers Trilogy

BY DEBBIE MACOMBER....

ONCE UPON A TIME, in a land not so far away, there lived a girl, Debbie Macomber, who grew up dreaming of castles, white knights and princes on fiery steeds. Her family was an ordinary one with a mother and father and one wicked brother, who sold copies of her diary to all the boys in her junior high class.

One day, when Debbie was only nineteen, a handsome electrician drove by in a shiny black convertible. Now Debbie knew a prince when she saw one, and before long they lived in a two-bedroom cottage surrounded by a white picket fence.

As often happens when a damsel fair meets her prince charming, children followed, and soon the two-bedroom cottage became a four-bedroom castle. The kingdom flourished and prospered, and between soccer games and car pools, ballet classes and clarinet lessons, Debbie thought about love and enchantment and the magic of romance.

One day Debbie said, "What this country needs is a good fairy tale." She remembered how well her diary had sold and she dreamed again of castles, white knights and princes on fiery steeds. And so the stories of Cinderella, Beauty and the Beast, and Snow White were reborn....

Look for Debbie Macomber's *Legendary Lovers* trilogy from Silhouette Romance: *Cindy and the Prince* (January, 1988); *Some Kind of Wonderful* (March, 1988); *Almost Paradise* (May, 1988). Don't miss them!

SRT-1

ATTRACTIVE, SPACE SAVING BOOK RACK

Display your most prized novels on this handsome and sturdy book rack. The hand-rubbed walnut finish will blend into your library decor with quiet elegance, providing a practical organizer for your favorite hard-or soft-covered books.

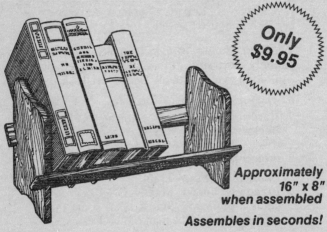

Only $9.95

Approximately 16" x 8" when assembled

Assembles in seconds!

To order, rush your name, address and zip code, along with a check or money order for $10.70* ($9.95 plus 75¢ postage and handling) payable to *Silhouette Books*.

Silhouette Books
Book Rack Offer
901 Fuhrmann Blvd.
P.O. Box 1396
Buffalo, NY 14269-1396

Offer not available in Canada.

BKR-2A

*New York and Iowa residents add appropriate sales tax.

Silhouette Special Edition

NORA ROBERTS'S 50TH SILHOUETTE NOVEL

In May, SILHOUETTE SPECIAL EDITION celebrates Nora Roberts's "golden anniversary"— her 50th Silhouette novel!

The Last Honest Woman launches a three-book "family portrait" of entrancing triplet sisters. You'll fall in love with all THE O'HURLEYS!

The Last Honest Woman—May
Hardworking mother Abigail O'Hurley Rockwell finally meets a man she can trust...but she's forced to deceive him to protect her sons.

Dance to the Piper—July
Broadway hoofer Maddy O'Hurley easily lands a plum role, but it takes some fancy footwork to win the man of her dreams.

Skin Deep—September
Hollywood goddess Chantel O'Hurley remains deliberately icy...until she melts in the arms of the man she'd love to hate.

Look for THE O'HURLEYS! And join the excitement of Silhouette Special Edition!

SSE451-1